COLD HEART

A STELLA LAVENDER MYSTERY

COLD HEART

KAREN PULLEN

FIVE STAR

A part of Gale, Cengage Learning

GALE
CENGAGE Learning·

Farmington Hills, Mich • San Francisco • New York • Waterville, Maine
Meriden, Conn • Mason, Ohio • Chicago

LIBRARY OF CONGRESS CATALOGING-IN-PUBLICATION DATA

Names: Pullen, Karen, author.
Title: Cold heart : a Stella Lavender mystery / Karen Pullen.
Description: First Edition. | Waterville, Maine : Five Star Publishing, a part of Cengage Learning, Inc., 2017.
Identifiers: LCCN 2016037255 (print) | LCCN 2016042135 (ebook) | ISBN 9781432832575 (hardback) | ISBN 1432832573 (hardcover) | ISBN 9781432834654 (ebook) | ISBN 1432834657 (ebook) | ISBN 9781432832469 (ebook) | ISBN 1432832468 (ebook)
Subjects: LCSH: North Carolina. State Bureau of Investigation—Fiction. | Drug enforcement agents—Fiction. | Murder—Investigation—Fiction. | BISAC: FICTION / Mystery & Detective / General. | FICTION / Mystery & Detective / Women Sleuths. | GSAFD: Mystery fiction.
Classification: LCC PS3616.U46 C66 2017 (print) | LCC PS3616.U46 (ebook) | DDC 813/.6—dc23
LC record available at https://lccn.loc.gov/2016037255

First Edition. First Printing: January 2017
Find us on Facebook– https://www.facebook.com/FiveStarCengage
Visit our website– http://www.gale.cengage.com/fivestar/
Contact Five Star™ Publishing at FiveStar@cengage.com

Printed in the United States of America
1 2 3 4 5 6 7 21 20 19 18 17

For my mother, Juanita H. Williams,
who would've liked it.

ACKNOWLEDGEMENTS

Invaluable feedback on the many drafts of *Cold Heart* came from patient writing friends Laurie Billman, Sam Brooks, Antoinette Brown, Toni Goodyear, Louise Hawes, Marjorie Hudson, Linda Johnson, Ruth Moose, Joanna Catherine Scott, Judith Stanton, and Frances Wood. Shirley Burch's advice kept my SBI agent reasonably well-behaved. I'm grateful to the Weymouth Arts Center in Southern Pines, NC, for several writing residencies, to Deni Dietz and Five Star for providing a home for Stella, and to Gordon Aalborg for his editorial guidance. I'm blessed with the encouragement of family, especially my husband, Mac. Thank you, all.

CHAPTER 1

Saturday night

Fredricks and I perched on stools at Clemmie's bar and nursed fizzy water. We were going to buy drugs, if we ever got a table.

Fredricks is a pudgy, bald cop, fifteen years my senior. My mentor, my instructor. I'm supposed to take direction from him. Usually I buy product and he backs me up. This night was different since the informant had sent us to a restaurant and Fredricks thought a couple would be less conspicuous. We didn't look like the other couples at Clemmie's bar, the ones sipping margaritas and lemon drops, furiously flirting. But no one seemed to notice us.

Fredricks loves eating in restaurants. In our idle moments, he bores me stupid with foodie talk, so naturally he was absorbed in the menu. After one look at it, seeing produce *babies*—beets, carrot, lettuce—and their prices, I closed it and glanced at the mirror behind the bar to study the couple sitting on my other side. The man had a lovely smell, clean like a waterfall, and every so often he'd lean into me, then apologize. I didn't mind; I was trembling, the way I always do before a drug buy, and his warm back steadied me. His attention was on his girlfriend, a stunner with the kind of white-blond silky-straight hair I will never have. Such is the unfairness of DNA. He reached out and smoothed her hair, tucked it behind one delicate ear. They smiled at each other, eyes locked. I sighed and turned to Fredricks.

"What're you gonna have?" he asked.

"What can I afford?" North Carolina state employees get eighteen dollars for dinner.

"Come on, Stella. Live a little." He read the appetizer list aloud.

I interrupted him. "What's a White Elf mushroom?"

"From the oyster mushroom family. Earthy, buttery flavor with notes of—"

"Stop. I'll have a salad. Caesar." Even that was over the allowance, up-priced by the addition of Parmesan and prosciutto crisps.

"I'm thinking the seared scallops with pea vines and cauliflower puree," Fredricks said. "Or maybe the pork loin. Turnips and baby kale." Listening to Fredricks talk about food was like listening to a football junkie review the weekend's games. Mind-numbing.

"Another club soda?" The bartender asked this without a flicker of irony, as if he were actually pleased we were taking up space with our two-dollar fizzy water.

"Uh, no thanks," Fredricks said, just as the restaurant's pager buzzed, signaling that our table was ready. He dropped a dollar on the bar, I added a second one, and we slid off our seats. I cast a fond glance at my neighbor in the mirror. He looked at me, nodded when he caught my eye. Approving of our fifty-percent tip, perhaps, or my leather miniskirt—my legs have been known to slow a man's breathing.

The dining room was decorated in happy Caribbean colors—teal, lime, orange. Hushed steel-pan jazz and the faint clink of silver on china permitted softly spoken conversations. Fredricks made small talk about his kids, ex-wife, and new girlfriend until our plates arrived and I had to watch him eat, a sight guaranteed to dampen one's appetite. Just as well, because, according to the plan, I was supposed to leave half my meal and ask for a to-go box. "Why make the sale right here in plain sight?" I whispered, crunching a Parmesan chip. "It's risky for him."

"Less risky, actually. No one gets robbed." He patted his mouth with the linen napkin.

We'd been told to ask for the manager. Here he came, walking swiftly, smiling as he drew near our table. His Claude Monet tie harmonized with his golden tan, white teeth, eyes blue as a Carolina sky. He was what my grandmother Fern—whose lifelong hobby is the male gender—would call a pretty one.

I crooked my finger, he bent down, and I smelled pine, like Christmas. I whispered, "Gift certificates, please. Twelve hundred dollars in denominations of eighty. And a to-go box for my salad."

His smile faded fast as he studied my face, then Fredricks's. "How did you hear about our gift certificates?"

"You come highly recommended. We have a mutual friend," Fredricks said, "from Ohio."

"Who is . . ."

"Benedict, actually." Fredricks was calm, scooping up a last morsel of pea vine and puree. No illegal drug transaction was going to interfere with his meal.

The manager handed Fredricks a black leather check folder. Fredricks signed the credit card slip and tucked it inside, along with an envelope containing twelve hundred dollars. I felt a little queasy, watching that much taxpayer money leave our control.

We waited. This was an iffy step in the exchange. Would he come back with the drugs? I sipped water. Fredricks buttered the last piece of bread and ate it.

The manager returned, handing Fredricks our receipt and me a styrofoam box.

I didn't open it until we'd climbed into our truck. Nestled under romaine and croutons and Parmesan was a little something special: fifteen eighty-milligram OxyContin tablets in a baggie.

"Check the video," Fredricks said.

I'd worn a tiny camera clipped to my collar, disguised by a scarf. My phone had an app for camera playback. "It's good," I said. "He's handing me the box. I guess I don't get to finish my salad."

"Ha. Can't eat the evidence." Fredricks burped quietly.

"Lincoln Teller owns that restaurant," I said. Lincoln was a Gardner University football All-Star who went on to play for the Washington Redskins, and a current darling of the Triangle media. "Think he's involved?"

"I hope not. Bad enough the manager's dealing right out of the dining room."

Our boss at the State Bureau of Investigation would want to control this case, which would attract significant media interest. Still, it would be several weeks before police could make an arrest. We'd attempt to insert an undercover into the kitchen, make more buys, and find the manager's sources. My most fervent prayer: Dear Lord, may that undercover be anyone but me.

"Are we done?" I asked.

"Evergreen." Fredricks started the engine and we rolled out of the parking lot.

"I hate that place."

"Residents want us to clean it up."

It was a beautiful night, the air soft on my skin and fragrant with honeysuckle. A night for hand-holding and slow kisses in the moonlight. And here I was, in the front seat of a rusty pickup driven by a squat middle-aged man, on my way into the shittiest building in Verwood. To buy drugs. I suspected every single apartment in Evergreen harbored a thriving drug business. And it was my job to patronize them.

I had to change. In my duffle, I found jeans, a t-shirt, and a hoodie, and wrestled myself into them as Fredricks looked the other way. I wiped off all my makeup, pulled my hair back tight into a ponytail. "How do I look?"

"About fourteen," he said. "Add some lipstick."

I painted my mouth dark red. The zombie look. I hooked the mike to my bra and ran its wire to the one-way transmitter in my back pocket. My Sig was concealed in a holster behind my back, under the hoodie.

"Where first?" I asked.

"Over by that mail kiosk. See what they're selling. Then you're going to hit an apartment—B215—belongs to some dude named Scottie. According to a CI, he's dealing heroin. Turn on the mike and let's test it."

Fredricks's earpiece squealed with feedback, and he pulled it away from his head. "Ouch. Works. You ready?"

Was I ready? The familiar stomach churn. An adrenaline tremor in my hands. Heart rate elevated, metallic taste in my mouth. "Here I go." I hopped down from the truck.

Evergreen had perhaps a hundred units, arranged in a "U" around a parking lot and mailboxes. Two teenagers lounged against the kiosk, smoking pot. Ugh. I hate pot; it makes my nose all stuffy. I bought a half ounce, and memorized their sweet faces. They were flirty, wanted me to smoke with them, and I felt a twinge of guilt. Undercover requires betrayal, and sometimes it gets to me. They'd be hauled into the sheriff's office later, based on evidence from Fredricks's film and my identification of them, charged with felonies, and given the choice of a year in jail or flipping—becoming informants. Making their moms proud.

I stuffed the pot into my hoodie pocket and walked around to a side entrance. The door was unlocked—broken—and I slipped inside, heard a woman's angry yells, TV, the cries of a

13

baby. A noxious smell of dirt, urine, frying meat. I climbed the steps to the second floor, took a deep breath, and knocked on the door of 215.

A big, big man opened the door. Tall and wide. He wore all black, like an undertaker, and a boatload of gold bling. His living room was a man cave, surprisingly neat for a heroin dealer. Leather sofa and recliner, oak coffee table sturdy enough for his massive feet.

He had an open, friendly face but I didn't trust him an inch. Faces lie. I took a deep breath and rolled my shoulders, tried to relax my expression. I knew I looked tense. Scottie was probably used to that look. "Hey," I said, "heard I could buy good stuff here."

He looked me up and down. "Do I know you?"

"I have cash. You sell china white?"

"Cute thing like you don't need cash."

The quicker this was over the better. I held out a handful of fifties. "How much will this buy?"

"Plenty," he said. He left the room, coming back soon with a bundle. As he handed it to me, he took hold of my arm instead of the money, pulled me over to the sofa. Jesus, I hate to be manhandled. "Quit," I said, curling in on myself. I wasn't going to tussle with him; he was too big.

He breathed beer fumes into my face. "What's a sweet kid like you gonna do with china white?"

"Same as anyone. Party," I said. Between his weight pressing me into the sofa corner and his hand clamped like a vise on my arm, I couldn't move. "Hey, can I get some space here?" Oddly, I wasn't terrified. Maybe because Fredricks was listening and would be on his way, maybe because of the Sig pressing against my spine. This was going to be resolved one way or another.

"Wait a sec." He heaved himself up, and I felt a momentary relief until I saw he was unzipping his pants.

"Jesus, no," I said. "Take the cash, man." I jumped up. He was big but slow, and I got around him and headed for the door. It was locked and as I fiddled with the deadbolt he grabbed me around the waist. His erection pressed into my backside, and he could feel my holster. Mutual alarming surprise.

"What's that, honey? You wearing a weapon?" He slipped his hand under my hoodie, I finally got the door open, and in burst Fredricks, fire in his eyes. Despite his bulky physique, my partner has moves. Within seconds Scottie was on his stomach, cuffed, and Mirandized.

"If you'd left her alone, we could've cut a deal," Fredricks said.

Scottie rolled onto his side and gave me a stink eye. "Damn. You a cop? I don't believe it."

"Thanks for this," I said, and slid the heroin bundle into an evidence bag. "I'll mail you a check."

Chapter 2

Sunday

Sunday was my day off, and I was antsy. I'd had a restless night, disturbed by thoughts of Scottie's bulk and the baby-faced kids.

I didn't want to spend the day at home, alone with puppy-sized dust bunnies and the neglected gloxinia dropping its shriveled furry leaves. It was an energy-sapping house, and I lacked the energy to do anything about it. I decided to visit my grandmother, Fern.

Merle, a yellow dog of indeterminate breed, watched my every movement for a sign he might be included in my day's plans. When I asked, "Want to practice?" he wriggled with rapturous delight and wagged his tail so hard it knocked a wine glass off the coffee table. "Practice" meant searching for socks scattered in my grandmother's woods. Each find garnered a chewy treat, thus combining Merle's two favorite activities— going out and snacks.

I grabbed my car keys and set off for Fern's farmhouse.

Five minutes later I crashed into a squad car.

Verwood's only traffic feature is a one-way loop around the county courthouse. In England, it would be called a roundabout. In Boston, a rotary. We call ours the Circle of Death. Sometimes it's tricky to join the flow of traffic, but once you are in the circle you can relax, since you have the right-of-way. So I relaxed, and reached for my water bottle in the drink holder, just as a county sheriff's squad car leapt in front of me, its siren shrieking. I slammed on the brakes. *Bam!* My '98 Corolla smashed into the rear of the squad car. Merle, all ninety pounds of him, thudded against the back of my seat.

I directed a few choice words at the puddle soaking my lap, blotting at it with some napkins I found in the glove compartment. The squad car's door opened and—oh no—my favorite Essex County cop stepped out. Lt. Anselmo Morales walked over to my window. His nice crooked smile was nowhere in evidence, and behind wire-rim glasses his black eyes flashed irritation.

"You okay, Stella?" He bent down to get a closer look at me, and I smelled soap and cloves. Merle began a full-body wiggle, begging for a pat on the head. I knew just how he felt.

"You didn't hear the siren?" Anselmo's voice was a no-nonsense baritone with a hint of Hispanic accent.

"I heard it. I was reaching for my water and didn't react fast enough. I'm terribly sorry." This humiliating story would tweet-percolate through the law enforcement gossip grapevine at the speed of light.

"There's no damage to either car but I've gotta write this up anyway. Right now I'm answering an urgent call, so you can pick up your citation at the law enforcement center. Next time, don't drink and drive." He took off, siren blaring.

Recently Anselmo and I had worked together on a homicide investigation. I worshipped him silently. He was intelligent, dedicated, easy to look at. But, alas, married. "Delicious," I said, turning to check on Merle. He gazed thoughtfully into my eyes, no doubt intrigued by the food adjective. "Such a lollipop." His tail thumped on the seat in agreement.

Fern lives on Clark Rudman Road, eight miles outside town. My car's shocks couldn't handle the ruts on her lane, so I parked next to her mailbox and walked two hundred yards to her house. Hillary and Bill, Fern's curious donkeys, peered at me over the fence as a rooster's rude cries disrupted the mid-morning quiet. Merle bounded ahead to harass the thousands of moles tunneling in her field.

Someone else had braved the lane's ruts. A car bounced past me on its way out. I thought I recognized the driver, Harry Edwards, a local lawyer. Only one reason he was leaving her house at nine a.m.—he'd spent the night with her. I'd always suspected he was one of her lovers, since he did her legal work for free. Fern's men tended to be a grateful bunch.

The dilapidated farmhouse looked nearly abandoned, except for the climbing roses she tended carefully, entwined around trellises. The house hadn't been painted in decades, and the rusty tin roof leaked under the eaves. The porch was hazardous, with water-rotted columns, missing balusters, and sagging steps. The farmhouse was a huge worry to me. I hated to see it deteriorate, but I couldn't afford the new roof it needed. I took Fern's trash to the recycling center once a week and paid a neighbor's boy to mow the weeds.

I tapped on the back door, then pushed it open. "Fern?"

People find it odd, even mildly shocking, that I call my grandmother by her given name. I always have. In the Lavender household there were no Nanas or Mommys, only my great-grandmother, Phoebe, grandmother, Fern, my mother, Grace, and me. We all grew up in this farmhouse.

"In here," she called. I found her in the kitchen sorting through a pile of cents-off coupons. My heart warmed at the sight of her cherubic face, framed with a white pixie cut. I leaned down and kissed her cheek. "Who was that leaving?"

"Harry Edwards." The lawyer, as I'd suspected.

"Ah. This is recent?"

"Oh, we go way back. He made me breakfast. A lovely omelet." Fern wore jeans and a red t-shirt, nondescript on any other sixty-two-year-old, but, with curves in all the right places, she was a man magnet. Both of us were exceedingly puzzled that I didn't inherit that exact gene. My attractive force was more like static cling—annoying and easily peeled away. "There's grits left, want some?" she asked.

"Not really. Just coffee." Congealed grits in the dented saucepan, worry over this falling-down farmhouse, and the reminder that my grandmother's love life was infinitely more exciting than mine—all combined to irritate me, a familiar feeling. I poured myself a cup and added milk.

"Can you shop for me? You can have these coupons." She seemed to live on toast and cheese, washed down with tarry coffee. She dug around in her black satchel and pulled out a five-dollar bill. "I need tomatoes, milk, and cheddar slices—real cheese, not the cheese food you got last time."

"I did? Sorry." I put the money in my pocket. Five dollars might have bought Fern's groceries twenty years ago, but I'd spend at least forty. We both knew it, and neither mentioned it.

"You have to eat. I'll make you some eggs," she said. She scraped butter into her cast-iron frying pan, heavy, black, seasoned to perfection. It, and the kitchen, hadn't changed in years. Checkered linoleum had been put down around 1950. The stove was antique—not the valuable kind, but the kind with two non-working burners. Knotty-pine cupboards held everything from plain ironstone to elegant porcelain, jelly jars next to crystal.

I wondered how much longer Fern could live like this. Her only income came from the painting classes she gave and an occasional sale of one of her pieces, so I paid her bills and bought the groceries. I wanted her to sell the property and move into a convenient apartment. The ramshackle farmhouse wasn't worth much, but sixty-eight acres on a state highway had to be valuable. Fern didn't want to live anywhere else. She refused to sell.

She handed me a plate of eggs and toast and we gossiped

about her neighbors and my job. Fern liked to hear about my work. She understood why I was a cop—she'd lost a daughter, my mother, Grace, to crime. We never admitted aloud that Grace was dead, but twenty-two years ago my mother had disappeared in a robbery-abduction. A cold case. I'd studied the case file enough times to know what happened to her would be a mystery until, some day, someone talked. Unlikely. A misery Fern and I shared.

Rain hit the tin roof, at first a patter, then a gushing downpour. Within minutes, water started dripping into a bucket placed strategically in the hallway. I sighed. I could ignore the leaks only when it wasn't raining. I rinsed my plate. "Before I put Merle to work, show me your new painting," I said.

Fern led the way to one of her front rooms, converted into a practical workspace. Canvases leaned against the walls; props and bespeckled drop cloths littered the floor. A regular "plop, plop, plop" into a bowl in the corner caught my attention.

"That's a new leak," I said. "Where's it coming from?"

Fern ignored me. Okay, stupid question. "I mean, is there water in the upstairs front too?"

"Sort of. It's drizzling down the wall. A trickle. Here, what do you think?" She pulled a canvas onto an easel.

In the past year, Fern's style had toughened, the brush marks more emphatic, wider, as if she didn't have patience for fine lines. A smudge of white for light, a swath of black for shadow, enough detail to show the subjects. This painting was a still life of my old toys—a dirty brown bear in a Cinderella crown, holding a magic wand, propped against a small rocking chair.

"Gosh, you remembered those?" I asked.

"Turn around. I dug them out of your closet upstairs."

Brownie, along with the crown, the rocker, and the wand, lay in a heap on the floor. "They look better in the picture."

Fern looked wistful. "I paint the memories, too. I miss that little girl. It's yours, of course. It wouldn't mean much to anyone else."

I put my arms around her. "It's a beautiful picture. Thank you. Now I have to hide some socks."

CHAPTER 3

Monday morning

Richard was absorbed in his latest management book, *Monday Morning Leadership*. My boss was going to ignore me whether I stood or sat, so I might as well be comfortable, and I sank into a chair. I studied him, looking for something to appreciate, perhaps what he was wearing, like his polished wingtips or today's crisp shirt of palest peach, a pleasing complement to his mocha-brown skin.

"I want a different assignment," I said. "It's dangerous out there. I feel like bait." My stomach churned as I waited for his response. A million dust motes danced in the sunlight slicing through his window blinds, striping the flat gray carpet and my favorite shoes, red slingbacks. The heels were worn. I tapped a reminder into my phone: *red heels*. I'd take them to the demented shoe-repair guy in his tiny cubbyhole at the mall, who ranted under his breath about the God Damn Government as he tore shoes apart.

I empathized. I, too, felt like ranting about the God Damn Government—my employer, the State Bureau of Investigation. Richard was the SBI special agent in charge of the capital district. I was a mere special agent, in charge of very little. I hoped Richard was absorbing leadership tips from his book that would work to my advantage.

His coffeemaker puffed out clouds of rich smells. When the puffing changed to hissing, as if it were a cue, he put the book down and swiveled in his leather chair. "Fredricks tells me you're good at undercover."

"Does he?"

"Before that you were working with the inter-agency bunch."

"Yup." I'd spent three months zooming around North Carolina in a helicopter with a thermal imager, looking for indoor pot gardens and meth labs.

"How'd you like it?" This was new, Richard caring whether I liked an assignment.

"Once I got over being airsick you mean? I learned a lot."

Richard spun again to enjoy his corner-office view of the parking lot. "You hated it, didn't you?"

"Every bleeping minute." I hated it from the first day—when the pilot, a state trooper twenty years my senior, grabbed my thigh, forcing me to express my need for personal space in blunt language—until the last day, when we raided a trailer full of thriving plants under gro-lights and arrested a man who wept as his four children wondered where they'd get their lunch money now. No, drug interdiction was not my favorite assignment.

He poured himself a cup of coffee and stared at me over the rim of his mug. "You're not a team player, Stella."

Ouch. I thought about volunteering to read last week's book, still on his desk, *Six Sigma Team Pocket Guide*. "I was good on the inter-agency team, wasn't I? I followed regulations. Were there complaints?"

"Hank didn't like you."

"The pilot? Hank liked me a lot. I had to make him not like me so much."

Richard frowned. He hated hearing about interpersonal conflicts. "You've put in a lot of overtime. Take the afternoon off. Maybe you'll feel different tomorrow." He opened his desk drawer and took out his cigar box. He selected one, laying it on his desk in preparation for ceremonial cutting and après-lunch smoking.

"I doubt it." I wanted to grab *Monday Morning Leadership* off his desk and find the page describing me: a Driver, not a Passenger; a square peg/round hole misfit.

He found a different metaphor. "I'd rather pitch to your strengths, Stella. I'll keep you in mind for a different assignment."

That was the first thing he'd said to me in a long time that I liked. Maybe those books were working.

I drove home, changed into jeans, and picked up Merle, planning to take him for a hike along the Rocky River. As I passed the high school, I saw a teenage girl hitchhiking. *Idiot.* I slowed to a stop and she got into my car, slinging a backpack onto the floor. She looked about sixteen, with small neat features, blond bangs covering her forehead, and a ponytail to the middle of her back. Silver hoops marched up her earlobes and a slim figure meant she could wear the skinny jeans I had to avoid.

"Thanks," she said. "Women never stop."

"Where are you going?"

"Silver Hills." An expensive gated golf community a few miles north.

"I'll take you there if you'll listen to these numbers." I was making an effort to keep calm, not throttle her for terminal stupidity. "There are almost six thousand registered sex offenders in this state. They've been convicted. But only one in seven men arrested for rape is convicted, and only one in twenty-five reported rapes results in an arrest. And most rapes aren't reported."

She closed her eyes and puffed out a breath, fluttering her bangs. "Spare me the lecture. I have to babysit, and the kid's dad didn't pick me up like he said he would. I waited at the school bus stop for an hour. What was I supposed to do?"

"Let me simplify. Predators look for girls like you. Girls are picked up and never seen again."

"Yeah, yeah. What makes you so smart?"

I showed her my ID. "What's your name?"

"Nikki Truly. You're a cop? You're no older than me."

"What makes you so smart?"

She laughed, showing even white teeth, transforming her face from sullen to cute. "OK. I get it. Next time I'll call a cab."

The entrance to Silver Hills was blocked by a red-striped boom, a flimsy barrier between its residents and undesirables. A spiky-haired guard emerged from his hut, nodded at Nikki, and raised the boom.

"He knows you," I said.

"I live here," she said. Wow. What would it be like, to have parents with money? Fern, a literally starving artist, had raised me. Many's the night she and I chowed down on oatmeal and beans, having exhausted our food stamps for the month. I drove slowly, past starter castles and baronial mansions with rock walls, each one landscaped at a price probably exceeding my salary. We passed a golf course, signs to a club house, tennis courts, a pool. "Where to?" I asked.

"The Mercers', where I'm supposed to take care of their kid." She directed me through hilly, curved streets into the driveway of a pink-brick two-story with a three-car garage. Compared to the houses around it, 1146 looked ill-tended. A patchy sod border encircled the house and a few small shrubs struggled in the muddy red earth of planting beds. "Come in with me," Nikki said. "I'll introduce you to the dad. You can give him the lecture so he won't be late again." I rolled down the windows, told Merle I'd be right back, and followed her to the front door.

There were no cars in the driveway but through a garage

window we could see a new-looking, burgundy SUV. "That's Kent's car. I wonder why he didn't pick me up," Nikki said. She tried the front door—it was unlocked. We walked into a high-ceilinged living room. Warm sunlight, tinted green from the trees outside, reflected from polished, oak floors. Stairs curved up to a second-floor balcony. The walls were covered with photographs—pictures of faces, hands, insects, babies, animals—living things. I didn't inherit any myself, but I recognize genuine artistic talent when I see it, and was drawn to photos of a toddler with delicate features, dark hair with straight-across bangs, hazel eyes. "This is the child who lives here?" I asked. "She's beautiful."

"Yeah, Paige. Her mom's a photographer. Kent?" Nikki called. There was no answer. "I'll see if Paige is here." She climbed the stairs.

I wandered into the kitchen, an acre of pickled-oak cabinets and black granite, cluttered with dishes and half-eaten food. French doors were open so I stepped onto the cypress deck, where a blue umbrella offered shade to a teak table. Below, a sandy path led through white-petaled dogwoods down to the shore of Two Springs Lake. A pretty postcard scene.

But on the patio below, something unnatural caught my eye. Bare feet, muscular legs.

Unmoving, still.

I leaned over the deck railing, recoiling when I realized what I saw.

A man lay on his back, probably dead, I thought immediately, based on the puddled blood that had poured from great gaping slices running from the crook of his elbows to his wrists. Under a golden tan, his skin was waxy, bluish. His hair was crinkly blond.

What was doubly shocking, I recognized him. Last night, this

man had sold me twelve hundred dollars' worth of oxys.
In a styrofoam to-go box.

CHAPTER 4

Monday afternoon

I called nine-one-one, then took a closer look at the body. It didn't look like a suicide because there was little blood on the man's torso or shorts. He couldn't cut one arm, then the other, and not get blood everywhere. Blood had spurted from the arteries in his arms onto the stones underneath, forming two distinct puddles. But there was no sign of a struggle, as though he had passively accepted his fatal injuries.

I had to tell Nikki, warning her it was a horrific scene. She leaned over the deck railing, and when she saw the man's body, she gasped, then screamed "Kent!" over and over, so loudly they probably heard it in the next county. She started down the stairs to the patio. I pulled her back and led her, hysterical and shaking, into the house where I parked her on a sofa.

As we waited for the police, Nikki clutched a pillow, rocked, covered her face. I sat beside her, patted her back, antsy to look for evidence, but not wanting to contaminate the scene. I'd spotted smudges of blood in the kitchen and on the deck. Nikki and I had probably walked on it. It was best we disturb nothing else.

The dead man was the father who was supposed to pick her up to babysit. I was itching to quiz her, extract every single byte of information from her skull. How often was she in this house? Did she ever visit for any other reason? What kind of person was he? Did he get along with his wife? Who else took care of

28

the baby? Did Nikki know he sold drugs? But questioning the teenager would be the investigators' job.

She took a shuddering breath, dropped the pillow, and stood. "I have to find something."

I had to stop her. "The police won't want us touching anything."

"Fuck them." She started down a hallway and stopped at the door of an office, now trashed. Files dumped, desk drawers opened and tossed, papers, folders, and supplies strewn everywhere. I saw a keyboard and mouse, a monitor, but no computer.

"Shit!" she wailed. She turned and ran up the stairs, charging into the master bedroom, an enormous room with two walk-in closets. I trotted right behind her. When she began opening drawers, I said, "Stop. This is a crime scene."

"You don't understand!"

"You'll be charged as accessory to murder if you mess with stuff. It's bad enough your fingerprints are everywhere."

Nikki looked at me, frowning. "Seriously?"

"Come on, let's wait by my car."

Deflated, she followed me downstairs. When I opened the front door, there stood my favorite law enforcement officer, Anselmo Morales. His eyes squinted, like he couldn't quite believe what he saw. "Stella?"

What could I say? *We have to stop meeting like this?* But it was no joke. "There's a dead man out back, on the patio. I was giving the babysitter here a ride. Nikki Truly, this is Lt. Morales."

We both looked at Nikki, who burst into tears again, either from grief or frustration that she couldn't find what she wanted. Or a ploy to elicit pity, in case she was about to be arrested for tampering with evidence? Something about her seemed calculated, not so innocent.

"Officer Chamberlain will take your statement," he said,

motioning a young deputy out of his car. They spoke briefly. Chamberlain was an African-American woman with pronounced cheekbones and reddish hair cut very short. She treated a sniffling Nikki gently as she took notes, walking us through the past half hour. She asked us to stop by the law enforcement center later, to provide fingerprints for elimination purposes, then let us go.

Nikki told me she lived about a half mile away, on the other side of Silver Hills, so I offered to drive her home. She had calmed down and even greeted Merle with a pat on his head. "I have a dog," she said, buckling her seat belt. "Tiny. He's my mother's, actually. He barks a lot. Bites people."

"Really? Bites?"

She held out her thumb to show me a tiny puncture, then leaned against the door, chewing her fingernails. "I bet you see a lot of dead people," she said. "In your work, I mean."

"Actually, no. It's rare. That was a terrible sight."

"Not my first dead body. My stepdad died when I was twelve. Insulin overdose. Or painkillers. They weren't sure which. I found his body."

"That's awful." So young, to be exposed to death, then and now.

"No great loss. I hated him. But I loved Kent." She sighed raggedly.

I was puzzled. She called him by his first name. "Was he a good friend?" A *special* friend, I wanted to ask but prying might shut her down.

Turned out I didn't need to be so delicate in my questioning, for she inhaled a big gulp of air and wailed, "We were lovers!" More tears. I handed her tissues, feeling a pang of pity for her genuine sorrow.

"The police will ask you about your relationship," I said. I would have to tell Anselmo. A teenage girlfriend—with all the complications that implied—could contribute to a motive for the murder. She'd told Deputy Chamberlain she was seventeen, over the state's age of consent, so the law couldn't have stopped their relationship. His furious wife, her dismayed parents, or an angry boyfriend—this particular match-up could have triggered rage in any number of hearts.

"I don't care who you tell," she said, and blew her nose. "My mom knows. People know."

"He was married, you said."

"I don't want to talk about it."

I recognized denial, but Nikki *would* be talking about it, sooner rather than later.

Her house was another mini-mansion, red brick with black shutters, white azaleas, and a koi pond surrounded by flagstone. She hauled her backpack out of my car. Her sad face was smudged with mascara. "I'd ask you in but my mom's home and you do not want to see her freak out over this."

I sped back to 1146 Fair Oaks Lane, warning Merle there would be no hike today. With a deep sigh, he stretched along the full width of my backseat, accepting disappointment graciously. The police will find Mercer's drug stash, I thought. Who else had bought from him? Had his killer been after his drugs? His money? Where did he get them? How much business did he do? Anselmo would want me to fill in the blanks.

A dozen technicians busied themselves in the victim's house, on the deck and patio.

"Let's talk," Anselmo said. "Away from the crowd." I followed him along a narrow path leading through scrub and pines, down to the lake. Mid-afternoon sun had converted moist air into a steam bath. He took off his jacket and loosened his tie. "Chamberlain filled me in on her interview with you and the babysitter. What else can you tell me?"

A rocky strip of sand encircled the lake. I sat on a fallen tree. "Kent Mercer manages a restaurant, Clemmie's," I said. "I bought oxycodone from him last night."

"That's Lincoln Teller's restaurant." Anselmo picked up a flat stone and skimmed it out onto the lake. One, two, three bounces, waking a turtle that disappeared with a splash. He tried again with another stone. Four bounces this time. "Nice place. Didn't know it was a drugstore."

"This guy seemed to be an independent contractor."

"I definitely need you on this case. Find out his sources, his customers. His murder might be a drug buy gone south." He turned to face me. "But. Keep yourself safe. I mean it. No more driving off bridges." He was referring to the last time we worked together, a case that ended with me inside my car, underwater.

"You'll have to call my boss at the SBI." Richard controlled my fate. But he was usually responsive to requests from local law enforcement, so I allowed myself to feel a surge of hope. Working with Anselmo, finding Mercer's killer—a dream assignment.

I threw my own rock into the lake. Plop. A breeze picked up, turning the lake's surface into sparkling ripples. An osprey cheeped overhead and, as I scanned the trees to find its nest, I noticed a metallic glint on the otherwise pristine lakeshore, about twenty yards away. Curious, I walked over and saw a new-looking mini-CD, the blank kind you can record on. *Clifford* was hand-printed on its label. Anselmo picked it up with a handkerchief and we started back to the house.

A door slammed. The ambulance had arrived. Two EMTs hopped out and came around the house to the patio. Chamberlain and I watched as they wrapped the body for transport to the medical examiner's office in Raleigh. She'd found a smear of blood on a decking support. "I think maybe the killer stood there," she said. "He had blood on his clothes, or his body, and brushed against the wood. There's a distinct fingerprint, a pocked loop."

"Good find," I said. I meant it. Under a deck wasn't a place for much of anything but spiders, but a bloody fingerprint was a five-star piece of evidence.

Chamberlain showed me pills she'd found on the floor of his office. "Seemed to be part of the contents of the dumped filing cabinet. Odd that they weren't taken." Also odd—they weren't in bottles but sorted into snack-size baggies, labeled with the pill's trade name, hand-written. Each baggie held small quantities of sedatives, tranquilizers, antidepressants, and painkillers. All prescription drugs, but without the bottle we couldn't contact a pharmacy, trace the script back to a doctor.

In the kitchen, an answering machine blinked. As soon as it had been dusted for prints, Anselmo pushed "play." The first message was Nikki—"Hey, I'm at school waiting. You're not answering your cell. Thought you were gonna get me."

The second was delivered in a familiar voice. "Hey, Kent, weren't we supposed to meet at two thirty? Get your butt over here."

"Sounds like Lincoln Teller. What's he got to do with this guy?" Chamberlain asked.

"He owns Clemmie's, where Mercer worked," I said. Just then the wall phone rang. Anselmo put it on speaker and answered it.

"Who are you?" The caller was a man.

Anselmo identified himself. "And you are?"

"Wesley Raintree. Kent's stepfather. What's going on? Where's Temple? Is Paige okay?"

Anselmo took his address and told him only that someone would be there soon to explain. This man was the closest kin to Kent Mercer we had at this point, since no one knew where Temple, his wife, was. I felt a twinge of misgiving at Raintree's mention of Paige, the toddler. Nikki had said Paige was supposed to be here. Perhaps she was with her mother.

While I waited for Richard to call Anselmo back, I went through the French doors onto the deck, to think. I had trouble with the scenario. Disarray in the office might indicate a robbery. A computer was apparently missing and shelves in the living room were bare. But why hadn't there been a struggle? Mercer looked well able to defend himself. The patio stones were damp from the mid-day rain but rain hadn't diluted the pool of his blood, so he'd died in sunshine, after it stopped. Lying there with open arms, as if welcoming the knife.

I heard a car door slam and went back through the house to the front door. A very pregnant woman stood in the driveway, glowering at Chamberlain. Her rosy cheeks and round belly contrasted with heavy black eye shadow, long hair teased into a pouf, and acrylic nails painted like silver foil. That rarely seen Blessed-Mary-meets-Jersey-Shore look. "What's going on?" she asked. "What happened?"

"You're Temple Mercer?" Chamberlain asked. "I'm so sorry. I have dreadful news. Your husband is dead. Agent Lavender here discovered his body about two hours ago."

Temple grasped my arm and I recoiled—those nails were like claws. "Who are you? What is she talking about?"

In jeans and a Haw River Festival t-shirt, I looked like a casual passerby. I dug out my ID and explained that I'd driven Nikki to this house when Kent didn't pick her up.

Her eyes searched my face. "What happened to him?"

I told her, as gently as I could, what I knew about her husband's death.

She closed her eyes. "Unreal. You're saying he bled to death? Where is he now?"

"The body's with the medical examiner," I said. "This must be a terrible shock. I'm so sorry."

"Is my daughter inside?" Her voice quavered. "Did your people take her somewhere?"

Dammit. I'd hoped she knew where the child was. "No," I said. "Nikki came here to babysit but found only your husband."

Temple frowned. "Maybe she's with her grandpa, Wesley."

I shook my head, remembering how Wesley, on the Mercers' phone, had asked if Paige was okay. "She must be with someone. Give me names." I handed her my notebook and a pen.

"Oh my God, this isn't real." She took the pen, closed her eyes in thought, scribbled names. "That's everyone I know. None of them would take her and not tell me. Unless they told Kent. Oh, what a nightmare. What should I do with this?" She waved the notebook.

I led her to Anselmo. I was not much more than a bystander at this point, not yet cleared to work on this case. Anselmo told Chamberlain to contact everyone on the list. "While she's calling," he told Temple, "tell me where you were today."

"Spa." She waggled her silver nails. "I was frantic to get out of the house. This baby's due any minute, and I am sick of looking like a manatee. This morning I was cranky enough to— . . . Never mind. Was it robbery? What happened?" We led her around the house to the patio encircled with yellow tape. She pointed to the blood stains. "That's Kent's blood?" She turned to face me. "I honestly don't know how I feel right now, sort of numb, like it's not real. Now I'm exhausted, can you blame me? I can't even—Kent's dead! Where's Paige? You're standing here asking stupid questions, and my child is missing!"

I showed her the mini-CD I'd found on the lakeshore, *Clifford* hand-printed on its label. "Do you recognize this?"

"Yeah, it's Paige's. Kent recorded stories for her, since he works evenings and misses her bedtime. She carries them in her boom box. Where'd you find it?"

I exchanged glances with Anselmo. How much more could

this woman take? "On the lakeshore."

"What?" Her voice rose. "Oh, my God," she moaned, rocking sideways. "Do something! What is wrong with you people?!"

I pulled Anselmo aside. "My dog's trained to track. He's outside in my car. What if . . ." He nodded, and I ran inside. Upstairs, in the child's room, I found a tiny sock in a laundry bin. Pink with white ducks on the cuff.

Merle's leather harness was in the trunk of my car. It was his signal to go to work. I buckled it around him and led him to the back of the house, to the patio. "Check," I whispered, waving the sock under his nose and removing the lead. Nose down, he circled the patio, ignoring the puddled blood, pausing at the foot of the stairs, then charging into the scrubby woods. I could barely keep up and called him to slow. He looked up for an instant but he was a dog on a mission, a little-pink-sock mission. He paralleled the lakeshore for a hundred yards, through brambly underbrush that scratched my legs. I could only imagine what it had done to a toddler's tender skin.

He paused in a clearing, over what he'd found: a disposable diaper, dry, recently dropped. A diaper? Why? He waited for me, then took off again, drawn by a scent that must have been strong. I pushed away dark thoughts and trampled after him, finally catching up at the rocky lakeshore where he trotted, nose down, one way, then another, then back. He'd lost the scent.

Shit. Shit shit shit.

A breeze rippled the lake's surface, disturbing the reflection of whipped-cream clouds and bluer than blue sky. Blue, despondent, wretched, downcast—pick any or all, that's how I felt.

Paige Mercer was probably in the lake.

CHAPTER 5

Monday afternoon

When I told Anselmo that Merle had lost the child's scent on the lakeshore, pain flickered over his face as the implication sunk in. "We might have to drag the lake but it's early days. Listen, I talked to your boss and he okayed it—you're officially on this case. I need you to take over the interviews. Start with Raintree and Teller. I've got to focus on the child."

Inwardly excited, I kept my face solemn. "Anything. Glad to help."

He wanted to keep Temple's car overnight for a forensic once-over, so I gave her a ride to a friend's house a few blocks away, and waited as she struggled to pull herself out of the car and trudged up to the door. I felt sick for her, for her tragic loss, the uncertainty about her toddler, giving birth alone. Though from what I was learning about Kent Mercer—dealing pills, unfaithful—he was a poor husband. Would she be better off by herself? Had she decided to do something about it? Her alibi would probably check out, I thought, but it wasn't impossible to arrange a murder. If you knew the right people.

I rushed home to drop off Merle and change into more suitable clothes—a black pantsuit and ankle boots, my work uniform—before I went to Wesley Raintree's house. The "someone" Anselmo had told him to expect was me.

Wesley, Kent Mercer's stepfather, lived ten minutes from Silver Hills, in a brick ranch with a lush green lawn, picture-perfect proof of the miracle of chemicals. Ex-military, I thought, observing Wesley's buzzed gray hair and a lean, muscular body held very straight—I could almost see the uniform.

"What's going on?" he demanded, waving me into a dust-free living room pleasantly furnished with chintz, dark wood, and plush carpet.

I'd heard that bad news should be delivered like removing a band-aid—quickly. "Mr. Raintree, your stepson, Kent Mercer, is dead. He was murdered today, at his home."

"Murdered? Really?" Disbelief flickered across his face as I nodded yes. "Well, he was a slime ball. Have a seat."

Bingo. I sank into a squishy chair covered with a cheerful floral. "Not what I expected you to say."

He spoke gruffly but decisively, like a man used to being listened to. "He's my wife's son from her first marriage. In her eyes, perfect. In mine, an all-around loser." Wesley counted off on his fingers. "One, he ruined my son Bryce—that's his half-brother. Two, he borrowed money from his mother countless times and never paid it back. Three, he cheated on his wife."

I could have added: four, he was a pill pusher. Wesley didn't hold back his feelings, and I appreciated that. No murky waters here. Where to begin? "Despite those feelings, you called him today," I said.

"I try to get along with him. I want to be part of Paige's life, not absent like I was with my son."

At the mention of the toddler, I tried very hard to keep my face expressionless. "Purpose of your call?"

"To see if Temple needed any help. She's going to have another baby any day now."

Something about the other son nagged at me. "Mr. Raintree, you mentioned your son, 'ruined' by his brother?"

Wesley stared at me, his self-discipline seeming to hold him rigid as he rubbed his face hard. "My son has issues. Of no interest to you."

I nodded. "Of course, but we'll be talking to him. Want to give me a preview?"

"He's eighteen. Dropped out of high school to be a body-builder." Wesley fell silent for a moment, as if deciding what I should know. "Bryce is smart. He could have achieved anything, but Kent taught him to cheat, slide through school, have fun, let someone else do the work." Wesley gritted his teeth, working his jaw muscles. "My wife indulged both of them, gave them anything they wanted. Then she got sick and I had to retire from the Navy to take care of her, after thirty-three years."

"Where is your wife now?"

He cleared his throat and for a moment sadness etched his face. "Sunny died eight months ago. Cancer. It's been tough."

His only son a loser in his eyes, his wife dead, a retirement he resents. "And Bryce?" I asked.

"Right this minute, you mean? No idea. He lives in a room behind my garage, but he comes and goes as he pleases. Right before Sunny got sick, she made us all go to counseling. She was afraid I'd kill him, I guess." Wesley flushed. "I mean, I was hard on the kid, fed up with him leeching off his mother. This therapist had us work out an agreement where Bryce pays rent. I don't bail him out of trouble, don't help him. He has to earn money for his gym. Be responsible for himself."

I wondered if that was Wesley's fingerprint under the Mercer house decking, though his disappointment in Bryce, blaming Kent Mercer, didn't seem a sufficient motive for murder. I asked him to go to the sheriff's office and get fingerprinted, to rule himself out.

Unless there was something he hadn't told me.

I called Richard to give him an update, confirm he'd talked to Anselmo. "Yeah, he called. No problem. Just keep me informed."

"I'm on my way to interview Lincoln Teller." I reminded him that the murder victim had managed Lincoln's restaurant, Clemmie's.

Richard hissed in a breath. "Any way to keep that under your bonnet?" His acute sensitivity to media interest in SBI cases bordered on paranoia.

"Short of an injunction, no," I said. "As soon as the press learns about the murder, they'll know where Mercer worked."

"Don't you mention it."

"I promise. Can you assign me a researcher?"

"I got you the best. Your boyfriend."

"He's not my boyfriend." A useless protest, since Richard said that only to annoy me. He meant Hogan. My ex-fiancé, Hogan Leith, dumped by me when I found he'd been secretly texting lassies he'd found on *stupidslut.com*.

Still, I had to work with him. Hogan was an SBI researcher, a gifted and talented information seeker. He could look up your cat's vaccination records, your electric bill, what you watched on cable. He was an online genius. Too bad he was so self-serving in the application of those talents.

Lincoln Teller's vintage Jaguar convertible was parked by Clemmie's front door. Raindrops beaded on its polished marine-blue finish. I peeked in the window to admire the immaculate black leather seats and walnut trim. At four thirty in the afternoon, the parking lot was nearly vacant, but crowds would begin to fill the place in an hour.

An African-American football hero who'd grown up in Verwood, Lincoln had spent a dozen years in the pros, then returned home to open Clemmie's, the restaurant named after his wife, Clementine. He'd been enormously popular in the community and throughout his career, a gentle giant who earned everyone's respect with his warm and courteous nature, reflecting his mother's firm training in civility and manners. It was hard to believe he'd spent years in such a violent sport. He and I were acquainted from a couple years back when I'd helped Clementine locate her father. The old guy had walked out on gambling debts, and she'd been afraid for his safety. With the help of my favorite researcher, Hogan, I found her father in— where else?—Las Vegas, trying futilely to improve his financial picture.

Clemmie's was quiet. Lincoln sat in a corner booth, dominating the room with his size, impeccable in a custom-made charcoal-gray suit, gleaming white shirt, and gray silk tie. Next to him a woman typed furiously on a laptop. Lincoln introduced her as Ursula Budd, his bookkeeper. I had seen her in one of Fern's art classes, and remembered her unusual looks—smooth pale skin and wiry orange hair, her features plain except for tilted greenish eyes, like a cat's. Ursula scooped up the computer. "I'll take this into the office," she said. She headed toward the kitchen. Lincoln watched her walk away, seemingly mesmerized by the movement of her long legs and swaying hips under her silky dress. Something else I'd heard about Lincoln— rumors about women.

I took her place in the booth and declined the beer he offered but accepted a coffee. He brought it to me himself, from a nearby cart. Tantalizing smells wafted from the kitchen, noisy with voices and laughter as the staff prepped for dinner. I decided to begin with heartfelt compliments. "I was here two nights ago. Fantastic food. And I love the happy colors." Soft-orange tablecloths, lime-green walls, vases of delicate, lemon-yellow lilies.

"Thank you, Stella, but I'm color-blind." He leaned back in the booth. "It's all gray to me. My wife gets the credit."

"But the restaurant was your dream, right?"

"Put everything I had into it. But it barely makes a profit.

41

I'm going to have to fire my manager."

"Actually, that's why I'm here, to talk to you about Kent Mercer."

Before I could explain, Lincoln jumped in. "*Lordy,* it is hard to get answers out of that weasel. Every time I look at the books I have a dozen questions he somehow can't answer right then, or the next time, or ever." He picked up a fork and rapped hard on the table. "The way Kent tells it, he has to comp people, but isn't sure how many, and the expense ratio is a little high, but maybe he's double-counting the retained tips or depreciating the wine cellar or some restaurant accounting thing I don't understand." His voice had grown strangled and quiet.

"Lincoln, Kent Mercer was murdered today."

He twisted toward me. "What?" He looked stunned. "Man, I wondered why he wasn't here. What happened?"

"We're not releasing details. It happened at his home, this afternoon." My intuition told me Lincoln had nothing to do with Mercer's murder, but I've learned the hard way that my hunches depend on my hormones and caffeine intake. A cup of strong coffee and Linc's pheromones had my intuition in a twist. So, for the moment, I pretended he was guilty as hell, perhaps even involved in Mercer's drug sales. "Tell me what you did today."

"Got up about six, went for a run. I go around Two Springs Lake. Takes me about an hour."

"You live on the lake now?"

"Silver Hills. Moved there in January. Clementine's idea. She feels more protected, you know—it's gated." His hands played with the fork, bending its tines like they were pipe cleaners.

"Silver Hills is where Mercer lived, too."

He shook his head. "Yeah. Maybe that's where my money went."

"After your run?"

"I had breakfast with Clementine and the kids. I drove my oldest to school and went by the chamber of commerce to review menus for a dinner. Went home, called around, and put together a golf game for the weekend. Talked to my agent about some upcoming events—charities, camps for kids . . . you know. Then I came back to the restaurant, to go over the books with Ursula. Kent was supposed to be here at two thirty."

He slumped back and looked at me. "Stella, I'm not a businessman. Ursula says the bills haven't been paid in months. She's prepared checks, but Kent's not signed or mailed them." He studied the randomly-pointed tines of the fork he'd been handling. "Darn it." He pressed them back into line, one by one.

"Were you home alone?"

"Yeah, Clementine had a doctor's appointment and the kids were at school."

I wished this big sweet man had an alibi. The phone calls might help; we could get his records and look at the times. But he was alone for the afternoon. He was in Silver Hills during the time window for the murder. He could easily overpower Mercer, who, it seemed, had nearly ruined him financially, cheating him and his family, on top of threatening his reputation with illegal drug sales.

"I may want to talk with you again, Lincoln," I said.

He shrugged, both hands in the air. "What for? I'm not a killer, Stella, you know that."

That's what they all say, though they're usually not as well-dressed.

I went to the cart and refilled my coffee cup, and Lincoln walked me to the office. He told Ursula, briefly, about Kent Mercer's murder. Her only reaction was a narrowing of her tilted eyes as she searched his face. In collusion? I couldn't tell. He left us to talk in private, and I asked her what her job was.

"I do payroll. I also print checks for unpaid bills, though Kent signs and mails them. But look." She showed me an invoice from a groceries wholesaler for over seven thousand, a bill from Marystone Meats demanding almost ten, and a letter from the seafood distributor threatening to cease deliveries if their account wasn't paid in the next five days. "He's nearly ruined this restaurant. Who do you think killed him?"

"Too early to say. I'm learning he didn't have many friends. You here full time?"

"Oh no. Just two days a week. I help a neighbor, June Devon. And I have my seniors. You know Paradise Keep—the senior apartments? I spent this morning in Paradise. *De*-pressing. I hope I *never* get the way those ladies are. There's Claudine— she's forgetful *and* paranoid. 'Why do you need my checkbook?' she asks, watching over my shoulder. 'Remember to pay the oilman,' she says, and her apartment is an all-electric! The other one, Olive, she's still in bed when I get there at eleven. She's wearing this filthy wrapper, an awful old rag. Can you imagine, not dressed at eleven?"

Ursula leaned toward me and her perfume hit me with a chemical smell like formaldehyde. I held my breath. "I didn't like working when Kent was here," she said. "He was always looking over my shoulder, telling me to change things. He'd reduce people's hours here and there, trying to shave a little money off a paycheck. I always changed it back. I know the cooks and waiters work hard for their money."

"Clemmie's is packed every night," I said. "It must be making a profit."

"That's the mystery—where's the money? Lincoln will want me to figure that out now."

I thanked her and left. I drove a few blocks, parked, and retrieved a fingerprint kit from the trunk of my car. "Just curious," I said to myself. "Won't prove a thing." I dusted the saucer from my coffee. I had picked up a second saucer when I refilled my cup, so I could leave one on the table. The dusting revealed Linc's prints were clearly whorls, like mine and one-third of all humans. The bloody fingerprint under Mercer's decking was a pocked-loop type. Not Lincoln Teller's.

I called Anselmo to update him. I asked about the toddler, Paige. He'd issued an Amber Alert and set up a search team command center in a vacant office outside the entrance to Silver Hills. The police were getting dozens of calls from people who wanted to volunteer or thought they'd seen her in a Topeka mall or on the beach in Florida. They were going to drag the lake.

The highway was backed up as usual, giving me an extra half hour to sit in traffic and ponder the vulnerability of baby girls. I tried to think of a positive outcome, but none came to mind. To blank out my thoughts, I turned on the radio. In Final Four basketball news . . . More rain tomorrow . . . In Silver Hills searchers are . . . Police say no leads.

CHAPTER 6

early Tuesday morning

Seven a.m. Fern and I sat on her back porch, in the fresh air, because her house was filled with a choking stench. She had run the washing machine and sewage had backed up into the lowest drain in her house, the downstairs toilet. We were waiting for the plumber.

Fern worked on my hair, taming my thick curls into a respectable braid. "I am in awe," she said, "the way you look all dressed up. I think, 'where is that sassy child who wouldn't take a bath?' Now she wears a suit, silk blouse. And heels! All navy blue, très chic!" She snapped an elastic around my braid.

"I get it from you, Fern. You're a vision even at dawn." In a pink terry robe with her white hair and rosy skin, Fern looked like strawberry shortcake.

"I can't afford a plumber," she said. "They charge sixty dollars just to show up."

"You can't afford not to have one. We'll work something out." I couldn't think what. My sad little bank account was starting to recover from the expenses of my move to Verwood. Perhaps Fern could get a small mortgage, though with little income, she wouldn't qualify and I'd have to cosign. I sighed.

Fern twisted my braid into a bun and pinned it securely. "There, all done. Where are you off to today?"

I told her about Kent Mercer and the missing child, and Fern turned on the TV. We watched the news from the porch, through a window. We waited through traffic, weather, and school stories until a report on Mercer's murder began. As the screen panned from his home to the streets of Silver Hills, a voice-over described the million-dollar homes and exclusive golf club. A cluster of nervous neighbors said they were counting on the police to solve the crime soon. "You buy into a gated community, you think you're safe," said a portly man in a golf shirt. At the playground, a woman clutched a toddler, declared she planned to get a gun. Searchers in the woods around Two Springs Lake looked for signs of Paige.

In a clip from last night's news conference, Richard reassured the public. "The Essex County sheriff's department and the SBI are going all out on this investigation." He introduced Temple, who begged for the return of her toddler. A picture of Paige flashed onto the screen, a photo I'd seen hanging on the wall of the Mercers' house. A delicate child, with her mother's dark hair, hazel eyes.

"That girl Temple—I know her," said Fern. "She used to come here for painting lessons when she was in high school. After you went off to State. Talented girl, and pretty. Guess she got married." Her tone implied that Temple's life had thereupon ended.

"She's expecting her second baby any day."

My grandmother frowned. "She had talent. I'll pay her a visit."

"She's staying with a neighbor." Sitting around, waiting for a plumber, made me twitchy. I checked email. Dr. O'Brien, the medical examiner, was a model of forensic efficiency. He had written me a synopsis:

Time of death: one to three p.m. Cause of death: exsanguinations, preceded by severe head trauma. Bruising on left shoulder. Both forearms exhibit multiple, deep, lengthwise incisions, made with a sharp, concave blade that severed radial and ulnar arteries. Blood test positive for cannabis; no other drug indications. Brain swelling and skull bruising indicate the concussion injury occurred approximately thirty minutes before death.

This explained why Mercer didn't struggle as he bled out—he was either unconscious or very confused and disoriented. For thirty minutes? That was puzzling. The blade described was unusual. I would ask Temple if she owned a knife like that.

The plumber arrived, took one look, and said he'd come back with a backhoe and a crew of four. Earth would be moved, lines uncovered, the blockage resolved. I told him to fix the problem, mentally shuddering as I added up the hourly cost for a backhoe and four plumbers, wondering if this was the first in a series of overdue old-house repairs.

I asked Fern to stay with me for a few days. She tipped her head, a gesture meaning that she planned something I might not approve of. "No, I don't want to be a bother."

"You won't be a bother—you can walk Merle."

"He's not easy to walk." This wasn't true. Hogan had trained Merle to heel beautifully.

"Then don't walk him. I have extra room. Please, Fern." If Fern was hiding something, I knew from experience she'd never tell. Stubbornness was her birthright.

"I'll go to June Devon's. She can always use a hand with her husband, Erwin. He had a stroke last month. Will you drop me off there?"

Ursula Budd, Lincoln's bookkeeper, had mentioned June Devon, too. The world kept getting smaller.

June Devon lived in White Pines, a secluded, woodsy development on a winding gravel road. Fern rang June's doorbell and I got out of the car to stretch. Spying a glint of water behind the house, I wandered down the driveway. The property dropped steeply to Two Springs Lake, and I saw activity on the other side, boats and divers. They were dragging the lake, looking for Paige Mercer, I guessed. A few hundred yards away, behind a bank of pale green foliage, I spotted the bright blue umbrella on Kent Mercer's deck. So much for Silver Hills gated security—anyone could get across the lake with a rowboat. Like the one tied up below that must belong to June.

"Stella?" Fern waved from the deck. "June is delighted to have me stay. Go on, don't worry about me."

I took Henderson Road over to Highway 64 and headed into Raleigh to the SBI office, to face my ex. I needed Hogan's help.

Hogan was glued to his computer monitor. I tapped him gently on the shoulder and he jumped.

"Dammit, Stella, you snuck up on me." His gaze swept me from head to toe, and he frowned. "Have you gained a little weight?" To my dismay, I had. Since I left him, I'd found nourishment from other men—Papa John, Big Mac, and the Colonel.

But Hogan had lost weight. His trim middle was accentuated by a slim-fit, gray herringbone shirt. Probably working out more often, trying to stay fit for his teenaged girlfriend.

I decided to respond with a rueful smile. "I don't know how you stay in such great shape, always in front of a computer, day after day." This was a jab at his paper-pushing desk job, hunting down the dangerous criminals who fudged accounting records to siphon off a few bucks for their kiddies' Christmas toys. When he wasn't trawling *meetaslut.com*.

He studied my face and decided to take me literally. Irritating. "Jasmine and I play a lot of tennis, and she's turned me into a vegetarian, practically. Hard not to be healthy under those circumstances. What do you need?"

"It's that murder case I called you about. Kent Mercer. Credit check and all of his bank and credit card transactions for the past six months."

"Got the subpoena?"

"Of course." I put a copy onto his desk. "Five o'clock?"

"I'll do my best." I knew he would. Hogan was methodical, knowledgeable, and thorough—admirable qualities in a husband. Unfortunately, he'd failed other sections of the test. I turned to leave.

Richard, my boss, stood in the doorway with an unlit cigar in his mouth. He chews on those cigars to offset his dimples. He ran his hand over his head to smooth down the wisps, then tugged his foulard necktie a millimeter to the left. It looked new, expensive.

"Thought you were in court," I said.

"What are you up to? Let's talk," he said. I followed him through the warren of cubicles into his corner office. He was grouchy. He's always being blamed for mistakes his agents made; not that we make lots of them, but a thorough investigation sometimes means stepping on toes. At least once a week he's called by a state legislator to explain where the hell the SBI got off treading on some constituent's rights, or usurping some department's authority, or prying into some agency's records. No one envies Richard his job.

I did envy his desk, unsoiled by paperwork. I filled him in on my interview with Lincoln Teller as well as the autopsy results.

He swung his mahogany leather boots onto the desk. "How is Lincoln Teller involved?"

"It seems that Mercer stole from his restaurant."

"Let's not go public with that, Stella," Richard said. "It makes Lincoln look like he had a motive, and the last thing we want to do is tarnish Lincoln Teller."

I told him about Mercer's oxy sale to Fredricks and me, and

his stash of small quantities, oddly packaged in hand-labeled baggies. "He's not on our radar as much of a dealer. But we don't have another motive yet. And the forensics are meager. Hogan's looking into his financials today."

He scowled and examined his soggy cigar. "What about the wife?"

"Shopping all day. And she's desperate to find her daughter."

"No note or ransom calls? What if mom's involved?"

"She wouldn't harm her own child."

"Don't assume. Remember Susan Smith? Andrea Yates?"

I didn't like it when he talked down to me so I wandered over to his coffeepot and inhaled. Today's brew was spicy-smelling, smoky. Oily beans spilled out of a brown paper bag, hand-printed with "Los Volcanes, Guatemala," as though he'd picked and roasted them himself.

"And we found a fingerprint," I said. "It's perfect evidence, in Mercer's blood. No matches in AFIS, though."

"How about friends of the couple? You know—look for instability or tension?"

"Good idea." I had already planned to do that, but it never hurt to let Richard think he was brilliant. "Hey, I saw your press conference this morning. You looked good." Richard's GQ-worthy clothes, dimples, and crusty resonant voice were perfect for TV.

"I look good when I have something to report. Don't blow this opportunity, Stella."

CHAPTER 7

Tuesday mid-morning

All was quiet in Silver Hills except for the drone of a distant airplane heading toward RDU, the fountain's splashing, and the creak of my shoulder holster as I poked the doorbell of Nikki Truly's house. I wanted to talk to her about babysitting the missing toddler, her affair with the toddler's dad, and any other subject she might be able to enlighten me on.

Inside the house a dog yapped, a white puff dashing back and forth to peer at me through glass sidelights. Tiny, Nikki had called him. Finally, a man wearing a uniform with the logo of a carpet-cleaning business opened the door. "She's in the garden," he said, pointing to a brick path leading around the house.

I tried to ignore the knot in my stomach, the unease I felt surrounded by Essex County wealth, and concentrate on the job. Ridiculous, this insecurity. As Fern often said, *we're all doing the best we can with what we have,* but obviously some *had* much more. Some had functional plumbing and leak-proof roofs, for example, as well as a landscaped garden—a confusing clutter of topiary shrubs, Roman statues, and rock gardens massed with white and yellow daffodils. Behind an obelisk, a woman kneeled on a foam pad and scraped at the earth with a claw-like tool. She was slender with frothy blond hair and looked about twenty, though since she was Nikki's mother she had to be nearly forty. "Mrs. Truly?"

She stopped scraping and looked up at me. "I haven't been

Mrs. Truly for years. I'm Zoë Schubert. Who are you?" Her peach skin was delicate, flawless. I wondered who did her peels in case I could afford one someday.

"I'd like to talk to your daughter." I showed her my ID.

She studied it and her smile faded. "Lavender. Are you related to Fern?" She spoke with a soft Carolina accent.

"She's my grandmother. How do you know her?"

"I've taken her painting classes. She's a wonderful teacher."

Every wanna-be artist in the county knew Fern, but that wasn't why I was here. "I need to talk to Nikki."

"She's sleeping. So sorry." She picked up the claw and attacked a dandelion.

"I'm investigating a murder, Mrs. Schubert. It's necessary that I talk with her."

Zoë blew out an exasperated puff of air, fluffing up her bangs. I suppressed a smile—Nikki had reacted the same way to me. "We'd like to have our lawyer present," she said.

Surprising. "There's no need for that."

She knitted her eyebrows together. Surely she knew frowning would engrave vertical wrinkles in her forehead, necessitating botox. "I meant, anytime we talk to the police our lawyer wants to be there. It's standard," she said.

One would think the cops called on her once a week. "How long will it take your lawyer to get here? I'll wait."

I guess she decided it wouldn't be a good idea for an SBI agent to sit on her front steps all day, because she changed her mind. "I'll get Nikki. But I'm warning you, if I think you are implying anything or leading her on, you'll be sorry."

You'll be sorry. A threat? I chose to decide it was simply the arrogance that comes with having a lawyer on call. She led me into her house and went upstairs to fetch Nikki. Tiny became hysterical, barking squeaks of fear as he scrabbled around me on the marble floor, leaving a trail of dribbles that explained the carpet cleaner. I scratched the dog's head, calming him. The creature was no more than a handful of coarse white hair with a wet, black nose. He continued to growl, vibrating like a guitar string.

The home décor was baroque, uncomfortable. Gold-curlicued lamps dripped crystals, naked gilt cherubs held up glass tables, knights chased foxes on wall tapestries. Every piece of furniture was upholstered in faux zebra or leopard or tiger skin. At least I hoped it was faux. I sat down on a furry white ottoman, possibly polar bear, and waited.

In a few minutes Zoë and Nikki came in. Nikki's sleep-creased face lit up when she saw me, her new cop friend. She had on flowered pajama bottoms and an Appalachian State sweatshirt. I wondered how comfortable it could be, sleeping in all those earrings and studs. She sat down on a zebra loveseat, and her mother squeezed in next to her. They looked like sisters—the same wide-apart gray eyes, the same petulant mouth. Tiny scrambled into Zoë's lap and stared at me suspiciously.

"A bit of background first," I said. "Are you from this area?"

"Originally, Texas. We've moved around." Zoë took Nikki's hand. "I came here about ten years ago after a divorce, to be closer to my brother, Erwin, and his wife. My only family."

June and Erwin Devon again. Kent Mercer's across-the-lake neighbors. "Mrs. Schubert, did you know Kent Mercer?"

"Only slightly. I talked to him about an upcoming party at Clemmie's, the restaurant. And Nikki took care of his child."

"Yeah," Nikki said. "What's going on with Paige? Did they find her?"

"Yes, we're very worried about her," Zoë added. The little crease reappeared between her eyebrows.

"You have any ideas I could pass on to the search team?"

They exchanged glances and shook their heads.

I asked Nikki how often she went to the Mercers' house to babysit.

"About twice a week? Sometimes in the evening. I've been sitting for them a year or so." Nikki seemed tense but calmer than yesterday, perhaps because her mother nodded supportively at each of her answers.

"Yesterday, after seeing Mercer's body, you ran around the house looking for something. What?"

Zoë looked at her sharply. Pursing her lips, Nikki finally said, "A book."

Really? A book? She wasn't in custody, this wasn't an interrogation, and her mother was holding her hand, so I let it go. "You told me you and Kent were lovers. Talk to me about that."

Squirming, Nikki didn't answer but turned to her mother. Zoë's face was cold. "A private matter," Zoë said, in a voice surprisingly flat. Gone was the sweet drawl. "Do not drag my daughter's personal life into this case."

"Not my intention," I said. "She's a minor and her identity will be protected. But if she knows something . . ."

"What could she possibly know? I want to consult an attorney before you ask her anything more."

So far Nikki had told me little, even though she'd been at the Mercers' house many times in the past year. From my babysitting era I remembered half the fun of the job was eating all the junk food Fern couldn't afford. The other half was snooping around in the parents' stuff. Had Nikki poked around? Zoë would probably consider that a leading question so I asked Nikki about other visitors to the house.

"I saw Lincoln Teller there a few times. Temple's friends."

"Ever hear anyone threaten Kent?"

"Paige's grandpa didn't like Kent. They had some blow-ups about money."

That would be Wesley Raintree. I was disappointed. The

information the girl gave me was superficial. I suspected the two women were holding something back, each protecting the other, and as long as they sat wedged hip-to-hip in the loveseat, clutching hands, I wouldn't hear much of interest from either one. Time to change the subject.

"What did you know about his drug business?"

Leaning forward, Zoë squeezed her daughter's hand so hard that Nikki pulled away. "Ow, Mom, quit."

"This stops now. Come with me." Zoë transferred her grip to the girl's upper arm, tugged her to standing. Nikki shrugged and rolled her eyes.

Silently declaring this interview incomplete, I followed them into the lofty hall and reminded Nikki to stop by the sheriff's department and get fingerprinted for elimination purposes.

"I'll check my calendar," Zoë answered, tugging Nikki up the stairs.

Crouched in a corner, Tiny vibrated a throaty growl. So scary. I let myself out.

Before I interviewed Bryce Raintree, I stopped by my house to pick up Merle. My dog softens people up, and from what Wesley Raintree had told me about his son, Bryce was a hard case—a steroid-fueled bodybuilder.

Bryce had told me he'd be at his gym. I got there a few minutes early, and stepped inside to observe. The gym was a huge open space with very high ceilings festooned with ropes and metal bars. Neatly stacked along the sides were tires, jump ropes, weight bars, wooden boxes, kettle bells, rowing machines. Bare walls held white boards with inspirational sayings and workout times. The place smelled like sweat, with undertones from the Chinese restaurant next door.

A class was in process. About twenty people were doing pushups, deadlifts, jumping on and off the boxes, squatting, throwing massive balls up against a wall. They grunted, groaned, and screamed encouragement at each other. Hip-hop music blared, barbells clanked, sweat flew. Body shapes ranged from pudgy to wiry, ages from twenty to seventy, but they all looked oxygen-deprived, hence confused, and after ten minutes of this, not a few were wobbly. One by one they screamed "time" and collapsed—chests heaving for air, streaming sweat—onto the floor, as a trainer wrote their times on a white board.

I had never met Bryce, so I didn't know which of the near-dead bodies was his, but after a few minutes the bulkiest of the young men staggered to his feet and waved at me. "Be right with you," he said in a rusty voice, toweling off his face, arms, and legs. He went into a restroom, then emerged wearing khaki shorts and a t-shirt. "Hey, sorry for the wait."

I know people who work out—some fellow agents are in the gym every day—but I'd never been up close to a body like his, bulging with muscle everywhere. His smooth, golden skin and even features, so much like his half-brother Kent's, must have come from Sunny. His hair was gorgeous: thick, honey blond, cascading over his shoulders. His expression was wary, neutral. He didn't have a record—I'd checked—but he gave off a suspicious vibe.

I shook his hand cautiously, and invited him to sit in my car. He slid the seat all the way back. Quivering with friendliness, Merle wedged himself between us, tilted his head to receive a pat. Bryce scratched between his ears.

"I'm very sorry about your brother's death," I said. "I want to find out what happened as much as you do."

"Thanks." Bryce reached under his t-shirt and lifted it to scratch, showing me his six-pack. Close-up, his skin wasn't so uniformly golden. Spots, chapped lips, and dark circles around his eyes hinted at a late-night lifestyle. I was surprised to see him take out a pack of cigarettes and a lighter. Bodybuilders are usually health-conscious.

"No smoking in my car, please. Tell me about Kent."

He frowned. "He was a cool guy. Helped me with stuff. Gave me a job at Clemmie's. Then he fired me." Merle pressed his chin firmly against Bryce's shoulder, focused on the sensations coming through his skin as Bryce rubbed his ears.

"What for?"

Bryce twisted his mouth into a smirk exactly like Wesley's. "I didn't show up a few times. It wasn't like anybody cared or anything. He was being a jerk." Bryce turned to face me. He didn't seem sad or upset. "So you're a cop? You don't look like one."

I ignored that. "Who do you think killed your brother?"

Bryce hesitated. "Dunno. Burglars?" He looked at me intently, as if to say, *you tell me.* His left leg jiggled. Bryce wasn't as cool as he seemed.

I shook my head. "Talk to me about Kent and drugs."

"Uh, ma'am, nothing there." Polite all of a sudden. He was knocking his knees together, like he had to pee. Merle, attuned to body language, retreated into the backseat.

"Come on, help me out here," I said.

He raised both arms. "Hey, I don't know. I stay away from that stuff. My trainer would kill me."

Yeah, right. I suspected his trainer had a good idea what Bryce ingested. "Did you find another job?"

Bryce nodded. "I'm working nights at a nursing home. Friend of my dad's owns it."

I wondered if Bryce would make it. He had little education and his ambition seemed absurd, but a father who cared was more than many kids had. "Do you know Nikki Truly?"

"Yeah. The babysitter. Why?"

"You ever see her at your brother's house?"

"I don't go there much. Kent said I made his wife uncomfortable." He upended his water bottle and drained it.

"How do you know Nikki if you didn't go to the house?"

"I met her a few times. Kent brought her to Clemmie's on her birthday. It was, like, a party. Right after I started there. August? I bussed. No one talked to me." He shrugged his shoulders, *I don't care,* but Bryce wasn't fooling me. His tough layer was a brittle scab covering confusion and hurt.

"One last question—where were you yesterday between one and three?"

"Right here, at the gym."

I let him go and he got into a shiny red Mustang with white leather seats. It looked new, and I wondered how he paid for it. Wesley didn't seem like the kind of dad who'd indulge his son's automotive fantasies.

I went into the gym and talked to a trainer. He clicked through yesterday's gym usage records and confirmed Bryce's alibi.

Anselmo called and updated me on the search for Paige Mercer. Since Temple's TV appeal, people had been swamping the call center and providing enough work for the police for weeks, once they sorted out the false leads and crank calls. "But help is on the way. The Feebies are sending a team," said Anselmo.

"How's the sheriff feel about that?" The last time the FBI "helped out" in Essex County, they were investigating the disappearance of a ton of marijuana in police custody.

"It's fine with him, as long as they buy the donuts," said Anselmo. He told me the divers searching in the lake had found nothing.

"Good." But Paige had been missing for a day and there'd been no ransom call. We both knew the odds were diminishing that she would be found alive. I felt a particular, familiar sort of agony, one I'd lived with for twenty-two years, ever since my mother vanished when I was five. The mixture of hope, fear, self-blame, frustration that Temple must be feeling was all too imaginable to me. But I was an instant believer in Paige's well-being when, an hour later, my phone chimed and I saw this text:

She's okay, listening to dad read goonight moon, sorry

"She" had to be Paige. "Listening to dad" struck me as creepy until I realized it must mean a recording, like the *Clifford* CD I'd found on the lake shore. How many people knew Kent had recorded himself reading stories for her bedtime? That Paige wouldn't be parted from her boom box?

I called Hogan right away with the sending number and asked him to trace it. Then Anselmo. "I think it's real," I told him. "OK if I contact Temple? She could verify the recording. *Good Night Moon.*"

"Or a hoax? Some jerk winding you up?"

"But why me? A random person following the case in the media wouldn't know to contact me, wouldn't know about the CDs Mercer made for his daughter. Ergo, it's genuine."

"Ergo?" He laughed.

"My pretentious side." I started to laugh too, and it came so easily I surprised myself. It had been a while since I felt like laughing. Surely the text meant Paige was alive. "I want to tell Temple."

"She's talking to the media all the time, and if it gets out, there will be copycats. Wait until we know more."

I had been handed a smidge of hope, but why? I thought a moment, then texted back:

Where is she? I'll come get her, no questions asked.

There was no reply.

CHAPTER 8

Tuesday afternoon

I drove to the farmhouse to check on the plumbers, a stop-and-go trip due to road construction. The highway between Silver Hills and Verwood was being widened to four lanes, and long stretches of raw red clay lay exposed. Sprawl around Raleigh was moving west to engulf Essex County, ruining the pleasant rural drive with a clutter of housing developments and strip malls. As a treat for Merle, I'd brought him with me—he loves the fields and woods, smells and creatures, of my grandmother's place.

I thought about Kent Mercer's murder as I drove, mumbling out loud to Merle now and then. "My instinct is asleep. No hunches. Family members? Temple's got an alibi. Wesley Rain-tree, the stepdad? Maybe. But he seems honorable, not the type to murder a fellow just because he doesn't like him, for pete's sake." I ruffled Merle's ears. "What's your theory?"

Motives for murder—greed, jealousy, passion—hovered in the background, though as my criminal psych professor used to say, murder doesn't have to be rational. Mercer's killer could have walked in and said, "I've had enough of your cheating-thieving-lying-irresponsible ways." Mercer might have laughed or shouted or yawned, triggering rage. The killer then forced him outside, onto the deck, down the steps to the flagstone patio, where he knocked Mercer unconscious, rummaged around the house for a half hour, then sliced Mercer's arms,

61

scooped up the toddler, and disappeared.

It didn't scan, especially the part about Paige and the interval between knocking Mercer unconscious and his murder. As for the motive—if being a jerk resulted in murder, a third of the population would be dead and another third in jail. I could only hope that investigation, lab work, and time would reveal a few more cold hard facts.

Three very muddy men stood in Fern's front yard, watching a fourth push dirt around with a small backhoe. Merle bounded up to them and barked a greeting, then dashed around the house to search for critters.

When the backhoe driver saw me, he grinned and cut the machine. "Chris, you're under arrest," I called to him. Back in high school, Chris and I had served after-school detention together. He was now married and the father of three. Or four? I'd lost track. Skinny, stubbled, he raked in dough as Essex County's busiest plumber.

"Howdy, Stella," he said. "We found the problem, look here." He picked up a piece of rusty iron pipe. "Collapsed drain. We're replacing the line. Be done tomorrow."

"Great. Do you need those three to stand around at seventy-five bucks an hour each?"

"That's funny," he said, "and you've got some other problems. Last time I pumped the septic, I noticed a leak in the flashing around a dormer. It's not been fixed. I'll show you."

He pulled off his boots and we went into the house. Fern had closed off the second floor and nailed up plastic sheets to save on heating expenses. I tugged the plastic aside and we climbed the stairs, then crouched through a mini-door to the attic, a musty, cobweb-swathed space running the width of the house. It smelled of mouse and ancient dust. Fern had placed a washtub in a dormer alcove to catch leaks. I could see daylight through the rotted siding and the window frame itself was nearly gone. The lower panes of glass had fallen out and Fern had tacked more plastic over them. Another repair problem she didn't want to deal with.

"Thanks, Chris." I felt glum at the thought of the cost. "That's gotta be fixed."

"Don't let it go, Stella. The framing gets wet, you've got rot and the place will start to fall down."

I hadn't been into the attic in years. It was full of the same dusty clutter I remembered from my childhood. A spinning wheel, a seven-foot-tall chifferobe. Filthy chairs with ragged upholstery. A stack of boxes probably contained old clothes and papers going back a hundred years. Was any of this junk valuable? I've seen *Antiques Road Show*—one woman's junk is another's collectible. Fern wasn't a hoarder, just couldn't be bothered. I decided to call her at June Devon's house, and went outside where I would get a better signal.

The phone rang and rang, and I was about to hang up when June answered. She went to get Fern. In the background I could hear a demented shrieking. When Fern came on, I asked her about the screeching noise.

"Oh, that's June's conure."

"Her what?"

"Her conure. It's like a parakeet. Right now it's tearing up a magazine, and that makes it happy and it screams."

"How is your stay going?"

"Okay. I'm trying to help her where I can. She has her hands full with Erwin. You know he's disabled. About your case—did you know June's sister-in-law is the babysitter's mother?"

"Say again?"

"The babysitter who found the body with you yesterday? Her mother is Erwin's sister. No love lost."

Of course. Zoë Schubert. She'd mentioned her brother, Erwin, and that she and Nikki had moved here to be closer to him. "Family tensions?"

"Zoë's super-rich, but she hasn't offered a penny to help June and Erwin. And there have been so many expenses! June had to remodel their bathroom, to make it accessible, and she had to quit her job to take care of Erwin."

"That's cold, to ignore her brother's needs. Guess she can't part with her money."

"Well, it isn't her money, it's her dead husband's. She's a parasite." That was a classic Fernism, believing women should earn their own money. It reminded me that my hard-earned money was going to a plumber. I told her about their progress, and the leak Chris had pointed out.

Fern sighed. "I didn't know what to do about that. Same old problem, you know."

"Would you consider selling anything from the attic? You could probably get enough to pay the plumber, do some repairs."

"There's nothing much up there, old furniture and clothes. I kept thinking I'd throw stuff out but never got to it. Go ahead, do what you can." Fern paused, then said, "I want to ask you a question. Something I've been thinking about." Her voice took on a cagey note.

"What's that?"

"What if someone took the child and then decided to return her. Would that someone be arrested?"

I couldn't quite believe what I was hearing. "Fern, what the hell . . . ?"

"It's just a question. Can you answer it, please?"

"Of course that someone would be arrested. Whatever are you saying?"

"I was thinking maybe everyone would be so glad to see the child they wouldn't be mad. They'd be thankful."

I took a deep breath. "Fern, you absolutely have to tell me everything you know. Right now. If you're withholding information, that in itself is a felony. Aiding and abetting is even worse. What do you know?"

"Nothing. I just have a feeling. Oops, there's the timer. Gotta run."

I decided she was being imaginative and we were back at cold reality. I wanted so badly to believe the child was alive that I dampened my hope. To a dedicated pessimist, all surprises are pleasant ones. I decided not to mention this conversation to Anselmo just yet. I hated to drag Fern into the investigation without a substantive reason. Besides, Anselmo didn't need the distraction of Fern's "feelings."

I made a call to a Verwood antiques dealer who said yes, she would be happy to come and look around, give us some appraisals. I could practically hear her drool—there's nothing more exciting to an antiques dealer than a dusty farmhouse attic. We agreed to meet at noon the next day.

I whistled for Merle. He bounded up, stinking of something he'd rolled in. As I hosed him off and dried him with paper towels, I told him about the potential treasure trove in the attic. "There's antiques! And art! And collectibles!" His long tail waved slowly. Any time I'm enthusiastic about something, he wants to believe he'll benefit somehow. I tried a sure winner, "Let's go see Hogan!" Merle wriggled with delight.

"I have good news and bad news," Hogan said. We were outside his office on Rowan Street, walking Merle, when a sudden shower began and Hogan whipped out an umbrella. The man was the ultimate Boy Scout, prepared for anything. We stood under a tree and waited for the drenching to end. I hadn't been that close to him in months, and his body heat, his caramel-salty, delicious smell, evoked happy memories—pre-Jasmine memories.

"Bad news first," I said.

He touched my chin, turned my face to his. "Your eyes are mes-mer-i-zing," drawing out each syllable.

Annoyed, I pulled back. "Quite the seducer, aren't you? Save it for your twiglet. News?"

"I can't help myself. OK. The text is untraceable. The sender paid cash for a burner and SIM card."

"What about location? Can you get the phone company to triangulate?"

"They tried. Only one tower picks up the phone's signal. It's somewhere in northeast Essex County."

A populated area, which happened to include Silver Hills and Two Springs Lake. "That's not terrible news. If Paige is with the text-sender, then she's still in this area. What's the good news?"

Hogan had acquired Kent Mercer's credit report and the bank had given him transaction printouts from two accounts in Mercer's name. "The guy was in debt up to his eyeballs, Stella. Credit cards maxed out. Behind on his taxes. Only about five hundred dollars in a joint account. But listen to this—he opened a second account a week ago and deposited fifty thousand dollars in it." He grinned.

Yes! That had to be a lead. "The bank is tracing the deposit?" I asked.

"They'll let me know in half an hour."

I looked at my watch. "I'll be back." I gave Merle water and put him in my car, parked under a tree, windows down. I wanted to report my three bits of good news to Richard—no little bodies in the lake, a hopeful though untraceable text, and fifty thou in Mercer's new bank account. Payment for services? Extortion? A horrible thought occurred to me—had he sold his little girl? Bizarre but not unheard of. I added it to my pathetically short list of scenarios.

Richard was in a conference room talking to the press. Temple sat next to him, looking haggard. Her dark-shadowed eyes scanned the room, searching each face for knowledge about her child, no doubt. I wondered if she'd been sleeping. She seemed calm at first, but after she held up the "missing child" poster, she dropped it and wept into her hands. The newscasters kept filming—they love the soap opera stuff. I walked out of the room. I could email Richard later. I felt guilty, an ugly feeling. I was sure Temple was terrified out of her mind and wished I could reassure her with solid facts.

My euphoria at the discovery of the money in Mercer's account evaporated twenty minutes later when Hogan told me the money was untraceable. The bank had microfilmed the deposit—five cashier's checks from a Cayman Islands branch of a Swiss bank, which had performed the service for an anonymous client with a numbered account. Unless we were investigating money laundering, the bank was under no obligation to reveal the name of the client.

Hogan was as frustrated as I was. "You'll have to get at it some other way. Who did he know with that kind of money? Ask around!"

"Brilliant idea," I said, irritated. Was Hogan still pushing my buttons, implying he could do my job better than I could? He claimed the only reason he wasn't a sworn agent was that his accounting and research skills were too useful. Even if it were true, I was tired of his patronizing tone.

But I did miss his superb cooking. Heading home, dispirited, I decided to forego the sandwich shop and cook. I got out the wok and made a huge stir-fry with everything I could find— peanuts, broccoli, chicken, green onions. It would have served six and I ate half of it. Running with Merle was the only reason I didn't turn into Stella Doughgirl. Not that I wanted Hogan back. Being single was in my genes.

My great-grandmother Phoebe had nursed a war-injured

soldier, then married him. Fern didn't talk much about her father except to say that he'd treated Phoebe like a servant, and she'd excused his behavior because of his wounds. Fern remembered tiptoeing around the house, trying to help her mother. When her husband's death freed Phoebe from the demands of an invalid, she took up her paints and music. She spent more time with ten-year-old Fern, who showed artistic promise.

On Fern's seventeenth birthday, Phoebe sent her to Paris to study art, wanting her talented daughter to experience more of life than she had. Fern returned two years later with the infant Grace, my mother. The baby's father? "An artist, naturally! But irresponsible," Fern told her mother. "We'll raise this child ourselves." Phoebe and Fern dressed her in clothing made from beautiful hand-dyed fabrics, pierced her ears for gems, encouraged her to be unconventional. No surprise, then, that teenaged Grace dyed her hair black, tattooed a dolphin on her chest, a skull on her thigh, and ran off to a commune in Virginia where open relationships were the norm. A year later, Grace brought her new baby—me—back to Verwood to live with Fern.

Pitying whispers followed me throughout my school years. Pity because my mother had disappeared and I lived with my grandmother in a tumbling-down farmhouse, whispers because unmarried mothers still carried a whiff of shame in our conservative small town. Nothing could make me feel good about the "bastard" label the seventh-grade bullies tagged on me. *Just kidding, ha. Ha.* Things got a little better in high school, because a crowd of kids was attracted to the tolerant freedom of Fern's house and her slightly scandalous ways. Misfits, underachievers, kids whose stepmothers couldn't stand their music or their mess—all crowded into her after-school art classes.

I poured myself a glass of wine and turned on the news and

heard what I already knew, an extensive search was under way for the missing child. I watched Temple sob into the camera again. It was damned depressing.

I felt stymied. The lab hadn't come up with much. Anselmo had told me the fingerprint under the deck wasn't made by Lincoln, Temple, Bryce, Nikki, or Wesley. The bloody tracks in the house matched Mercer's blood type. Precious few clues, no way to trace the money, no witnesses, and no motive.

I ran a bath and dripped in some lavender oil. Lavender's supposed to calm and relax, and I gave it ten minutes to work, studying my toes and grinding my teeth as my dark thoughts churned. Bryce grunting as he pressed a massive kettlebell over his shoulder, his blond hair dripping sweat. Nikki's gray eyes watching her mother. Plumbers and a backhoe. Buckets in Fern's attic. Fern might know something about the missing toddler. I would get it out of her one way or another.

CHAPTER 9

Wednesday morning

At six a.m., my phone chimed. Anselmo's voice was gruff. "Lincoln Teller was in a bad car accident about thirty minutes ago. Chamberlain's there. Graham Parkway, Silver Hills. She said he's hurt but alive. Thought you'd want to know."

"Sure. Thanks." My brain felt like cold mashed potatoes as I tried to process what Anselmo had said. I went into the bathroom and brushed my teeth. Merle clack-clacked across the floor, expecting a run—the only reason in his mind I'd be vertical at dawn. When I pulled on slacks and a leather jacket instead of running shorts, he sighed and jumped onto the bed, stared at me gloomily. I put my arms around him, fighting an urge to crawl back under the covers. "Sorry, buddy. Wish we could trade places."

Deputy Chamberlain was taking pictures of Lincoln's blue Jag convertible, its passenger side crumpled like tinfoil. "I don't understand," I shouted over the whomp-whomp-whomp of the ambulance helicopter as it took off.

"Me either," Chamberlain yelled back. We watched the helicopter turn and head north to Community Hospital. Lincoln had lost control on a sharp curve, spun nearly one-eighty, and slammed into a recycling truck. What made it odd was the location. In Silver Hills, the speed limit is twenty-five. Only the suicidal would speed in this neighborhood of hilly, narrow streets with slow-moving, random traffic.

"How bad is he hurt?" I asked. There were no air bags in the vintage car.

"Hard to say. He couldn't move his left arm. He was conscious but incoherent—concussed, I'd say. He didn't want to sit up, which made me worry about spinal cord damage, so I called airlift."

I hated to ask the next question, but it was important. "Alcohol?"

"Didn't smell it." Chamberlain knelt down to peer underneath the smashed car. Her camera flashed three times.

I walked up Graham Parkway. I didn't see tire skid marks. Maybe he was on the phone or texting. Maybe the brakes failed. Maybe he had an argument and was steamed up, not paying attention.

I drove to the hospital. I doubted they'd let me see him, but maybe someone could reassure me. Lincoln had always seemed heavy-duty, tougher than us ordinary mortals. Surely he'd be all right. In the emergency room, I learned Lincoln had been wheeled off for scans. I made my way through a fluorescent-lit maze of corridors to the radiology waiting room, deserted at this hour of the morning except for two little boys and their mother, a tall African-American woman wearing a softly wrinkled linen pantsuit the color of butterscotch pudding. She was slender, elegant, confident, and had to be Clementine Teller, Lincoln's wife. According to a recent magazine article, she had a law degree and was the brains in the family.

She talked with the receptionist while her two boys rolled on the floor. The younger one was on top, pummeling the older one as they both roared until their noise distracted their mother.

"Come over here and settle down now," she said, untangling them. She led them by their arms to sit on either side of her, where they proceeded to make faces at each other.

I introduced myself. "I talked with Lincoln just yesterday. I'm so sorry to hear about this accident."

"I don't understand it. He's gone down that hill a thousand times. The deputy said he'd been speeding? Nonsense. Lincoln drives slow. You know how laid back he is. Now me, I like speed. I like to get where I'm going."

"Has he been troubled about anything? Preoccupied?"

"He's always worried about the restaurant."

The receptionist came over and told Clementine that Dr. Newell wanted to talk to her.

"Okay, give me a minute." Clementine looked at me and grimaced, her dark eyes shadowy.

I offered to watch the boys. "Thanks," she said. "That'll help. I have a hard time with doorways."

I must have looked quizzical because she explained, "Going from one room to another." She puffed out a breath. "I have to get through the door. May take me a while." She walked to the door and patted the door frame with her left hand, then her right, over and over again, her head nodding in unison with the taps. The boys stopped their play and watched her. She must have tapped the door frame over fifty times. Obsessive-compulsive disorder, it looked like. OCD hadn't been mentioned in the magazine article. I wondered how else the illness manifested itself, and whether she was being treated. Finally she walked through.

The boys watched her struggle. "She made it," said the older one, who looked about six. "Made it," repeated his younger brother.

"She sure did," I said. "What're your names?"

"I'm Jimmy and he's Ben," said the older one. "Can I see your gun?"

Right now I needed to occupy them with something that wasn't wrestling. I thought back to my babysitting days, recalling the lessons I learned from the Sampson twins, four-year-olds with two behavior modes: walkabout and destroy. "Okay, let's play a quiz. You have to guess what animal I am." I stood up and started zooming around the room. "Bzzzz . . . bzzzzz . . . where's the flower? . . . Bzzzz . . ."

"You're a bee," said Jimmy. "That's easy."

"Bee," said Ben.

I got down on my knees and started pretend-licking my hands and rubbing them on my face. "Let Ben guess first," I said. "Meow!"

"Kitty!" said Ben.

"Right! Okay, what's this?" I got on my hands and knees and growled, "I'm king of the jungle! I'm the baddest cat there is! Grrrrr!"

"You're a lion," I heard, a voice that could only be Anselmo's. I looked behind me and saw him standing in the doorway. I hoped he wouldn't notice my full-body blush.

"A lion!" yelled Jimmy.

"A lion!" echoed Ben.

"Can I play too?" Anselmo asked. He quacked and the boys yelled "Duck!"

With his uniform and willingness to play, he was an instant magnet for little boys. We'd cycled through Old MacDonald's farmyard and started on the Serengeti when Clementine returned. She found it just as challenging to come back through the door into the waiting room, with much tapping and head nodding. How difficult her life must be, I thought.

I introduced Anselmo to her and he stood up, with difficulty, a boy attached to each leg, all three of them laughing. It was an endearing picture. He liked kids, I could tell. Probably had some. With his lucky wife.

He untangled himself from the boys. "How's Lincoln doing?"

"Two broken ribs and a broken clavicle. A subdural hematoma. He's going into surgery soon."

"A summer . . . toma?" Jimmy stammered.

"Like a bruise on his brain." She knelt and rubbed his head. "He's going to be fine."

"That's good news," I said.

"Keep it to yourself? Anything you say will be headlines the next day. We talk publicly only through Lincoln's press agent."

"Of course." I gave her my business card. "Anything I can do, let me know."

"He chose the public life, not me. Some days I have to dig pretty deep, you know, to find the strength? Now, I'm going to stay here. My sister is coming to pick up the boys."

I offered to stay with her until the sister arrived, but she shooed us off. "Go on, there's nothing wrong with me. Appreciate your help just now."

We took the elevator down. "Cute kids," Anselmo said. "Sure hope he'll be okay."

"She didn't seem too worried."

"Was that OCD, her coming through the door?"

"Looked like it." I felt self-conscious because my hair was so wild. The helicopter-wind had turned me into Medusa. I dug in my purse and found a hairclip to subdue the mane.

"Don't," he said. "I like your hair like that." He reached out and smoothed an errant curl. "Mermaid hair."

I laughed. *He likes my hair.* A small joy.

Next on my list—ask Temple about the money in her husband's bank account. The gum-smacking guard at the Silver Hills gate waved me through. Temple was staying with her neighbor in a Tara wanna-be with two-story white columns. A huge spider had spun an impressive web at the top of one of them. It looked like prime real estate for a spider.

Temple motioned me to a rocking chair on a screened side

porch. She'd put on makeup but fatigue had hollowed out dark shadows under her eyes. She wore black leggings and an oversized white shirt, looking more chic than any nine-months-pregnant woman had a right to. She wore a pin, a circular disk with Paige's picture, a website, and in bold print, "Have You Seen This Child?" She gave me one and I fastened it to my jacket.

"Paige Central," she said, pointing to a window. Inside I could see a dozen people at computer screens or huddled in small groups. "They've been here all night."

"Family?" I asked.

"Neighbors and friends. My sister can't get away from work, and my mother is in a mental hospital." Temple rubbed her belly with her small, pale hands. One of her fake nails had broken off, exposing a chewed nub.

"Couple of questions. Did your husband have a life insurance policy?"

Temple twisted her bulky body and pushed her face close to mine. "Yes, he did. Did he make the payments? I sure as hell hope so, or I'll be celebrating Mother's Day in a homeless shelter." Her face sagged.

"Did you know about your husband's second bank account? Fifty thousand dollars deposited last week?"

Her eyes widened. "Fifty thousand? I thought we were broke!"

I believed her, since their joint account held less than five hundred dollars. "Any idea where that money came from?"

She snorted. "I'm not surprised he had a separate account. To tell you the truth, Stella, we were about through. I'd had enough. Kent was always out for himself, taking the easy way, sliding through life with a wink and a smile. Well, his smile was fake and his winks made me want to throw up."

"I met him at Clemmie's. He was charming."

Temple ran her fingers through her hair. "Yes, that's how he got me. I mean, he could be irresistible. No woman could hold out. But it only lasts as long as he wants something. Then he moves on to someone else."

A behavior I recognized. On to someone else, the bums. I wanted to say *Temple, you deserve someone decent,* but it wasn't the moment. "Can you give me any names?" Wouldn't be the first time a scorned woman turned on her lover.

"I didn't want to know. Ouch." She shifted herself into a half-lying position. "This one's a real kicker."

"Who had a reason to kill him?"

"He kept things secret. I don't know where he got money from. He blamed me for spending, but he picked out the house we couldn't afford, he leased expensive cars." She stood and arched her back. Her white shirt billowed like a sail. "We were broke, really broke. Our landlord was threatening eviction. And we couldn't talk about it—Kent would yell at me about credit cards."

"So you were stuck."

"Yeah. Though mostly I didn't think about it. I was a mom who took pictures. That was—is—my life." She laughed though her words were bitter. "Fifty thousand dollars, huh? I'd give it all to have my baby back."

"The medical examiner said Kent's wounds were made with an unusual knife. Curved like this." I curled my finger to illustrate.

"I have a little knife like that. A bird's-beak paring knife. It's purple, blade and all. It's very sharp." She shuddered. "Can I go back to my house?"

"They should be finished later today. Temple, my grandmother remembers you. Fern Lavender."

Her face lightened. "She's your grandmother? She is so cool! And I loved her old farmhouse."

"With its picturesque falling-down porch?"

"Who cares? Artists are supposed to be broke. None of that bourgeois worry about appearances."

Easy for you to say. Us bourgeoisie had worked thirty hours a week after school serving pizza to pay the artist's electric bill. "Fern said you two were good friends."

"I hung out there nearly every afternoon, just to talk to her and watch her paint, my senior year, the year my dad left us. Such a warm, safe place to be. I'd love to see her again."

"I'll bring her to the memorial service this afternoon."

Temple winced and rubbed her back. "I keep thinking about Paige. She's a picky eater—do they know what to feed her?"

I wanted to tell Temple about Fern's what-if and the anonymous text, but Anselmo had forbidden it. All I could manage was, "I'm hopeful," as a fat tear spilled out of her eye.

CHAPTER 10

Wednesday midday

I picked up Fern for our appointment with the antiques dealer. It was drizzling rain and the wipers' swipe-swipe was aggravating the hell out of me, but Fern was also to blame. She refused to tell me whether she knew anything.

She held up her hands. Her fingernails were painted watermelon pink. "Fuchsia Fling. Don't you love it? I did my toes too."

"Don't change the subject. Is it someone in your painting class?"

"Can't you be patient a little longer?"

"Not when a child is missing and a murderer is wandering around Silver Hills."

"Hmm," said Fern. "I see your point."

Fern was good at keeping secrets and I was so furious I didn't speak to her for the next ten minutes, and having to stew in silence made me even madder. Finally I mentioned that I'd seen Temple. "She's all alone, Fern. No family. I don't know how she's getting through this."

"Did you know her mother's in a mental hospital?"

I nodded. "This must feel like more insanity."

"Well, I hope she gets her baby back soon. I'll call her." She pulled down the sun visor and applied lipstick. More Fuchsia Fling. I wanted to throttle her.

Chris and his crew had left a muddy hill of red earth in Fern's front yard. The antiques dealer stood next to it, waiting for us under an umbrella. Jane was a petite white-haired dynamo, often seen jogging the streets of Verwood at six a.m. Her store, The Treasure Trove, occupied several rooms on two floors in a downtown building. She sold everything—Civil War–era furniture, vintage linens, Depression glassware, old books, kitchenware from the Fifties. If Jane couldn't appraise an item, we'd have to go to Atlanta to find the expertise.

Jane and Fern wandered around the attic while I searched downstairs for a light bulb so we could see. Even after I replaced the bulb it was dim as a bat cave.

"Where to begin?" Fern murmured. "All this stuff!"

"Tell me about the chifferobe." Jane ran her hands over its carved doors. "Cherry. Beautiful."

"It was my mother's, but I don't know much about it," said Fern.

"It's a fine piece. Can I open it?"

Fern had stashed some paintings inside. She helped Jane take them out, one at a time. "Ugly things, aren't they?" Fern said. "All cubist crap."

The paintings were abstract, with harsh lines and colors. They didn't look like her work at all. "Who painted them?" I asked.

"When I was in Paris, friends gave them to me in exchange for meals or a few dollars. Back then it was all abstract—blocky, puzzle-piece stuff. They fooled people into thinking it was art. I thought maybe someday they'd be worth something."

Jane nodded. "You could be right, Fern. These are signed and the names are familiar—Michael Reyes and Everett Klein. I'm going to get an art appraiser over here."

"Mick and Ev—now that takes me back." Fern closed her eyes and smiled. "The Place du Tertre in Montmartre. We sold our paintings to tourists. They were both in love with me, always hanging around my apartment hoping the other would leave. It's quite possible one of them was your grandfather, Stella."

" 'Quite possible'? Or perhaps someone else?" Jane and I exchanged looks of mock-dismay but I'd quit being embarrassed by Fern years ago.

I went outside to make calls. Picking my way through the muddy ruts of Fern's drive, I was pondering how to get around a particularly wide and mucky patch when Anselmo called with news about Lincoln Teller's accident.

"Chamberlain noticed brake fluid on the street and a trail of it back to Lincoln's garage up the hill," he said. "So she went to the tow yard and crawled underneath his Jag. Guess what she saw?"

"I'll let you tell me."

"Brake lines were cut."

"That's a movie cliché," I said, the smart-ass response masking my alarm. Someone wanted Linc Teller's car to speed uncontrollably down the hill and smash into any luckless passer-by or parked car. A catastrophe for Lincoln and his family.

"Yes, but an efficient way to cause an accident. Especially on a car built in 1963, before dual brakes. So when he started down Graham Parkway . . ."

"Deliberately cut?" I asked. "Not worn away?"

"Neatly sawed. No accident."

"There must be a connection with Kent Mercer's death," I said.

"You're the investigator. Tell me who would want to kill both of them."

I laughed as though Anselmo were joking. I didn't have the slightest idea.

★ ★ ★ ★ ★

Around eleven, I was on Highway 64 halfway to Raleigh to meet with Richard when my phone chimed. I slowed to take the call but didn't recognize the number.

"Miz Lavender?" The woman's voice had a definite Carolina twang. "My name is Kim Grady, and I'm the manager on duty at Roll's Grocery, up in Essex Junction? How are you today?" A southern conversational trait—it's rude to get to the point too quickly, as though the only reason you called was to conduct business. "Gosh, it's so exciting to be talking to an SBI agent!"

I was mystified. "What can I help you with?"

"Well, one of our customers went into the restroom and found a little girl all by herself in a shopping cart. She has a note pinned to her shirt with your name and number on it. Says to call you and only you."

Could it be . . . ? An adrenaline rush gave me head-to-toe goose bumps. "What does she look like?" I checked my rearview mirror. A Coke truck was in the passing lane.

"She's the cutest little thing. She's got on a little hat and seersucker shorts and won't let go of a boom box. Her t-shirt has a monkey on it, Curious George. He's one of my son's favorites. Ryan's older than she is, though."

God give me patience, she was a talker. "Age?" I asked.

"This child? About one and a half, I'd say."

It had to be Paige Mercer. "Was there anything else in the note?"

"No, just to call you. She was in the restroom in a cart, like I said."

I moved across the passing lane, rolled onto the grassy median for a U-turn, and looked at my watch. "I'll be there in fifteen minutes. She O.K.?"

"She looks fine. I gave her some juice."

"Great. Thank you, Ms. Grady. Thank you very much." As I

sped the twelve miles back to Verwood, I called Anselmo and told him about Kim Grady's call. Was Fern right and the kidnapper had changed his mind? Now would Fern share what she knew?

At Roll's I pulled into the fire lane and ran into the store. Deputy Chamberlain from the sheriff's department was already there, beaming such a wide smile I thought she'd levitate from happiness.

"Stella," she said, "it's her. Paige Mercer." Chamberlain led me into the store office where a tiny girl grasping a Hello Kitty boom box sat in a grocery cart. She had grape juice on her chin, but there was no doubt it was the same child whose face had been plastered all over the TV news and internet for the past two days. With those delicate features and dark-lashed hazel eyes, she was clearly Temple's toddler. I felt nearly airborne as chains of fear and worry dropped away.

With an inquisitive "ahh-siss?" Paige pointed to a pair of sunglasses lying on a desk. Chamberlain picked them up and slid them onto Paige's face. The child grinned like it was hilarious. Joy surged through me. She was alive.

"Now what? This is a first for me," Chamberlain said.

"We take the child to the doctor to be checked over."

"I have a car seat," said Kim Grady. "You can borrow it. I'll need it back before four." I almost kissed her. State car-seat law exempts emergency vehicles, but I didn't want to take any chances reuniting this child with her frantic mother. I called Temple with the great news. "We found Paige. She's fine."

"What? Oh Stella, thank you, thank you. I knew it! I knew she was all right! Where is she? I want to see her!"

"We're at Roll's in Essex Junction. She'll have to be checked over by a doctor."

"Wait there, I'll go with you."

"I'll wait. Bring a change of clothes for her."

I asked Chamberlain to secure the store. "You know what to do now?"

She nodded. "Question all employees and talk with everyone currently in the store. No one goes in or out. I've already impounded the store's security tapes, though they just film the cash register area."

The child was all right. She looked fine; her color was rosy and she was alert. In fact, she was a wiggle worm—while waiting through my conversations, she had climbed into my lap and was trying to unbraid my hair.

"Okay, let's go, cutie pie." I hugged her close and carried her out of the office, avoiding eye contact with any curious onlookers. I didn't want to answer questions, neither deny nor reinforce any rumors. Kim installed the car seat like a pro and fastened Paige into it. A few minutes later Temple flew into the parking lot. When Paige saw her mother, she burst into tears but soon calmed down as Temple covered her face with kisses.

I told Temple how she'd been found. "The sheriff's department will interview everyone who was in the store when we got there. But I suspect whoever put Paige in the restroom left the store right away."

"Fern called me, did you know? She was certain Paige would be found. And she was right!"

"Yes, she was," I said, though I suspected Fern's certainty was based on more than the power of positive thinking.

On the way to the hospital I phoned Richard to let him know the good news. For once Richard wasn't grouchy. He congratulated me, though I insisted I had nothing to do with her recovery.

"Why did you get that text? Why was your name pinned to her shirt? Someone felt you could be trusted," he said. "But this doesn't feel like a kidnapper's move."

"Maybe taken to keep her safe," I said. "Someone witnessed Mercer's murder, and worried about the baby being in danger.

Or saw the body, found her afterwards."

"A felonious Samaritan. Interesting." He seemed to like that idea.

Listening to my side of the phone call, Temple turned to her daughter. "Where have you been, Paige? Who's been taking care of you?"

Paige punched a button on her boom box and a man's voice begin to sing. Her father. Whatever Kent Mercer's crimes, his singing would make his daughter's memories. *This old man, he played one* . . . Paige and Temple joined in and I bit my lip hard to stop the tears filming my eyes at the sound of the three gentle voices. "Where" and "who" meant nothing to the toddler singing along with her parents, restoring her world with each tuneless phrase.

At the hospital the doctor pronounced Paige healthy and unharmed. I put the Curious George T-shirt, seersucker shorts, and denim hat into an evidence bag. Temple dressed Paige in clean clothes, and I drove them back to Roll's parking lot.

I hoped these two would be spared any further suffering. But the attempts on Lincoln's life did not bode well for this being over. Desperation, revenge, or greed was still driving someone to murderous acts. I needed better evidence—or a witness. I knew where, how, and when Kent Mercer was killed. Who and why were unanswered questions.

CHAPTER 11

Wednesday afternoon

Pleasant Grove Methodist Church perched on a slight rise, a simple, white building with a cemetery to one side, a playground on the other, and developers pressing in relentlessly as the Chapel Hill and Raleigh suburbs drifted outward. The afternoon sun shone through stained-glass windows high on the west wall, sprinkling drops of color on wide-plank floors. From a loft, an enormous organ boomed out a somber dirge to begin Kent Mercer's funeral service.

Agents don't usually attend a victim's funeral, but Fern wanted to see Temple, and I had to drive her. We were late because I had driven her to the farmhouse to find something to wear. Fern owned nothing in muted colors. She claimed they were unflattering. She'd fretted as she dug through her closet, finally deciding on a wrap-around jersey dress, teal green with a subtle black print, and fringed scarf.

We took a seat behind Nikki Truly, her mother, Zoë Schubert, and a man I didn't recognize. He was lean like a distance runner, fifty-ish and bald. Zoë wore an oddly cheerful red dress and black hat. I wondered why she was there—perhaps to keep her daughter company. In front, Temple sat between Wesley and Bryce. There were maybe fifty people in the pews.

The minister's words, full of platitudes and Biblical quotes, seemed hardly to apply to Kent Mercer's life. Then he invited us to speak, and Bryce stood. His navy blazer was tight across his back, and he had loosened his tie. His long golden hair was pulled into a ponytail, revealing a small silver hoop in each ear.

"My brother was someone who loved life," he said in his rusty voice. "In spite of his violent end, he was a gentle man who did many good deeds for others. I wish he had not died, but it is a comfort to me and my dad that Kent is with our mom now. Thank you all for coming."

Then Nikki stood. Zoë flinched and tugged at her daughter's arm, but Nikki tugged back and said, "When I first met Kent I thought he was the nicest person I ever met. He, like, paid attention to me? I loved him. I would do anything for him." Then she wailed, "Whoever killed him is a monster!" She stamped her foot and sat down.

Responses to this outburst were mixed. Temple bowed her head, Wesley stared up at the ceiling, and Zoë exchanged looks with the lean bald man next to her. I wanted to know who he was, and was glad to hear the minister say there would be refreshments after the service, giving me a chance to talk to them.

In the church hall, Wesley handed me a cup of punch. "You look nice," he said, referring to my indigo linen suit, giving me a bone-crushing handshake. I introduced him to Fern; the way she filled out her dress would cheer him up. She gave him her irresistible smile. "I can tell you were a military man," she said, and I knew he would soon be another fly in her sticky web.

I noticed Nikki, Zoë, and the unidentified man drifting toward the door. I got there quickly and grabbed Nikki's hand.

"Lovely words, Nikki, so meaningful," I babbled. "Oh, hello, Mrs. Schubert, how nice to see you again."

The little vertical wrinkles appeared as Zoë frowned. "I'm sorry. I don't remember your name."

"Stella Lavender. How are you?" I put out my hand to her companion.

"This is Dr. William Newell, my fiancé," Zoë said, clasping his arm and flashing an engagement ring with an almond-sized sapphire.

"Oh!" I said, trying to remember where I'd heard his name before. "Congratulations! The ring is new, isn't it?"

"I proposed last night," the doctor said. "Begged and begged until she finally said yes." He beamed at his bride-to-be.

"William is chief of staff at Community Hospital." Zoë squeezed his arm against her side. The mention of Community Hospital triggered my memory. Dr. Newell was the doctor Clementine had talked to about Lincoln's injuries. "We're both on the hospital board."

"I didn't know you were interested in health care," I said.

"Oh, my career was in nursing, and it's a real concern of mine."

The cynical me thought that snagging a chief-of-staff husband might rank higher on her agenda than controlling hospital operating costs, but perhaps I misjudged her. I wondered how Nikki felt about her stepdad-to-be. "Nikki, are you going to be a bridesmaid?" I asked.

"No," she said. "Certainly not."

Zoë's little frown came back. "What Nikki means is the ceremony will be a simple one, no attendants."

"Yeah, fourth time around it better be simple," said Nikki.

"Fourth?" asked the doctor.

"Sweetheart, third; you know how she exaggerates. Good to see you, Stella." Zoë squeezed his arm some more and propelled her family out the door. Darn, she hadn't invited me to the wedding.

I went to fetch Fern, and found her deep in conversation with Wesley, already Lancelot to her Guinevere. "I'm moving in with Temple for a while," she said. "I can't go home because of the plumbing repairs. Wesley tells me the poor girl needs some company, and I can help take care of Paige."

In principle it sounded like a good idea, but I didn't like it. As long as Mercer's killer was roaming around and someone was cutting brake lines on expensive automobiles, Silver Hills didn't seem like a safe place for my only living relative. On the other hand, Fern's ability to ferret out information could be useful right there at the scene of the crime. I gave her a little lecture on being alert and taking care of herself. She laughed, and fluttered her fringe at me. "Sweetheart, you worry too much!" She took Wesley's hand. "We'll be fine! And when the new baby arrives, Temple will need lots of help."

Temple edged between them. "Did someone mention a new baby? I predict . . ." She clutched Wesley's arm and stood very still for a moment. "Soon."

Fern gasped, "Oh honey," Wesley whispered, "Oh my," and the two of them supported her as they walked slowly out the door. I leaned against a wall, marveling at what this day would mean to Temple. Her child's safe return, her husband's funeral, her new baby's birth.

She was long overdue for a breather.

CHAPTER 12

Thursday morning

Fern and I rocked on her bouncy porch, waiting for the art appraiser. Yellow forsythia and daffodils, frothy pink redbud trees, and purpley-blue wisteria had brightened her yard, but I wasn't in the mood for Easter-egg colors. Gloomy brown better suited my headachy thoughts about Mercer's murder, Lincoln's "accident," and an abducted-then-mysteriously-returned toddler.

"False alarm yesterday," Fern said. "They sent her home, told her to rest. Poor girl's been through so much."

"Can she rest? Taking care of Paige?"

"Soon as I get back, I'll take over. Oh, and she told me to tell you—she can't find her purple knife." I filed that tidbit away to tell Anselmo: a knife fitting the ME's description of the murder weapon might have been grabbed from Mercer's kitchen.

The appraiser had picked up a dozen or so paintings yesterday, Fern said—the ugly cubist ones, not her mother, Phoebe's, delicate botanicals. "He's Dutch and has a very strong accent. Jane says he consults for art museums."

"Did he like the paintings?"

"Hard to tell. He didn't seem too excited."

The porch floor felt like a trampoline. Termites? Rot? I stopped rocking. "Maybe he didn't seem excited because he was trying to look cool. Maybe he was all aflurry underneath the surface."

"If we can get a few hundred bucks for them, I want a new stove."

"While we're waiting, this would be a good time for you to tell me what you know," I said, not expecting anything.

"Kent Mercer was having an affair with Nikki Truly."

Not news to me, of course, but how did Fern find out? I couldn't hide my surprise. "Who told you?"

"June told me. June and Erwin both saw them, across the lake. They were bird-watching."

"Who—Nikki and Kent?"

"No. Erwin and June are bird-watchers. They saw Kent and Nikki together outside."

"So what? Nikki babysat there all the time."

"They were naked, Stella! They were doing it on the deck in front of everyone!"

I laughed. Although an advocate of sexual freedom, Fern could be a prude. She giggled. "It sounds funny, but June and Erwin were appalled. They both watched with binoculars."

"That sounds kinky, Fern."

"Well, it's their darling niece! I don't mean they watched. I mean they looked enough to know what they were seeing. Erwin had his stroke the next day. June is certain his anger caused it."

"Nikki's mother knows," I said, remembering how protective and controlling Zoë Schubert had been when I tried to ask her daughter about her relationship with Mercer.

"Yes. June told her. Then Zoë took Nikki to a psychologist. You remember Dr. Soto?"

"Of course." Fern had sent me to Emilie Soto for counseling when I was sixteen. I'd hated the idea, of course. Fern insisted, driving me there and waiting until she was sure I was safely in the psychologist's office. My bi-weekly visits to that sunny room, full of contemporary art, colorful rugs, and fresh flowers, became my lifeline in a year when I was nearly drowning—

skipping school, getting high, making plans to drop out and travel the world with a thirty-eight-year-old biker I'd met at the state fair. Fern had found out what I was doing when the police came to the farmhouse looking for him. Chuck was wanted for a shopping list of crimes including burglary, resisting arrest, and failure to pay child support. Chuck went to jail and I went to Dr. Soto.

She was warm and sympathetic and entirely on my side in my battle with the rest of the world. I loved her straight talk, delivered in a rolling Italian rush. She called me "Biker Cheek." She understood what a difficult time I was having, living in a small town with my unconventional grandmother and poverty-stricken lifestyle. Dr. Soto wouldn't share what she knew about Nikki, but I would love to be a bug on her wall for any session with the teenager.

The art appraiser carefully picked his way over the ruts in the gravel drive. Joseph was androgynous, with smooth skin and a mop of curly graying brown hair. He looked at Fern appreciatively—she was wearing a silky sea-blue shift batiked with tiny fish and shells. A silver starfish dangled from each ear. He kissed her on both cheeks—smack, smack—but not me, probably inhibited by my gun.

"Yer peexters er mervlus!"

His voice was high, almost feminine, and he had such an accent I couldn't understand a word he said. Puzzled, I looked at Fern to translate.

"He says my pictures are marvelous."

"Yer vas not misteekin, em er Reyes un Klein."

"I told you who painted them, Joseph," Fern said. "I wondered whether Reyes and Klein had any value these days."

"Zowzands, meenie zowzands."

That I understood. "How many thousands?" I asked.

"Ee tek zeem to auction. Each zeem peexters get hunna zow-zand eese."

I was astonished. "A hundred thousand? Fern, how many did you have?"

"He took two by Mick and one by Ev. Ugly old things. Hard to believe anyone would want them."

"Zee museums vant zem. Ver, ver valabel. Zay er zeind."

"Zay er what?" I asked.

"Zeind. Zeind!" Joseph was impatient with my ignorance of the English language.

"Signed," Fern whispered to me.

"Ee vel shit sem to zee auction zouse."

"Shit sem?" I whispered to Fern.

"Ship them. He'll ship them to Christie's."

"Wait a minute, please, Joseph. We need to talk this over." I led Fern inside, into the kitchen. "Do you trust him? Do you want a second opinion? I mean, this sounds big."

"Oh, he's fine. I asked Harry to draw up some papers and everyone has signed them. We're all covered. I even have insurance."

"Insurance? When did you get insurance?"

"Um, eight years ago. I saw where one of Mick's paintings had sold for nearly seventy thousand dollars. I thought I better insure mine in case we had a fire, you know. That old kerosene heater in the parlor could just go boom!" She laughed and the starfish danced against her cheeks.

I was speechless, too overcome to say the obvious. When she bought insurance, she had appraisals. So she knew all along what the paintings were worth. She knew she was sitting on a fortune. She let me buy her groceries, and pay someone to mow the fields? She watched the roof rust and the porch sag?

Fern knew what I was thinking. She patted my shoulder. "They were for you. I didn't want to sell them. I thought they'd appreciate, and I was right. Don't be angry."

"I'm calling a contractor tomorrow, Fern. The bank will give you a loan against those paintings and you can do all the repairs you've put off for thirty years."

"Can I have real air conditioning?" Fern got through the summer with floor fans that hurled dust bunnies from wall to wall.

"You'll have central heat and air conditioning, I promise." I too had been worried about the kerosene heater, a monstrous metal box that came on explosively, heated red-hot, and left a noxious greasy film on the walls and furniture. I suddenly felt twenty pounds lighter as the realization sunk in: Fern's money problems were over. I was so happy I startled Joseph with a smack-smack as he left. Fern and I stayed another half hour, making a list of the necessary repairs. Roof, porch, kitchen, HVAC. Then I took her to the bank.

CHAPTER 13

Thursday early afternoon

Bad news comes in threes, but so does good. Paige Mercer was OK, Fern had resources, and now—Lincoln Teller was conscious and able to talk.

The ICU waiting room was a bustling, noisy place. Visitors and medical staff walked in and out, passing through a hall where an elderly man slept on a gurney, attached to an IV and an oxygen tank. After a while an orderly pushed the gurney around a corner. I waited for a few minutes, then wandered into the ICU. No one stopped me.

The well-lit room contained eleven beds, each occupied by a patient. Assorted machines whispered, hummed, beeped, and whooshed, an out-of-sync cacophony like a fifth-grade orchestra tuning up.

A swarm of white coats surrounded Lincoln Teller's bed. I didn't recognize him—his bruised eyes were slits and his ears were nearly lost in the puffiness of his swollen head. The swarm, however, knew exactly who he was, and I guessed they would be asking for autographs as soon as he could hold a pen.

A candy-striper handed him a water bottle. Lincoln took a long sip and winked a puffy eye at the teenager, who glowed happily.

"Okay, folks, show's over," said a white coat, Dr. Beckert according to his name tag. He had gray eyes behind rimless glasses and a patch of hair like a tarantula on his chin. "Let Mr. Teller have a little peace and quiet. He's doing very well. No need to gawk."

The swarm wished Lincoln good luck and a speedy recovery, and slowly dispersed, except for a nurse who examined his head bandages.

"Not much under there, I bet," Lincoln said in a raspy voice.

"The doctor left most of it," she said. She was a forty-ish plump woman who moved quickly and efficiently. "I've connected a morphine pump. The doctor prescribed it for when you woke up." She showed him how to use it. "You can't overdose. The pump won't let you."

"Here we go, then," he said, and pushed the button. Rolling the medication cart out of the room, the nurse waved me over to his bed.

"It's really good to see you," I said, though he looked terrible. "Do you feel like talking a bit?"

"Hmm. Throat hurts. How long was I out?"

"About a day. I understand you have a new hole in your head."

"Not another one!" His cheeks twitched as though he were trying to grin. It was hard to watch.

"What do you remember about your accident?"

"Nothing." His gaze shifted to the doorway and his face lit up. I turned. Clementine stood there, a slender teenage girl behind her.

"Ooh, poor baby. You look awful," Clementine said.

"I think he looks great," the girl said, starting to cry. I decided she was their oldest child, Sue. She pushed her way around her mother, who had started her tapping and nodding ritual at the doorway. Knowing they didn't need me hanging about, I left them and took the elevator to the lobby café, where I got a cup of coffee and sat down to think.

How could Lincoln's engineered accident be related to

Mercer's murder? Mercer worked for Lincoln and they lived in the same neighborhood. Was a disgruntled employee at Clemmie's getting even with the management, one by one? A serial killer targeting male residents of Silver Hills? Perhaps a woman, scorned and furious, one who knew how to cut brake lines.

The lobby bustled with people trotting, limping, and pushing wheelchairs in and out. Automatic doors wheezed open, swished closed. Outside, a group of smokers shivered in the chilly shadows while cars waited in a queue to pick up discharged patients. I watched a dad struggle to fasten an infant carrier into his car as the baby wailed and a nurse hovered, murmuring instructions. I sipped my coffee until I saw Wesley Raintree striding through the lobby.

"Hey, Wesley," I called. "You here with Temple again?"

He pulled out a chair and sat down. "Not yet. No, I was here for a hospital board meeting. Man, what a waste of time."

"Oh?"

"The staff tells us what they want us to hear, then certain board members ask stupid questions and get misleading answers. Mostly it's about getting money out of my friends. I tell you, there's nothing I hate more than a fundraiser. Everyone gets drunk and the noise gives me a headache."

"Something tells me you miss the Navy," I said.

"I'll admit retirement is tough for me. I want to be useful."

"Volunteering?"

Wesley shook his head. "Can you see me serving corn bread to the homeless? Look, here comes the rest of the board."

They were easy to spot on the escalator, a well-dressed group, obviously not patients or staff. Zoë and her Dr. Newell led the way. Behind them I spotted Dr. Emilie Soto, my former therapist. I hadn't seen her in ten years, but she recognized me immediately. She beamed and held out her arms for a hug. She was rounder than ever, and the mass of curls spilling onto her shoulders had turned silver, but she still wore gold ear-hoops and jangling bracelets.

Wesley put his arm around her shoulders. "This woman is a saint. When my wife was sick, Bryce was unmanageable. I think I would have killed him if Dr. Soto hadn't helped us."

"Well, I have a little saying—there's nothing wrong with teenagers that reasoning with them won't aggravate." She laughed, a throaty chuckle, and I remembered how much fun she was. "Stella, come and see me. I want to catch up with you."

"Of course," I said, thinking I might quiz her about Nikki Truly. "What's a good time?"

"After work tomorrow? Around six. I'll fix your Lemon Zinger!" Drinking tea in Dr. Soto's office—a good memory.

"Excuse me? Agent Lavender?" said a man's voice behind me. I turned to face Dr. Newell and Zoë Schubert. Zoë had changed the clothes she'd worn to the funeral, into a tailored charcoal-gray suit and matching shoes, livened up with an apple-green scarf. Her board look. "We were glad to hear the Mercer child has been found," Dr. Newell said. "What happened to her?"

I shrugged, hating how little I knew. "It's a mystery."

"Stella, my friend," Dr. Soto said, slipping her arm around my waist and squeezing, "see you tomorrow at six. Gotta run now." She walked quickly through the lobby, her curls bouncing.

"I thought you might be here because of the child," Zoë said to me.

"I was visiting someone."

"Oh?" She tilted her head and raised her eyebrows a millimeter. I could almost hear her wondering who it was.

"How's Nikki doing?" I asked.

97

"Well, you know. She's glad about Paige."

"She's found somewhere else to go," said Wesley. We all looked at him. "She's been hanging out with Bryce."

Zoë's face turned pink. "What?"

"My son. The two of them were together yesterday afternoon. I saw them leave his place together."

"That was Bryce who spoke at the service yesterday, wasn't it?" she asked.

"He seemed like a nice young man," Dr. Newell said. "Perhaps they are a comfort to each other."

The rest of us looked at the floor.

My cell phone chimed and I stepped away from them. It was Clementine, her voice panicky. "Stella, you still here? They think Lincoln's stopped breathing!"

I ran back up the escalator and down what seemed a mile of corridor to the ICU. Through the door I could see a crew of nurses and doctors surrounding Lincoln's bed, inserting tubes and needles with a hushed urgency.

Clementine and Sue huddled just outside the ICU. Clementine patted her cheekbones rapidly; Sue leaned against her, peering through a glass window.

"What happened?" I asked, trying to catch my breath.

Sue must have realized that her mother was in no shape to talk, as she answered me. "After you left, we talked with Daddy for a while. He wanted to sleep, so we went to the cafeteria for a snack. When we got back, a nurse wouldn't let us in. She said he was having trouble breathing!"

We waited and listened, trying to assess what they were doing to Lincoln and what the outcome would be. The number of staff busy around him was reassuring. The plump middle-aged nurse who'd set up the pump came into the hall, so I showed her my ID and asked what happened.

"I just don't understand it," she said. "As soon as I saw he was having trouble, I checked the morphine pump. It was fine, all settings normal. But somehow he overdosed."

"Who was with him after his wife and daughter left?" I asked.

"I was monitoring the equipment, if that's what you mean."

"Anyone in this room besides patients?"

She looked around. "Well, sure. Visitors. I was getting meds ready."

Clementine finally stopped tapping and put her arm around Sue. "The poor man's had some bad luck lately," she said.

No. Not bad luck, or bad karma, or being in the wrong place at the wrong time. Maybe I was paranoid, but possibly someone had tried to kill Lincoln a second time. I said nothing to Clementine, though. She didn't even know about the severed brakes; Anselmo had wanted that kept confidential for a few days.

It had never occurred to me that a second attempt on his life would be made in the ICU. Lincoln could blame me for not protecting him. It wouldn't happen again. I called the police department and asked them to send a security detail. Until it was set up, I would guard him myself.

A white coat separated from the crowd around Lincoln's bed and came toward us. "Ladies," said Dr. Beckert, "we pulled him back. The man was heading toward the white light, but we performed a miracle."

Clementine's cold expression and mottled cheeks told me she was unimpressed by his bedside manner. "Someone made a mistake. As a lawyer, I know malpractice when I see it."

Dr. Beckert's chin patch quivered as he looked over his shoulder to see who was listening. He patted her shoulder as you would a child's. "Now, now, Mrs. Teller, calm down. The hospital will thoroughly investigate this incident."

"Calm down?" She gripped the doctor's arm with both hands. Her voice carried down the hall and people turned to look.

"Lincoln Teller nearly dies in your hospital, and all you care about is calming me down?"

He blanched and pried at her fingers. "Please let go of me. He's going to be all right. We injected naloxone and he's being closely monitored. You can see him in a few minutes." He finally succeeded in loosening her grip and trotted down the hall.

Clementine sagged against the wall and stared at the floor, rolling her head from side to side. Sue crept into the ICU, to her father's bedside, and took his hand.

Once more I had to tell Clementine I was sorry. This time, I felt personally responsible. I should have known Lincoln was in danger.

A police officer arrived and I filled her in. She promised to vet every person who came near Lincoln Teller's bed, but anyone with a white coat could walk into the ICU, stick a syringe into an IV port, and walk out. The setup was ideal for murder.

An hour later, I sat on Fern's rickety porch steps as a soft gray mist fell gently. For a few peaceful minutes, entertained by Merle out in the field, I forgot my worries. He was pouncing and digging feverishly, probably after a mole, one of the thousands heaving up tunnels every spring. From the hemlock next to the porch steps, a Carolina wren warned me with a raspy buzz to keep my distance from her nest. A slow drip, drip into a bucket reminded me why I was here—to meet a contractor for a bid on the repair work.

Axles squeaked as a truck bounced over the driveway ruts. *Sam Norris General Contracting*, it said on the side. Sam Norris himself emerged, sturdy and rugged as ever, though his brown curls that once begged to be tousled were now thinning a bit. I'd had a serious crush on him in senior high, post–Biker Cheek, but the only time he'd ever noticed me was at a party after too much beer. We both lay on the floor and talked about me. I didn't remember much of the conversation, just that he said I would have an interesting life. He was kind and hunky and I wanted to kiss him, but his girlfriend Emma was passed out behind us on the couch and someone would have told her.

Sam was now affluent, I'd heard. I shook his hand. "I didn't think you'd come yourself," I said. He had a sixty-home development going up near Big Pine Road, and I'd seen his sign on the site of a recently completed office building in Verwood.

"I'm glad you called. I wondered when you were going to get around to the repairs on this place. It's such a great old farmhouse," he said. We wandered around and he took lots of notes. "I can have a crew here tomorrow, if you want to get started. You and Fern go to the plumbing supply showroom, tell them you've hired me. They'll give you the contractor price."

"Tomorrow? That's amazing. Usually it takes weeks to get remodeling started around here."

"There's an open window for one of my crews right now. And if we wait another day, this place might fall down." He seemed in no hurry to leave and accepted my offer of iced tea. He told me he got a divorce a year ago. "I hate it, Stella," he said. "I feel like such a failure sometimes. Twenty-seven and already divorced."

I didn't want to be nosy but he seemed to want to talk. "What happened?"

He shook his head. "Emma started grad school, and I was building my business, and both of us got to where we liked working more than we liked being together. The only time we talked was to fight over who would watch our son, Garrett."

"Bring him over here. He can help Merle find gopher holes."

Sam laughed. "I heard you're with the SBI. I was right about the interesting life, wasn't I?"

"I can't believe you remember that conversation."

"You told me you were poor and would have to work hard. I remembered, because my folks didn't have money either. The working hard part is still true, isn't it? And you had the sense to stay single."

"Not for want of trying." I told him about Hogan, our engagement, our breakup. My phone chimed, rescuing me from recounting miserable details. I told Fern I'd call her back in a few minutes. Sam took the interruption as a cue to leave. He promised to phone me with a bid the next day. I watched him drive away, pleased that my high school crush now felt more like warm friendship.

The rain had stopped and a rainbow of coral, gold, and plum dressed the sky. I called Merle in from his hunt. He was wet and muddy so I splashed him with rainwater, then rubbed him down with an old towel—he loved it.

When I called Fern back, she reminded me about a dance Saturday night, a fundraiser for the schools' arts program. "Remember, Stella? At the Mill? You bought a ticket. Also, can you make some dip? We're getting people to bring appetizers so all the money can go to the schools." I had pushed the event out of my short-term memory because it meant dress-up for the second time in a week.

"Everyone who's anyone will be there," she said. "And I made you a dress."

"What does it look like?" Fern was an excellent seamstress, though her taste in formal wear was bolder than mine. I hoped it wasn't strapless, backless, and slit to the hip.

"It's red, very conservative. It's here at Temple's."

Even though the dance was a fundraiser, I wasn't sure whether my appearance at a public frolic was wise, with no arrests in Mercer's murder and two attempts on Lincoln Teller's life. I guess I could claim I was working, even carrying a bowl of guacamole. You never know what's going to happen at a dance when *everyone* who's *anyone* is in attendance.

CHAPTER 14

Thursday early evening

Dr. Emilie Soto had asked me to drop by at six. Her office occupied a small frame house on a quiet Verwood street, across from a graveyard dating back to the Civil War. I looked forward to seeing her, telling her that her guidance had put me back on the right path. So much had changed in the last ten years. Back then, at sixteen, I had been poised to escape—to just about anywhere, as long as it took me away from Fern's flirting and paint-dabbing and bills she couldn't pay. I had wanted to attack life with the outrage and anger I had carried since I was five, since the day someone abducted my mother while I, unwitting, waited in her car.

Some grain of self-preservation made me listen to Dr. Soto when she told me to turn my rage into a positive force. I listened, and decided to make homicide investigation my life's work. If that sounds melodramatic—well, it was.

I arrived just as a group of women of varied ages was leaving. "My relationship group," Emilie told me. She wore a mango-colored linen dress and a necklace of shells—tiny shrimp- and pearl-colored conches. Today her silver curls were pulled back into a shell barrette. She was round, colorful, and I loved her. "A support group. I try to keep them focused, remind them what's healthy."

"I should join."

"You'd be welcome. But that's not why you're visiting! Here's your Lemon Zinger. Sit down and tell me all about yourself. I must tell you how happy I was to see you yesterday. You looked so professional, so successful."

"Fooled you, did I?"

She clasped her hands over her heart. "I knew you'd achieve your goals. Fern must be proud."

"I think she's reconciled to it."

"And you chose law enforcement."

"Not exactly. It's the investigative part I like, the search. That's why I wanted to join the SBI rather than a police department."

"Finding the bad guys. And hopefully removing them from circulation."

I had removed my shoes out of habit, and now, curled up in the overstuffed chair, I sipped my tea. The antique clock ticked softly in the corner, and I smelled vanilla and some other spice, cinnamon or nutmeg, from the bowl of potpourri on her desk. What a safe-feeling place she'd created. "I probably never told you how grateful I was for you, back then," I said.

"No need to say it. You trusted me, such a gift. Tell me, how did you get into the SBI?"

"I was lucky."

"No, you worked for it."

"I got a BS in criminal justice from State, and then I interned with the SBI. I guess I made a decent impression. That's the lucky part." I told her about the training, my assignment as an undercover drug agent. "And now I'm working on the murder of Kent Mercer."

Emilie's smile faded. "Ah, yes. I have been following that case. The missing baby, such a worry. And a relief, when she was found. Her poor mother . . . what she's been through."

"Do you know her? Temple Mercer?"

She nodded. "I do."

Temple might be a client, but I knew Emilie wouldn't confirm it. "Funny thing," I mused. "Fern told me the child was okay. I don't know if she knew something, or was just an optimist."

"This is a small town, Stella. You can't keep a secret around here."

"You must know secrets." I sipped my tea.

"But I can't ever share them, unless I think someone's life is in danger. I do know a secret connected to your case."

I set my mug on the table. "Tell!"

"I'll talk with my client. Perhaps." She clasped my hands in both of hers, pulling me closer. "Be patient?"

"There's a murderer out there thinking up new ways to kill Lincoln Teller. I can't be patient. I want to stop this."

Emilie looked puzzled. "This has nothing to do with Lincoln Teller. It's a delicate situation. I'll let you know if I think anyone is at risk."

I had to accept that promise. I stood. "Come say hello to Merle, the well-adjusted one of the family."

She laughed. "You turned out all right." We walked outside. The bakery a block away had filled the air with the aroma of warm bread, making me hungry. I let Merle out of the car to greet her. He sniffed her hand politely, and wagged his tail as she leaned down to scratch his ears. The shells of her necklace swung above his head.

"Merle's a lucky fellow to have you as his person." She rubbed between his shoulders.

"You have it backwards. I'm the lucky one."

"What good manners he has," she said. I felt a surge of gratitude toward her, and Merle, for being in my life.

Then a gunshot shattered our peace forever.

I felt the first bullet, a whoosh of air pressure inches from my head, as I heard a rifle's *crack*. I dropped to the ground, pushing Merle down under me, reached up for Emilie, too late, for a snapping pop sprayed her blood everywhere and she collapsed. The three of us lay in a gasping whimpering knot for an instant. We couldn't stay there. I had to get us to the other side of the car, to put it between us and the shooter across the street in the graveyard.

I dragged Emilie around the car, waiting for the next gunshot to finish her, or hit me, or Merle, who bounded into the open, barking angrily at the sound of the gun. I screamed his name but he wouldn't come, and I had to go out there and pull him, angry now because he was being a stupid dog, risking us both. Then someone hit me in the head with a baseball bat—at least that's what it felt like.

I lay on the ground, stunned, not sure what happened until I touched my forehead and my fingers came away bloody and I realized a bullet had grazed me. Adrenaline took over and I scuttled around the car, dragging Merle after me. He whined and wriggled and I took deep breaths. I knew my injury had to be superficial—I was conscious, rational, terrified.

But Emilie's injury wasn't superficial. Her breathing was a harsh choking, and no wonder—she'd been shot in the throat and I guessed blood was running into her lungs. There was blood everywhere, filling the little conch shells of her necklace, sprayed onto her silver curls. I eased her onto her side, thinking it might help her breathe.

I slid into the backseat, onto the floor, reached for my phone, and called nine-one-one for officer down, backup, and an ambulance. I pressed my jacket to Emilie's neck, listened to her bubbling attempts to breathe. I stroked her hair and watched her eyes. "Hold on," I whispered, "they're almost here." She looked up, into the clouds.

What just happened? She wouldn't die, would she? Where was the goddam ambulance?

After a short eternity I heard sirens, and Anselmo called on my cell.

"We're here. Are you all right?" he asked. "Where are you?"

"In my car. I'm OK. Hurry, Dr. Soto needs help."

"We have to secure the area before the ambulance can come in, so hold on. We'll keep talking."

"Hurry. Thanks. Please," and it was true, I was grateful, more than he could possibly realize, to have another human being who could hear me if I had anything to say like *help come get me*. Emilie's breathing had become harsher. I whispered meaning-less encouraging things to her. *You'll be okay soon. Here they are. Just hold on.*

"We're encircling the graveyard across the street now," he said. "Did you see a person or a car?"

"No, with the first shot I got down."

"We're not seeing anything over here. It's deserted. The shooter is gone."

I heard the vehicles pull up. Paramedics began to work on Emilie with skill and urgency. One asked me, "Are you hurt?" I held up my hand and shook my head, no.

Anselmo gently pulled my hair back. "It's just a graze, right at the hairline," he said. I could feel the blood trickling down my face. I was still jumpy, and wanted to tell him to drop and hide, so that no bullet would pierce his chest and dull his warm black eyes. I kept my cowardice to myself and slowly pulled myself out of the car. I looked over the EMTs' shoulders at Emilie. Her eyes were open, her breathing ragged. I knelt and took her hand, her plump, freckled, warm hand.

"I'm sorry," I said. "I'm so sorry." *Sorry for your suffering. Sorry you came out into the parking lot with me. Sorry I visited today.* Why did I bring Merle, anyway?

They eased her onto a stretcher and slid her into the ambulance. Then my legs buckled and I sat down on the gravel.

Merle nosed me, whimpering.

Anselmo handed me an icepack. "You're okay, Stella, it's shock." He twisted the cap off a bottle of water and offered it. "I called Richard. He's going to take you off the case."

"Over my dead body."

"Well, yeah. Almost. Tell me what happened."

"We came out of her office. We were standing by the car, she was patting my dog. Three shots were fired. It sounded like a rifle."

"Yeah. We found the bullets—.25 caliber. Were the shots intended for you?"

That had occurred to me. We had been standing close together, about a foot apart, Dr. Soto leaning down as she reached for Merle. "I don't know. She'd told me she knew a secret, something to do with the Mercer murder. I want to look at her files."

"You'll have to specify the files you want, to get a subpoena."

He was right. Dr. Soto's patient records were privileged and confidential, unless I had names, dates, and a good reason. Well, I had a damn good reason—she had just been taken away in an ambulance. Names and dates would be in her appointment book. There were two ways to go. The legal way—get a search warrant in the morning, research the appointment book, get a subpoena for specific files, and wait until they were retrieved for me.

Or another way.

I would come back later, by myself, and browse. I wouldn't be collecting evidence, not exactly—just information, a pointer to a person or an event. Hardly legal procedure but I didn't care. Dr. Soto knew a secret, and someone had tried to kill her, or me. I didn't want to wait another day to find out what it was. Whoever fired those rifle shots could easily pick off another target at any time. "Can you put a guard on her room?" I asked.

"I'll see to it. And you—avoid open spaces."

"Yup," I said, though a sniper can work at any distance. "I'm going inside to clean up." At the restroom sink I wiped my arms and face with dampened paper towels and studied my injury in the mirror. Right at the hairline, an ugly lump had formed, a groove in my skin. Minor. Another centimeter and I'd have a cracked skull, or worse.

I went into Dr. Soto's office and found keys that unlocked her desk and filing cabinets. Her appointment book was in her desk but I couldn't very well walk out with it, so I put it back and shut the drawer. Finally, I went to the restroom again and opened the window an inch. I was still in there dabbing at my shirt when Anselmo came to find me. "I'm going to give you a ride to the ER."

"If we'll drop my dog at home first." Normally I would try to be stronger, able to handle this. But today's events were so shocking, it felt right to let Anselmo take care of me for a little while.

On the ride, he told me he'd been shot once himself.

"On duty?"

"Yep. I had to serve papers on this paranoid old guy, divorce case. His wife was afraid of him and asked us to help. He opened the window and blasted me with a shotgun when I rang the bell. I've got a couple of holes in my back still. Here, you can feel them."

He pointed to his shoulder blade, and I eased my fingers along his back. Two little depressions, flaws in the warm hard muscle of his back. My hand lingered no more than a second.

"You were lucky," I said.

"Yeah. I dropped when I saw the gun. You were lucky too, Stella. I think you were the more likely target back there."

I wasn't sure. What did Emilie know? I hoped she took good notes.

Chapter 15

Thursday midnight

The paramedics got Emilie to the hospital fast and she was whisked into surgery to stop the bleeding and save her life. But she had nearly died, either because of a secret a patient had told her or because she had the bad luck to be standing next to me. I had to find out why. I was waiting until the wee hours to return to her office and search her files.

My injury had been treated with antiseptic and stitches. The doctor predicted I'd always have a little scar at the hairline that could be repaired with minor plastic surgery. I said I'd think about it. I might keep it as a reminder. She gave me painkillers that I didn't take because of the drowsiness warning. My head ached, a manageable pain as long as I didn't move too fast. I spent an unpleasant hour on the phone convincing Richard I was fine, that it was ridiculous to take me off the case. He finally gave in.

Suffering survivor's guilt, I treated it with a hot bath, the gift of doing nothing, trying to silence the self-blame I felt when I thought of Emilie Soto, alive, in critical condition after surgery, absolutely no visitors allowed. Emotionally I felt numb, like that instant when the air is knocked out of you and just before you have to breathe. Yes, oxygen was necessary for life and yes, my lungs weren't working.

I added lavender bubble bath to the tub. Might as well smell good when you're planning to fracture the law.

★ ★ ★ ★ ★

At one a.m., I dressed in all black and clipped a leash to Merle's collar. Should anyone ask, I was obviously walking my dog. We walked through the quiet, dark streets of Verwood, a half-mile from my house to Emilie's office. I didn't see a living soul. A sniveling, cowardly part of me didn't want to be anywhere near her office, across the street from that moonlit graveyard. I kept hearing the crack of a rifle and seeing her eyes as she struggled to breathe.

I approached the back of the building, avoiding the well-lit street and parking area. In the moonlight, a slow-moving creek flashed silver, and white blooms of azaleas glowed, luminous. I looped Merle's leash over a shrub branch, pushed up the bathroom window, and climbed through.

Someone had been—or still was—in her office. A flashlight lying on the floor cast a beam to several open file drawers. The damp night air pressed into the room, and I realized the front door was ajar. I stood very still, feeling my heart thump, listening to the peeper frogs croak outside. A sound, or a sixth sense, warned of danger and I dropped to a crouch just as a gun fired, deafening me, starting an adrenaline flood that sent me scuttling into the bathroom. I wrenched my Sig from its holster, trying to sense the whereabouts of the shooter. I couldn't see any outline or movement to give me a target. Outside, Merle barked angrily with notes of fear.

"Police!" I yelled. "Give it up!"

A second gunshot hit the mirror over the sink, shattering it into shrapnel. My survival instincts kicked in as slivers of glass cut into my face, neck, and chest—stinging, fiery—and I slammed the door shut and scrambled through the open bathroom window, landing in a crouch as my heart pounded nearly out of my chest.

A car door slammed, an engine revved. I ran around the

building in time to see a car squeal down the street, spitting gravel. It was a mid-size SUV, narrowing the suspect population down to several million residents of the Triangle. I took a few deep breaths to slow my heart and patted my face, felt a couple slivers of mirror glass. Ouch. I called Anselmo. He said he'd be there in fifteen minutes.

Plenty of time for what I needed to do. I was on automatic, pushing down my visceral reactions, rubbing my arms as I scanned Emilie's appointment book.

I found several names I recognized—Wesley and Bryce Raintree, Nikki Truly—and also one more name associated with my case—Clementine Teller. I rifled through the files until I found the Raintree family. A quick scan of Emilie's hand-written notes told me they corroborated Wesley's description of events: Bryce lifting weights and goofing off; Wesley nursing his dying wife round the clock, under enormous stress, helped only by an occasional visit from a home-health aide. Bryce shut himself in his bedroom when he wasn't out partying, unable to face his mother's frailty and pain. One fact caught my eye—Wesley had administered meds to Sunny, morphine injections "whenever she seemed to need it," the notes said. Wesley had been in the hospital yesterday, for the board meeting. Had he slipped out? Wandered over to visit Lincoln in the ICU with a syringe and a few leftover vials?

Clementine Teller had visited Dr. Soto four times, most recently two months ago. Her compulsive disorder, the tapping and nodding I'd observed in the radiology waiting room, was more extensive than I thought. She was a compulsive cleaner, arranger. It was getting worse, taking longer and longer before she could perform the most mundane act. Recent life events had triggered the disorder. Clementine's father, a ne'er-do-well absent during her childhood, had recently surfaced asking for money. I felt like a snoop until I read that Clementine blamed

Lincoln's cash-flow problems on Kent Mercer. Might her obsessive nature find an outlet in violence?

Nikki Truly's file was missing. I rummaged—even looking under Schubert, her mother's name—but didn't see it. Nikki had visited Emilie only once, according to her aunt, but still, the doctor seemed to be so meticulously organized that even a one-time client should have a file. A missing file—did the intruder take it?

Outside, a car door slammed. I quickly stuffed folders back into place. I had no business looking through them without a subpoena. Anselmo would disapprove, the last thing I wanted.

He came in, a welcome sight in t-shirt and jeans, his hair mussed. He scanned the room, taking in the open drawers, the flashlight, me. "What the hell?" He cupped my chin, tilted my face to his. "You're cut up. Hold still." As he studied the nicks and gently tweaked out a sliver of glass, then another, his breath was soft on my face, his body so close I could sense his heat. I stood still, captured by his black eyes and warm hands, not wanting the moment to end, ever.

"Your poor face," he said.

"Thanks, I'll be okay," I said. "You're very kind."

"What brought you back here?"

"I was out for a walk with my dog, saw the flashlight beam."

"You didn't get enough of this place this afternoon."

"Right. Drawn to the scene. The door was open so I searched around. When the intruder started shooting, I ran into the bathroom and a shot hit the mirror." This story was ninety-five percent accurate. Okay, eighty-five.

"Seems like you get shot at every time you come to this place. Maybe we should stake you to the front door as bait, catch the crook that way." He smiled to show it was a joke.

I smiled back, ever the good sport, but it wasn't funny. I already felt like a goat in a Komodo dragon trap, not knowing what would happen next but suspecting I wouldn't like it much.

"Techs and a locksmith are on the way," he said. "I'm going to give you a ride home. Do you have to walk your dog at midnight?"

It was only a few minutes' ride to my house. Anselmo looked around outside, then came in with me for a brief walk-through. Shaky as I felt, I had enough mental energy to feel distressed for the state of my house. Except for Fern's colorful paintings, my abode was a sorry sight. Bed sheets covered the windows, a jumble of boxes crowded the dining area, and a collection of plants on the kitchen table had dried and gone to heaven. A fine layer of dust covered every surface, and Fern could have knitted mittens from the dog hair. I knew this atmosphere was sad and depressing but Anselmo tactfully said nothing. As we reached the door to say good night, he paused. "Put some antibiotic on those nicks. And quit pushing your luck at midnight."

"Will do." I thanked him again. "Go home. Go back to bed." Back to sleep with your wife. Hope she knows how lucky she is.

After he left, I checked my locked doors twice. I'm not normally paranoid but nothing seemed normal. "Just this once," I told Merle, as he jumped onto my bed. My face ached, but not as much as my pride, or my heart, and it took a long time to fall asleep, to erase gunshots, choking sounds, and bloody shell necklaces from my mind.

CHAPTER 16

Friday morning

I took my coffee outside, hoping the soft morning air and bird-song would pull me out of an exhausted funk. A familiar wave of helplessness washed over me, this time a fear that I couldn't find the killer/kidnapper/brake-line cutter/shooter, even with my shiny gun and fancy lab and official ID. Running sometimes improves my mood so I put on shorts and sneakers. The jingle of Merle's leash woke him from a twitching sleep in a nanosecond and propelled him nose-first to the door, dancing, his nails clacking on the floor like castanets. Sometimes I think the purpose of Merle's life is To Go Out; everything else is just waiting.

I added a couple of miles to our run but halfway into it, I had to sit down behind a tree to quash sobs threatening to break through. There was no need to analyze my feelings. I knew very clearly where all the sadness came from, and it wasn't the stinging glass punctures. I'd almost lost Emilie, like I'd lost my mom. I leaned against the tree, closed my eyes, and listened for Emilie's wisdom. I heard nothing, no warm, accented voice telling me what to do. Merle sat patiently. After a while, however, he stood and whined at me, softly, conversationally. He couldn't be more clear. Get up, let's go, there's treats to be eaten and socks to be found and the day is going to be fabulous.

★ ★ ★ ★ ★

Merle was right. The day, and my mood, improved.

Fern called to tell me Temple had given birth to a baby boy, John Franklin Mercer, eight pounds, four ounces. Mother and baby doing well.

Before anyone else frightened her with an exaggerated report, I gave her a brief version of yesterday's parking-lot shooting. "Emilie Soto was badly injured but I'm okay."

"What on earth! Are you sure?"

"Just worried about Emilie." I promised to keep her posted.

Then Sam called with his bid. It was lower than I'd expected, for the whole job. I told him to get started. What a nice guy.

I drove to the hospital to see Emilie, and on my way through the maze of corridors, I poked my head into Temple's room. Wesley was there, beaming widely at the baby in Temple's arms. "A perfect ten on his Apgar," he said. "The first of many perfect scores."

Temple looked remarkably fresh. Someone had un-poufed her hair, and it streamed onto her shoulders. "Want to hold him?" she asked me. "Just support his head."

I took the tiny bundle and sat down. I couldn't remember ever holding a newborn. He was warm, solid, and wriggly, even swaddled tight as a cigar. He fastened his deep-blue eyes on my face, seeming to be interested in the scratches.

Temple noticed. "Are you all right? You look pale. I heard about the shooting yesterday. How terrifying."

"Yup. It's nothing, I'm fine," I lied, though a couple of ibuprofen every three hours kept me functioning. I had picked a dozen glass slivers out of my face, neck, and shoulders last night, and each tiny puncture was now a puffy oozing bump that itched like a mosquito bite. I had camouflaged the bandaged lump on my head by gathering my hair into a tousled updo. It worked well—I have enough hair to hide a basketball.

"I was shocked to hear about Dr. Soto," Wesley said. "Sure hope she'll be all right."

"Dr. Soto is the best," Temple said. "You know how when you're a kid you think everything is your fault, except for the things that really are? I was sure my dad would have stayed if I'd done a better job of covering up my mom's illness. Dr. Soto showed me how ridiculous that was."

"I went to her too, in high school. She put up with a lot of whining from me," I said, recalling the hours I spent complaining about Fern as Dr. Soto nodded. Gradually she led me around to the real issue—my life was too precious to damage by partying with bikers. Such words from any other adult would have been rejected as just another lecture. From Emilie Soto, they felt like high praise.

"She helped us end a war, literally. I didn't think it was possible," said Wesley. "My wife was very ill, and Bryce was being a punk. I wanted to kick him out."

"Sunny wouldn't let you," said Temple.

"Right. Dr. Soto helped us find a middle ground. She was tough too, told me how it was going to be. Sure hope she's going to be okay."

Suddenly I yearned to be there in Emilie's office, curled up in the overstuffed chair, sipping Lemon Zinger, listening to her bubbly chuckle. "Here, your turn," I said, and handed Wesley the warm bundle.

I left the obstetrics ward and wandered through the labyrinth of corridors until I reached the closed door to Emilie Soto's room. A bulky guard blocked my entry. Thank God someone was keeping Emilie safe. Too safe—he wouldn't let me in. "No visitors. Only medical personnel," he said.

"How's she doing?" I asked.

"You'll have to ask her doctor."

A nurse pointed Emilie's doc out to me—Dr. Beckert of the

chin patch, who'd so annoyed Clementine Teller. He was even less forthcoming than the patrolman until I explained I'd been standing with Emilie when she was shot and showed him my ID.

"She was very lucky," he said. "The bullet missed her arteries and spine. EMS created an airway, they were fantastic." His gray eyes roamed over my face, studying the tiny nicks, lingering on my hairline bandage. "You have lots of ouchies."

"When can I see her?"

"Check back tomorrow. Say, you want to have a drink sometime? Can I call you?"

Maybe Fern's man-magnet DNA was finally kicking in. "Uh, sure," I said. Our schedules would never mesh.

Later on I stopped at the grocery store for dog food and coffee, loading up my cart with about eighty dollars' worth of stuff I couldn't live without. I got into a checkout line right behind Ursula Budd, Linc Teller's bookkeeper, catching up on the latest celebrity weddings in *People*. Next to her, a striking young woman loaded groceries onto the conveyer belt. They had to be related—the girl had Ursula's above-average height, tilted eyes over wide cheekbones, and frizzy hair, a darker red than Ursula's.

"Ursula!" I called. "Hi!"

She turned, then scowled when she saw me. "What happened to you?"

"Accident." I stuck out my hand to the girl, curious to find out who she was. "I'm Stella."

"Lauren," the girl said. She shook my hand. She was perhaps twenty, slender, with a gangly grace.

"Stella's grandmother teaches the painting class I was telling you about," Ursula said to Lauren.

"You two look so much alike, you must be related," I said.

119

They looked at each other. "Well, yes," said Ursula, nodding firmly, "we're related. Sorry we can't chat." She turned away, busied herself with paying, then wheeled her cart towards the store entrance.

I felt vaguely snubbed, realizing they didn't want me prying into their relationship. Hmmm. Fern would know. I called her.

"Did you see Temple's baby?" Fern asked.

"He's perfect," I said. "Very wiggly."

"I can't wait till she brings him home. Well, Paige and I have been playing. And guess what we found."

"What?"

"Some mini-CDs you might want to listen to. The box was in Paige's closet, but they're not children's recordings, Stella, they're odd—just people talking. They sound like phone conversations."

I couldn't imagine a few poor recordings could help me, but I trusted Fern's instincts. "Sure. I'll come over. What are you playing them on?"

"Paige has a boom box. I put in new batteries."

I waved my ID at the guard at the Silver Hills gate and a few minutes later parked in Temple's driveway. Her car, a dark green Toyota minivan, sat in the driveway. I looked in the garage window—Kent's burgundy SUV was still there. Had I seen it last night, screeching through the streets of Verwood? I didn't know. In the dark, I couldn't tell one of the boxy cars from another.

Fern opened the front door and waved. Paige stood beside her, clutching a fraying, much-loved stuffed dog. Their outfits made me laugh—both Fern and Paige wore negligees, several strands of beads, and crimson lipstick. "We're being movie stars today."

"Hollywood, watch out," I said.

Fern studied my face and I could tell she didn't like what she saw. "I'll be right back after Paige goes down for a nap. The CDs are in the kitchen." She picked up a bottle of milk and led Paige up the stairs.

There were five mini-CDs, each a Memorex eighty-minute disc labeled in green marker with a date—February 10, 16, 20, and March 4 and 9. It might take hours to listen to all of them. I'd have to take them with me. I waited until Fern came back downstairs.

"What happened?" she asked. "It can't be chicken pox, you had that when you were four."

I gave her a version of the midnight events at Emilie Soto's office. I dreaded telling her about my brushes with violence— Fern feared the risks of my job even more than I did.

"Oh, honey!" Fern lost her winsome smile and, for a moment, looked her age. She put her arms around me and squeezed. "I hate that you're hurt."

"Very superficial injuries." I smiled reassuringly. She didn't need to know about the lump underneath my piled-up hair.

"And poor Emilie! Will she be all right?"

"She will." Optimism was called for. I motioned to the handful of compact discs. "Which of these is useful?"

She shrugged. "Can't tell. Paige's dad singing and reading stories, then other voices just talking. They sound like phone conversations."

"I'll have to listen to all of them to see whether they're helpful or not."

I was pretending very hard that I should take the CDs and listen to them. With no reason to suspect they were related to a crime, I couldn't get a search warrant. But they probably contained nothing useful, so who would care? If I found anything, Fern could ask Temple to give them to me, conveniently forgetting to mention I'd already heard them. I thought briefly about calling Anselmo to come and listen with me, because two heads are better than one. But he'd question the legality of my possessing them. I decided not to involve him until I knew more.

One more question for Fern. She knew everything. "Who's the young woman hanging out with Ursula Budd? Named Lauren, looks like her daughter?"

"She is." Fern pulled out her knitting, a square of powder-blue yarn. She was making a blanket for Temple's baby. "Ursula gave her up for adoption at birth. The daughter's twenty-one now and she got her birth certificate, sought out her birth mother. Lovely, isn't she?"

"It's a happy reunion then."

Fern bound off the square and started another, this one green. "Ursula wasn't sure how George would take it. But he's been fine so far. Did you know they've been married eighteen years? I've never understood that, they're different as two people can be."

"Come on, Fern, any marriage is a mystery to you."

"She's so lively and interested in doing new things. He's dull as a tree stump, just fixes cars and goes fishing."

"Who can explain love?" I mused, thinking about all the feelings I wasted on Hogan.

It was a rhetorical question, but she chose to answer it. "You're right, Stella. They are genuinely fond of each other. And they both dote on their boy, Phillip. He's a handful. Even Emilie Soto would have her work cut out with that one."

I couldn't respond. Emilie's near-fatal shooting had scared me more than I wanted to admit, even to Fern. But I swear Fern could read my mind. "You should talk about it, Stella. It wasn't your fault."

I wasn't so sure. "I want to find whoever did it."

Fern knew how much Dr. Soto had helped me—with her careful listening, cajoling, and humor—to talk about my mother,

Grace. She'd told both of us that my grief would be lessened if the killer were found, that having someone to blame would crystallize my sadness into anger, then satisfaction once justice was served. Well, justice for Grace hadn't happened. Yet.

Before I left, I held Fern close. She was strong, fearless, and all the family I had. I wanted to put her on a cruise ship until this case was over. "You'll be careful, won't you?" I asked her.

"Stella! You're sweet to worry about me," she said, planting a sticky kiss on my cheek.

I took the five CDs home. Mixed in with recordings for Paige—Temple reading a story, Kent singing nursery rhymes—were hours of phone conversations. I heard Lincoln Teller telling Clementine he'd pick up Sue after soccer practice, arranging a golf game, and talking to Clemmie's chef about special events. Ursula Budd, Lincoln's bookkeeper, argued with her husband, George, about money, about their son's school problems. The restaurant's office phone must have been bugged. By Kent Mercer? Why? And why had he burned the CDs?

Listening didn't improve my mood or help my aching head, and the only way I could stay awake was to keep busy. It was as good a time as any to make a dent in my neglected home environment. Though kind to hide his thoughts after one glance, Anselmo must've been horrified. I picked up all my dirty laundry and started a load of wash, then ran the vacuum. Cleared the kitchen table—junk mail, dirty dishes, ATM receipts, and one dust-covered zucchini, a present from my gardening neighbor. I found the box with the cooking pots and made marinara sauce with red wine—a favorite recipe that calls for a glass for the pot and a glass for the cook. After two glasses and two bowls of spaghetti my head ceased throbbing. My mood, while not glowing rosy, flushed faintly.

It abruptly improved when I inserted the fifth CD and heard

a brand-new set of phone conversations: Bryce Raintree's rusty voice arranging sales of prescription drugs, drugs freely available from Wisteria Acres, the nursing home where he worked. I sent a silent "thank-you" to Fern for her discovery of the five mini-CDs. This last one made the preceding dull hours worthwhile.

It sounded like Bryce was the source of the oxycodone I bought from Kent Mercer at Clemmie's almost a week ago. Why did Mercer bug Bryce's phone? Was he blackmailing Bryce? How far would Wesley go to keep Bryce, his son, from prison?

Since Bryce's phone had been bugged illegally, my hands were tied.

But Fredricks might have an idea or two. Surely, mentoring your undercover drug agent must include a discussion of inadmissible evidence. Surely, Fredricks wouldn't be annoyed that I'd traded our delightful evenings together for a homicide investigation.

I picked up my phone and called him.

"What's up?" he answered, shushing the background video-game noises from his two rowdy boys. Skipping the small talk, I summarized my Bryce pills-and-illegal-recordings dilemma.

"He's not using scrips?" Fredricks asked.

"No." I knew where he was heading. Bryce was very small potatoes. We couldn't flip him, because he was a one-man show. There was no unethical pain clinic to shut down, no unscrupulous doctor writing reams of prescriptions.

Fredricks was chewing something crunchy. Cheetos, probably. He'd always kept a stash for us in the truck, claiming the orange dust on my fingers added to my disguise. "When are you coming back to the streets? Your work awaits. Evergreen needs you."

"You're changing the subject," I said.

"There's an ocean of gray between black and white. Is the kid salvageable?"

I thought about Bryce, suffering through his mother's terminal illness, the trauma of his brother's murder. Hurting under a thick veneer of muscle. "He's salvageable."

"Best not to involve me, actually."

"So you're saying . . . don't pursue an arrest?"

"Think of the system resources you'd save. Lawyers, court time, body-cavity searches. You'll think of something." He rang off, claiming a stovetop emergency.

I pondered. Where could Bryce take his muscles, besides jail? Where would they tame his flowing locks and lazy ways, teach him skills and respect for authority?

The answer was obvious.

CHAPTER 17

Saturday morning

June Devon had been in Fern's classes for years, but we'd never met. Her name had popped up all over this case. She was Fern's friend, Nikki Truly's aunt, Zoë Schubert's sister-in-law. Everyone knew June except me. Time to pay her a visit.

I called her to ask if I could stop by. "Sure," she told me. "I get up with the sun. Come on over."

Like Silver Hills, the White Pines development where June lived fronted Two Springs Lake, but there the resemblance ended. White Pines homes were modest, not mansions; the trees loblolly pines, not Japanese maples; the driveways gravel, not paved. Septic tank requirements gave each house two or three acres, spreading the houses apart. June's house had a new-looking handicapped ramp.

She was a robust woman in her mid-fifties with the erect posture of a dancer and graying brown hair pulled into a ponytail. A petite parrot with green, orange, and yellow feathers—"a conure," June told me—perched on her shoulder, head tilted as it peered at me with black beady eyes. It cried a rusty screech, a startling sound June ignored. I told her I was investigating Kent Mercer's murder.

"You're Fern's granddaughter, right? You have her sea-blue eyes." She tactfully didn't mention my scabby face. Her home was furnished with dark, gloomy antiques but the paintings were colorful—soft, near-abstract but recognizably birds, a subject she clearly loved.

A loud groan from a nearby room startled me.

"That's Erwin, my husband. You know he had a stroke last month? He can't talk. Come, meet him," June said. "I hope you don't mind if I keep working. Lots to do."

I followed her into a bedroom, musty with sour smells. Erwin lay on his back, watching us through bleary brown eyes. He was a large, gaunt man with stiff gray hair combed back from an expressionless face. He would have looked less alarming if he'd had a shave recently.

"Morning, sweetheart!" June kissed Erwin's brow. "Ready to rise and shine?" Erwin grasped her arm as she helped him into a wheelchair. She wheeled Erwin across the hall and into a bathroom, leaving the door open. "We had to add this whirlpool tub. Cost a fortune, but it was that or the nursing home, even more money we don't have. The tub's good for his circulation." She turned on the tub's jets and the floor vibrated. She seemed careless of her husband's privacy as she stripped off his pajamas.

Uncomfortable watching, I stepped back into her kitchen. The bird hopped around, from the sink to the stove to an open drawer. It seemed to have the run of the place.

June joined me. She took out a box of oatmeal and measured some into a bowl. "Erwin has to have food he can swallow without choking. He barely chews."

"It's a lot of work for you," I said. "Do you have help?"

"He has a speech therapist three times a week, and a physical therapist for walking. They say he's getting better. I guess he is. He can walk a bit now. A neighbor comes by so I can get out. Ursula Budd, do you know her? She helps with the insurance stuff. I don't mind the work. I'm angry because my husband is gone. That's—" she jabbed her thumb at the bathroom "—a wasted shell." She put the bowl of oatmeal into a microwave. "I'll tell you the truth. I'm jealous of women with husbands who drive, mow the grass, feed themselves, for Christ's sake. I'm even jealous of widows for their freedom. No nursing, doctors, watching the money hemorrhage away." She stared at me as if to make sure I got the full picture, then disappeared into the bathroom for a few minutes. The bird hopped about the table. When I held out my finger, hoping it might hop on, it pecked me gently, like a warning not to get personal.

June wheeled a dampish Erwin up to the table and placed the oatmeal in front of him. The bird nibbled a raisin from his bowl. An unsanitary practice, but I wasn't the health inspector.

"Ursula's coming this morning. She's a doll, isn't she, Erwin?" As June spooned the oatmeal into his mouth, he tipped his head back, either in agreement or to make swallowing easier, I couldn't tell which. "I'll take a walk while she's here. There's a hawk down by the lake. I want to find its nest." After a few bites, Erwin pressed his lips together, shook his head, so June gently washed his face. She wheeled him into the next room and helped him into a recliner in front of the TV, tuned to a kids' channel.

She returned to the kitchen, drained a pot of boiled potatoes, then began to sharpen a knife on a stone, whisking it back and forth. The conure perched on her shoulder, muttering as it preened her hair. June said, "I had to quit my bookstore job to take care of him. I loved my job—talking to the customers, meeting writers. My only pleasure these days is the few minutes I can slip away and watch the birds." She started cutting the potatoes into dice.

"Fern said you could see Kent Mercer's house from here. That's why I'm here, it's the murder case I'm investigating. She said you saw Mercer having sex with your niece, Nikki."

"She told you that? It was the day before Erwin had his stroke. He was outside bird-watching, and called me. I could tell he was disturbed—his face was white as this potato. He

Cold Heart

didn't say a word, just handed me the binoculars and pointed across the lake to the Mercers' house. I looked, and saw Mercer standing there naked. Wrapped around him was a woman who wasn't his wife. I knew the wife had dark hair. This woman had long blond hair. I couldn't watch what they were doing; it seemed so twisted, that they might be having sex outdoors, in full view of everyone. Then Erwin said, 'It's Nikki.' I can still remember how sick and angry he sounded." June contemplated her husband lying in the recliner, his mouth slack and open, his eyes glazed. Flickering light and mindless noise from TV cartoons washed over his blank face. "I could tell he wanted to go over there and beat Kent Mercer's brains out. You know, Stella, if Erwin wasn't so disabled now, he'd be your prime suspect. He was furious."

"What did you decide to do about it?"

"We told Nikki's mother, of course. And then Erwin had his stroke the next day, and I had other things to worry about."

"Was Erwin close to his niece?"

"Yes, very close. She always spent summers with us, and we've done what we could for her. We sent her clothes and toys when she was little and her mother was struggling. Even when Zoë was married to Oscar Schubert, wealthy as he was, he didn't want a penny spent on Nikki. We paid for her braces, her bicycle, her clothes—everything. Oscar Schubert was a nasty, cheap piece of work."

Muttering what sounded like bird-swears, the bird hopped from June's shoulder to the table and marched around. I put my hands in my lap lest it think I had treats. "That's Zoë's second husband?"

"Her third. A radiologist, richer than Trump. If you want to hear about my sister-in-law, it'll take a while."

Ah. I remembered at Mercer's funeral what Nikki said about her mother's upcoming wedding—*fourth time around, it better be*

129

simple and Zoë correcting her: *third, you know how she exagger-ates.* Amusing, that Zoë had deleted one of her marriages from her history.

"Zoë and Erwin were raised in Salt Flat, Texas. Dusty, hardscrabble ranch, no money, shooting squirrels for food. Their parents worked themselves near to death, trying and failing in one harebrained scheme after another. Never enough money. I bet Zoë started looking for a way out before she was ten years old. She married Tommy Truly 'cause he had a pickup and a business. Gas station. He was a good mechanic and the two of them worked like mules. Then Nikki was born, the bills piled up, and the fights started. Zoë left. She waited tables and somehow finished nursing school. She married again—an Air Force guy—it lasted six months. He liked his pretty wife, but not the brat—Nikki's always been a handful. That's when Erwin started sending Nikki clothes and toys, and paying for the child to visit us."

The bird startled me by flying onto my shoulder. June smiled. "He doesn't take to everyone. You should be honored." She took a head of celery from the fridge, broke off a few pieces for chopping.

"She has money now," I said, thinking of Zoë's Silver Hills mini-mansion.

"Zoë married her boss. She inherited half his estate."

By now I'd nearly forgotten why we were discussing Zoë. Perhaps some of this was relevant to Mercer's murder, so I decided to let her go on. "Schubert, right?"

"Oscar was almost thirty years older, with married kids, grandkids even. Erwin and I used to call him three-D— divorced, depressed, and drunk. Nikki hated him." June scooped the celery into the bowl with the diced potatoes, added a glob of mayonnaise, mixed vigorously. She held out a spoonful. "Taste this, will you? Does it need more salt?"

"Yummy. I'm glad you didn't put any pickles in it."

"I worry about Nikki. That creep Mercer took advantage of her. Zoë took her to the psychologist, Dr. Soto." June covered the salad with plastic wrap and put it in the fridge. "Three weeks ago. She was due for another appointment tomorrow. What a terrible thing, that shooting yesterday. You were there, weren't you? Is Dr. Soto going to be okay?"

"I hope so," I said, wondering whether she was accusing me of something or whether my guilty conscience saw blame everywhere.

June put her finger up to my shoulder and the bird hopped onto it. "Who knows what Nikki told the doctor."

Someone knows, I thought, remembering the missing file.

CHAPTER 18

Saturday midday

Richard had asked for a meeting.

"What for?" I asked. I'd been texting him updates, not that I had much to report.

"See where we're at. Clarify the scene. Get on the same sheet of music. You and the lieutenant. Bring your boyfriend the researcher, let's all get up to date."

"Hogan's not my boyfriend."

"Whatever."

So there we were—Richard, Anselmo, Hogan, myself—in Richard's office. Hogan took a look at me and frowned. "Looks like you broke a windshield with your face."

"Something like that," I said, not wanting to explain at the moment. I'd tried to camouflage the bullet graze at my hairline with artful hair design but the dozen-plus glass sliver scratches were now scabby. Not a good look.

Diplomatically promoting inter-agency harmony, Richard offered Anselmo a cigar. "I've played you. Essex team, right?"

Anselmo turned down the cigar. "Yeah. And you?"

"Raleigh West Side."

"Tough team. You've got that pitcher—" Anselmo mimicked a side-arm throw.

"Amos. The Bulls drop-out."

"You nearly shut us out that last game, man."

"Nobody gets a hit off Amos."

Hogan sat patiently, scrolling through texts from his girl-friend—what was her name, Gardenia? Daphne? some sort of odorous flower. I hoped he would behave himself in case Anselmo found out he was my ex-fiancé. I wanted Anselmo to think I used good sense picking boyfriends. Hogan was prone to spells of bitter jealousy, one of our sore points since I worked with so many men. He had no right or reason to be jealous, but a man like Anselmo—tough, confident—would trigger his insecurities.

Richard felt secure. He and Anselmo were already arranging a multi-team beer fest for the next time they played. Preliminaries over, Richard asked me to summarize. I handed out a page of notes.

Saturday 4/7. SBI Agents Lavender and Fredricks, under-cover, purchase oxycodone from Kent Mercer, Clemmie's restaurant manager.

Monday 4/9. Mercer found dead at his home in Silver Hills, from blood loss; radial and ulnar arteries of both arms were severed by knife. Death occurs within minutes. Head injury thirty minutes prior. Why a thirty-minute interval between the head injury and the injuries that cause his death? Computer, phone, and personal family items miss-ing from the house. Drugs stash not taken. Unidentified bloody fingerprint under deck. Mercer's 20-month-old daughter, Paige, is missing.

Tuesday 4/10. Text sent to Agent Lavender says Paige is okay. Hoax? Untraceable.

Wednesday 4/11. Brake lines of Lincoln Teller's (owner of Clemmie's) car are severed, resulting in serious injury to him. Paige Mercer is found in grocery store, unharmed; note pinned to her shirt says to call SBI Agent Lavender.

Thursday 4/12. Someone enters Teller's hospital room and injects a near-fatal morphine dose into his IV. Why is he a target? Who is trying to kill him?

Parking lot shooting critically injures Dr. Soto, slightly injures Agent Lavender. Who is target & why? Midnight break-in at Soto's office, more gunplay, files in disarray . . .

Leads: Fifty thousand dollars in Mercer's bank account; relationship of this money to his murder?

"Stella, these aren't notes, these are questions," Richard said.

"Right."

"It doesn't look good that someone keeps trying to kill Lincoln Teller. I don't want you in *People* magazine as the agent who goofed around while North Carolina's icon of black achievement was in danger." He gave me a hard look, crossed his arms, and leaned back.

"Right."

"Stop agreeing with me."

"Right," I said. "Er, I mean sorry. We've interviewed a number of people with ties to the victim, but no leads developed. Six crimes—Mercer's murder, the kidnapping of his child, two attempts on Lincoln's life, shooting of Dr. Soto, and her office break-in with more shooting."

"Are the crimes even related?" Hogan asked.

Richard trimmed the end of his cigar. Good Lord, was he going to smoke it? Our building was a no-smoking facility but more than once I'd caught a whiff of cigar stink in here.

"I think the child was taken to keep her safe. Possibly by someone who saw the killing," I said.

"A witness? Or an accomplice?" Hogan asked.

I shook my head. "I don't know. Maybe the killer took her. Felt sorry for the little girl alone in the house."

"Plenty of people disliked Mercer," Anselmo said. "But the money's a factor. Was he paid to do something he failed to do? Or sold something he didn't deliver?"

"That kind of money usually means drugs," Richard said.

"Was he dealing at that level?"

"No," I said, remembering the baggies of pills with hand-written labels. "His stash was relatively minor, all prescription. But he needed money—his wife says they were about to be evicted."

"Talk to me about Lincoln Teller." Richard stood and straightened the pictures, awards, and mementoes displayed on his wall. They didn't look crooked to me. I thought he just liked to touch them.

Anselmo answered first. "That's a tough one. The restaurant connects him to Mercer, so maybe it's a disgruntled employee. My team is talking to everyone who works there. They're also interviewing visitors to the ICU who may have seen something."

Richard rolled his cigar between his hands to warm it. "He has security?"

I nodded. "Moved to a private room, guarded round the clock. When the hospital releases him, he's leaving town with his family."

"Leaving? He can't split. He's involved in this case."

"They're going to his wife's sister's house in Durham. Now that's a secret, sir."

"Indeed. He's already used up two lives. I don't want to hear about strike three."

"Why don't you pull him in for questioning?" Hogan asked.

"I'd like to have him hypnotized," I said. "I think the person who killed Mercer is trying to kill Lincoln too. He thinks Lincoln knows something. And Lincoln doesn't know—or won't say—what he knows."

Anselmo said, "And if he has nothing to hide, he'll go along with it."

"Why are you so sure he's innocent?" Hogan asked.

I held up my fingers one at a time. "One, the bloody fingerprint under the deck. It's not Lincoln's. Someone else was

there. Two, the attempts on his life. Three, no compelling motive. Four, I mean . . . really. You know Lincoln's no killer."

Richard scowled. He hates it when I get intuitive. "Five," he
said, grimacing, "it's Lincoln Teller and we can't afford to be
wrong, for his sake and ours."

Hogan handed out a description of Mercer's assets, debts,
and business dealings. "Except for the fifty thousand deposited
right before he died, the guy had negative worth. He and his
wife owed back rent on their house in Silver Hills. A load of
credit card debt. His bank deposits show an income of about a
hundred thou a year. He was living way beyond that."

I couldn't sympathize with Mercer's money woes since my
income was a third of his, a trifling amount that kept Merle in
dog food and Fern in watercolors. Hogan went on. "As I told
Stella, we can't trace the deposit unless the Feds get involved,
and they require proof drug money is being laundered."

I thought briefly about mentioning Bryce's drug dealings,
that he'd been supplying Mercer, but knew the muddy morass
I'd be diving into if I tried to explain the CDs. *Uh,
my grandmother found them in the victim's playroom and I took
them* . . . So I kept mum.

Anselmo said the brake lines of Lincoln Teller's Jag had been
cut with a saw by someone who knew something about cars,
but wasn't an expert—he'd also severed the rear brake-light
connection. "Just sort of hacked away. Unfortunately, nothing
was damaged that would have warned Lincoln something was
wrong."

"And the hospital incident?" Richard prompted.

"It appears someone deliberately added morphine through
an injection port," I said. "Fortunately his depressed breathing
was noticed right away."

Richard tipped his chair back. "Ideas? Anyone? Time to think
out of the box. Find the cheese." I didn't get the allusion until

he held up his new management self-help book—*Who Moved My Cheese?*.

Anselmo said, "What if the crimes were independent? Different killers?"

"We're still nowhere," said Richard.

The only things I could add—CDs and confidential psychologist's records—would horrify Richard, repel Anselmo, and fuel Hogan's belief that he is more competent than I. But I wanted desperately to solve these crimes. I wanted to come back into this room and tell these three men the full particulars—who, how, and why. Lay out the confessions and the timeline, show them the weapons. Wrap it up, so families could move on, away from fear and anger. I wanted Lincoln's children to wave goodbye to their dad each morning without the shadowy thought that it might be the last time. Kent's kids, Paige and baby John, should know who killed their daddy. I wanted to give them the peace that had been missing from my life for twenty-two years.

CHAPTER 19

Saturday evening

I don't cook much but I can make guacamole. Four ripe avocados, the juice of two lemons, a few drops of Tabasco, mash with a fork. I spooned it into a yellow bowl and sprinkled a chopped tomato on top. I gave Merle a dab on a cracker—he liked it, not a surprise.

Tonight's dance would raise money for Essex Arts, a nonprofit group that organizes showings for local artists. Fern wanted me to attend, to show support. Perhaps the event would temper my frustration. Or take my mind off my worry about Emilie Soto. These seemed like good reasons to go.

Fern was still staying at Temple's house, waiting for her house repairs to be completed, so I drove there to pick up the dress she'd made me. Fern looked fabulous in a dress of shimmery peach fabric threaded with gold. With matching gold heels and eye shadow, she fairly gleamed.

Paige pushed "play" on her boom box and started bouncing to the beat of a pop tune. "Dance!" she demanded, and Fern obliged, sending her dress twirling.

Temple and her new baby had come home from the hospital. She held him on her shoulder, patting his back as his head bobbed. A pacifier and stained dish towel lay in her lap. "Your dress is in the coat closet," she said, her voice quavery.

Dismayed, I asked, "What's wrong?"

"I'll never go to another dance again." Her face was puffy

and blotchy with fatigue. "Look at me! I'm a mess!" She held out her once-crisp white shirt, now wrinkled and sporting spit-up stains.

Fern sat beside her, held her shoulders. "You most certainly will go to a dance again. I promise you."

"Sorry, sorry, sorry. I need a good night's rest," she said, wiping her eyes. "It's fine in the hospital, everyone visiting and making a fuss. But I can't sleep there, and then I come home and the baby wants to eat every two hours."

Paige pressed her nose against John's. "Bad baby," she whispered, and Temple laughed.

"I don't have to go," Fern said. "I'll watch your children so you can rest."

Her face crumpled. "Oh God, I don't know what's wrong with me. Someone says something nice and I fall apart."

"You know it's those awful old hormones," Fern said. "Up and down like a roller coaster."

"It's Kent's death, too," said Temple. "Not that he'd be any help right now like you are. But I look at this little baby and wish he had a daddy, you know?"

"I know," I said.

She looked up, distressed. "Oh, Stella. I didn't mean . . ."

I waved my hands. "It's nothing! It's completely different, anyway. Your son will have pictures and stories and a name. A grandpa to teach him to throw a football."

She made a face. "Or play golf. I'll teach him to draw. Now go put on your dress. I want to see what it looks like."

It looked like tomato soup, a creamy red satiny fabric that Fern had stitched into a simple sheath dress that fit perfectly. A stole of sheer black organza slithered around my shoulders. "Well, they'll be able to see me anyway," I said. "No pockets— guess I'll have to leave my gun in the car."

"You need jewelry," Temple said. She put the sleeping baby

139

into a bouncy seat and went upstairs, returning with a string of onyx beads.

"I feel like Cinderella," I said. "Where's my pumpkin?"

The dance was in the old Essex textile mill, a cavernous brick building converted to a business park. Part of the mill was still empty, with exposed beams and dusty floors—the perfect place for a dance. Strands of little white lights had been hung overhead, like tiny stars, and candles flickered on the small tables dotting the edges of the room. A five-piece band was already playing the typical Essex County blend of folk, rock, and bluegrass with a touch of Cajun and a whiff of Celtic to confuse the purist.

Hogan and his girlfriend were doing a mean jitterbug. She wore a black dress so short her undies flashed as Hogan twirled her around, flinging her toothpick arms and legs this way and that. If I watched long enough he'd hurl her into the air and spin her like a plate. He could never have tried it with me, but Jasmine was little enough to be flingable. I started feeling a bit jealous and strolled away toward the wine table, where Fern and my favorite contractor, Sam Norris, were pouring drinks.

Sam wore bartender's garb, a black vest and white shirt. In the shadowy light, he looked better than ever. How easy it would be to revive my puppy love for him. He was waiting on Ursula Budd, Lincoln Teller's bookkeeper, and a physically powerful man who must have been her husband. Sam mixed red wine with cranberry juice for Ursula. She took her drink and turned around, flinching as she saw me. "What are you doing here?" she said, then caught herself. "I mean, I didn't know you'd be here. This is my husband, George."

George held out his hand. I put my hand into that big mitt with trepidation, but he was gentle as he tipped his head and said, "How do you do?"

"I'm fine," I said, smiling at Ursula, wondering why I made her nervous, for she was inching sideways and trying to pull George with her, not an easy task, as he said, "Nice to meet you," tipping his head again, backing away.

"Likewise," I said. It was odd—I knew quite a bit about George from the recorded phone conversations—what he wanted for dinner, how much the new TV cost, his son's school problems. He seemed like a decent guy, kind to his wife and hardworking. They worried a lot about money.

Sam poured me a glass of red wine. "Great dress," he said, and I was glad the lighting was dim because my blush was no doubt highlighting the nicks on my face.

"You've cleaned up nicely yourself," I said.

"Cleaned up is right. I spent all day at Fern's place." He put his arm around her shoulders. "We're making progress, just the usual surprises."

"Can we come by tomorrow?" Fern nestled up to Sam.

"If each of you will dance with me after our shift."

Fern winked at me and I sipped my wine. "It'll be a pleasure," I said, looking forward to resting my hand on that broad shoulder, feeling his hand on my waist, and following his lead, moving my body with his. To me, slow dancing is like foreplay with rules, though it was dark enough in here that no one would know if we broke a rule or two.

I sauntered over to the food table, laden with potluck hors d'oeuvres, and found a spot for my guacamole between plates of baked brie and Rice Krispies bars—a three-course meal right there. I was hungry, and it all looked delicious. Wesley Raintree appeared at my side. "I didn't recognize you at first," he said to me. "Is your hair different?"

"Well, I'm wearing it up. Usually it's freestyle."

"Nice dress. I like red. Sunny used to wear a lot of red."

"It's good of you to support this group," I said.

"Your grandmother sold me some tickets. I gave a couple to Bryce, too. He knows the band so maybe he'll even show up. Here, I brought this brie. Baked with raspberry jam. Want some?" He spread a generous blob on a cracker and handed it to me.

The band started playing a bluegrass-flavored polka and I pointed to the dance floor, my mouth full of cracker. Wesley was a skillful dancer, weaving us past other couples. I asked where he learned to dance.

"At the Naval Academy, of all places. Mandatory ballroom dancing class. They also taught us etiquette and protocol."

"Very useful things to know."

"Wish I could teach Bryce some manners."

"Guess he's not interested in the Navy?" I asked, pleased I could simultaneously make conversation and twirl along with Wesley.

"That's right. He has a hard time with authority. Wish I had the clout to force Bryce to join up. He shuts down when I mention it."

"Let me tell you, you have plenty of clout." Our dancing slowed as I told him about Bryce's theft of pills and the "phone taps," evidence that had mysteriously come into my hands. "I'd prefer not to waste everyone's time with an investigation and arrest," I said. "Let's get Bryce into the military."

"How's that?" said a rough voice behind me, and I nearly fell off my shoes, turning to see Bryce glaring at me. His thick golden hair, loose on his shoulders, looked soft and touchable, but his expression warned me he was angry.

"Hi, son," said Wesley, "we were talking about you. Your future."

"Oh yeah? Well, don't bother, Dad. My future's not your problem." He shook his head to flip his hair back.

"You here by yourself?" I asked. I was curious who his friends were.

He looked behind him. "Uh, no, my friends are over there." He waved his hand toward a remote corner. "That dress is hot."

"I'll tell Fern. She made it."

"My mom used to sew a lot. She made me a cool fleece jacket last year, right before she got sick."

It seemed tragic that these two men, with their common feelings of love and grief for Sunny, were so far apart otherwise. I knew how to fix it, and though this wasn't the best occasion, it was an opportunity. "Bryce, want to dance?"

He grinned. "Sure. I don't think I've ever danced with a cop before."

We joined the other dancers on the floor. He held me tightly as he rocked from side to side. I looked him right in the eye. "What's your plan, Bryce? What are you going to do with your life?"

"Work out, compete. Good times." He shook his hair back.

"Don't waste these years. Before you know it, it'll be too late."

"You sound like my dad."

"He's right."

"I don't want to give him the satisfaction."

"Think about this." I pulled back from his too-familiar hold and told him how his brother, Kent, had bugged his phone; the conversations I knew about; the quantity of pills he had sold; the money he had made. He listened carefully, but when I said I'd have the recordings destroyed if he'd join the military, he got agitated and grabbed my arm, attracting attention from nearby dancers. "That'll never happen."

"Let go," I hissed. When, instead, he pulled me toward him, I pressed my heel into the top of his sandaled foot. "Ow, that hurt!" he growled, and jerked away.

I whispered in his ear, "You can get some training, become a useful citizen. It's like a get-out-of-jail-free card."

"You can't use those tapes," he growled. "I know my rights." Unfortunately he was correct. He limped slowly toward his friends. I noticed Nikki in the group, in a skimpy white halter top and low-riding jeans that exposed a foot of skin and a sparkling navel ring. She took Bryce's hand and spoke to him, then looked over at me, frowning, her mother's expression exactly, with that worried wrinkle between her eyebrows.

I returned to the drinks table where Wesley was talking with Fern. "What happened?" he asked.

"We had a little chat about his joining the military."

"And?"

"He's going to give it some thought. Right now he's kinda negative, doesn't want the haircut."

It took me a few minutes to find the women's restroom, down a deserted corridor in the back of the building. Jasmine, Hogan's *slut.com* find, leaned into the mirror, applying eyeliner with the care of a Chinese calligrapher. She looked up. "Stella Lavender!" She had a loud harsh voice.

"That's right," I said. "How do we know each other?"

"Oh, Hogan talks about you all the time. It's 'Stella's so smart' and 'Stella's so brave.' So I asked him to point you out. 'The girl in the red dress,' he said, and I knew exactly who he meant, everyone is looking at you. I'd be jealous if I didn't know my Hogan!" Jasmine dabbed powder on her perfect nose and picked up her clutch purse. "Isn't it dangerous being a cop?"

I nodded. Never far from my mind was the sensation a bullet causes as it flies by, that firm push of air, as fresh a memory as the taste of strawberries.

"He doesn't tell me anything; so annoying! Anyway, we're

about to leave. I'm in a tennis tournament tomorrow and need a good night's sleep."

I wished her luck, washed my hands, and checked my appearance—same old me. Some might say I needed my eyebrows waxed, hair straightened, and makeup advice from a pro, but I liked the way I looked—like my mother.

Fern came into the restroom. "There you are, Stella. Sam is looking for you." As if reading my mind, she said, "You look more like Grace all the time. You've always had her hair and eyes, but these days, when I look at you, it's like I see her. Same strong shoulders, straight back. When you talk, you sound exactly like her. You're taller though."

"I'm older than she was, too," I said. It was hard for me to fathom, that my mother disappeared when she was only twenty-five. "See these wrinkles?"

"Oh, what nonsense." Fern kissed my cheek.

"Did you dance with Sam already?" I asked.

"Yes. He's hunky."

He was waiting by the drinks table and I slipped into his arms, determined to forget Hogan, forget Anselmo. Sam wasn't only hunky, he was nice and smelled divine, like rain. Neither of us seemed to want to talk. It was during our third slow dance that we somehow ended up kissing—his idea? My move? It didn't matter. I was transported, reliving a long-ago high-school moment, when Hogan tapped me on the shoulder.

"What?" I asked, opening my eyes and trying to focus.

"Get lost, pal," Sam said, pulling me closer. I didn't object.

"Come over here," Hogan said. "I want you to see what Wesley Raintree found sticking in his cheese."

Regretfully, I took a last sniff of Sam, pulled away, and followed Hogan to the food table. There, in the brie, was a bird's-beak knife with a purple handle, purple blade. Like the unusual knife missing from Temple Mercer's kitchen. Like the knife used to murder Kent Mercer.

With the discovery of the knife, the dance ended for me. I had to take it to the SBI lab in Raleigh.

Outside the mill, my car was parked next to a Mustang I recognized as Bryce's. I was about to start my car when I heard voices and saw the Mustang's interior light come on. I eased down in my seat.

"Leggo of my door," Bryce said.

"When you tell me what the hell happened in there." Wesley stood outside Bryce's car, leaning down to talk to his son. "What did she want?"

"She's a cop. What do they always want? Put you in jail."

"What for, Bryce? What are you involved in now?"

"Leave me the hell alone."

Wesley pounded on the car roof. "I care about you. Do you want to go to prison?"

"Do you, Dad? Shall I tell her what you did?"

"You wouldn't! No one would believe you!"

"I really wanted to talk to Mom before she died. Thanks to your heavy hand with the dope, she didn't talk to anyone."

"Bryce, don't go there. She was in agony."

"The doctor said she'd live another month at least. But no, under your excellent care she went fast!" He spat. "Now leave me the hell alone! You fuck everything up!" Bryce started up his car and spun out of the parking lot.

"Goddammit," Wesley muttered. He walked slowly back to the mill.

I sank lower, not wanting Wesley to know I'd overheard their argument. Was it significant, that he hadn't denied killing his wife with a morphine overdose? A common accident when a caretaker doesn't want to see a loved one suffer. But Bryce seemed to imply it was criminal. I wondered whether Kent Mercer had made the same accusation, perhaps backing it up with evidence. Such a charge, added to Wesley's bitter resentment of Kent's influence on Bryce, maybe even blackmail threats around Bryce's drug deals, might have been sufficient motive for Wesley to kill Kent. Though the guard gate had no record of Wesley entering Silver Hills the day of Kent's murder, perimeter security was minimal. Wesley could have parked a quarter-mile down the road and vaulted over a fence.

I dropped the knife off at the SBI lab to have it tested. I didn't see any fingerprints on it—it was shiny clean—but a few stray molecules of blood were enough for a DNA match with Kent Mercer's blood. Unfortunately, it would be weeks before the lab could give me any results.

Hogan and I had questioned Wesley, but he said he didn't know how the purple knife got there. Someone had stuck it in the cheese at the last minute, at the end of the evening. Why? Taunting the police? Trying, crudely, to draw suspicion to Wesley? Someone at the dance was directly connected with Kent Mercer's death.

CHAPTER 20

Sunday morning

It had been three days since Emilie Soto was shot in the throat and nearly died. When I peeked into her hospital room, I was astonished to see her sitting up and eating breakfast. Granted, breakfast was liquid, and she was sucking it through a straw, but knowing she could swallow made me smile.

Bandages swathed her jaw and neck, so I couldn't tell whether she smiled back at me. But when she winked, I felt enormous relief. She was alive and alert and communicating, even if it was only an eyelid twitch. Her curls were pulled back into a scrunchy, and her hospital gown was faded, shapeless, and wrinkled, but she looked beautiful to me.

I pulled a chair up to the foot of her bed. "Can you talk?"

She shook her finger, no, and picked up a tablet. She typed, then showed me: *not yet soon*

"You'll recover then. That makes me so happy."

Her warm brown eyes widened as she typed. *me too* ☺ *meanwhile . . . what happened?*

"It was a sniper, from the graveyard. He got away. I'm so terribly sorry."

not your fault

"I might have been the target, not you."

not much of a marksman, then

I smiled at her joke. "I feel guilty, though. I asked you to go outside, remember?"

i would have gone out eventually right? don't forget guilt is a use-less emotion

"Oh yeah. Let's find out who did this."

of course

"The day of the shooting, you said you knew a secret that might be relevant to my case. The murder of Kent Mercer. Can you elaborate?"

A frown. She didn't want to talk about anything confidential. I tried another approach.

"Just tell me—was it related to Nikki Truly? Her file is missing from your office."

i heard you discovered the break-in quite a coincidence

"You know it. So, Nikki Truly? You remember, a teenager with long blond hair, having an affair with an older man?"

She noisily sucked on her straw. *you know that much, then*

"Since her file is missing, it must be important. Someone came back in the evening, after the shooting, and took Nikki's file. Nothing else."

Stern brown eyes over white gauze. *privileged*

"I can't get a court order—I don't know what to ask for."

She squinted, typed, *privilege belongs to the patient and how do you know her file was missing?*

Mentally I squirmed. "Her aunt told me she'd been a patient. Your file drawers were disturbed, and Nikki's was obviously missing." A partly-true answer. I hated lying to Dr. Soto. No more. "I'll ask Nikki, then. No need to bother you."

would be best With her fingers she signed *I love you* and I didn't feel quite so guilty. "I love you too," I said, and it was true.

Accompanied by Merle, I drove to Temple's to pick up Fern. We were going to the farmhouse to see how the improvements were coming along. I knocked on the door and when Fern opened it, Wesley stood close behind her. She breezed into my car as he watched her fondly, smiling.

I was in jeans and a t-shirt but Fern wore a filmy purple tunic with matching leggings. She was the butterfly; I, the caterpillar. "New conquest?" I asked, not sure I liked the thought. Wesley was too involved in my professional life.

"A gentleman's rare these days."

"Oh, please. You have a dozen at your beck and call. Now buckle up."

The air was softly warm, the sky a cloudless blue. Redbud trees had burst into bloom, their pink-flocked branches reaching for the sun. "I dreamed about you this morning," I said. "You were trying to separate me from Hogan." In my dream, Hogan and I were in bed together—a canopy bed, draped with yards of smothering linens. He tugged at my ruffled flannel nightgown, twisted around me like a mummy's wrappings. "You pounded on my door and told him to go home."

"Breaking up was the wise thing to do," Fern said. "Hogan is wonderful, but if you'd married him, he'd expect you to behave like a *wife*." She implied a *wife* endured unreasonable expectations and irrational restrictions. I'm not sure how she knew this, having never *been* one. She and Grace had both skipped matrimony on their way to motherhood.

"It's odd to be dreaming about him, though," I said. "It's been months."

"You miss him?"

"I run into him at work all the time. It's awkward."

"Behave nicely. Otherwise you embarrass yourself. That's one of the first things I think about when I meet someone new. How will he behave when it's over? You want to be able to remember them fondly. Do you remember Bruce, summer of '96?"

"Pickup truck Bruce, or short Bruce with the log cabin in Asheville?"

"The log cabin was much later, you were in high school. Bruce with the pickup truck. He still sends me roses every birthday, the sweetheart."

We reached the farmhouse and my car jounced along the long driveway. "Let's get this graded," she said. "My friends don't like walking all the way up to the house, especially when it rains."

"Will do. Have you heard from the art appraiser lately? Joseph?"

"Zee auction iss een seeks wicks."

"Hmm?"

"The auction is in six weeks. He sent me a fancy brochure. Oh, will you look at that." A new tin roof shone silver, reflecting sunlight back into scattered puffs of clouds. New windows looked out of the dormers. Saws, worktables, and wood littered the yard. A pile of debris—bricks, flooring, rotted lumber—drew Merle's interest. He sniffed around a bit, then headed for the back field.

Sam made his way toward us. From his dusty face, protective glasses, and grimy t-shirt, I could tell he worked alongside his crew. I smiled at him, remembering last night, our slow dance, the way he smelled, the lovely gentle kiss. "Sorry I had to leave so quickly," I said.

He took off the glasses and wiped them on his shirt. His eyes were clear and friendly. "Yeah, me too."

Fern pointed to the bricks. "Seems like you're working fast. Thanks so much."

"You're welcome. You could repay me by entertaining me over dinner when it's all done."

"We will!" I said. An evening with Sam—all cleaned up—hardly seemed like payment. Merle bounded up, greeted him with a spasm of wriggling. Sam knelt and let Merle give him a slobbery kiss. I fished in my pocket for a tissue, and gave it to

Sam to wipe his face.

"Thanks," he said. "Come on in. I'll show you what's happening. Watch your step there."

We went through the front door for the first time in years, into the living room. Something was missing. "Old Ironsides is gone!" I said. The rusted brown kerosene heater had vanished. Sam tapped a switch and gas logs lit up with flickering flames.

"Looks real," Fern said. Her face lit in astonishment, like a child's watching a magic trick.

In the kitchen, a new oven stood in the corner, still in its carton. "The flooring's being installed tomorrow," Sam said, "and the countertop will be delivered the day after. Sure you don't want a dishwasher?"

"I have one," Fern said. "Me. I can wash my cup and plate in the evening."

"And you want to keep that sink?"

She nodded. "It's been in this house for eighty years, and will last another eighty." The iron sink was a single shallow basin, its porcelain worn from Fern's daily scrubbing. The rest of the house could collapse in ruins, but that sink was always spotless.

"I'll have it re-glazed," said Sam. "Now come see the bathroom." He led us through Fern's bedroom.

"Wow," I said, "this is beautiful. So bright." Shiny buttercup-yellow tile surrounded a new tub. The floor was tiled in black with a yellow border, and a white pedestal sink stood in the corner. I flushed the toilet, gratified to see the bowl empty promptly.

I looked at Fern to see if she liked it. For so long she had claimed to want things the way they were, had resisted changing anything in the farmhouse. Her eyes were big with excitement and pleasure. "You know, I could never clean my old linoleum floor," she said. "This tile will wash up well. But that sink's too pretty for my paintbrushes."

"Well, take a look in here," Sam said. He led us across the hall into the art room.

Fern gasped as she saw the closet where Sam had installed a janitor's sink and floor-to-ceiling wire shelving. A narrow, tall cabinet held a dozen drawers.

"This is wonderful," she said. "How did you know what I needed?" She gave Sam a hug, and he winked at me over her shoulder.

"Had to do some detective work," he said.

Let's see—he hugs my grandmother, smells intoxicating, and lets my dog kiss him. Did I mention his biceps?

CHAPTER 21

Sunday afternoon

When I took Fern back to Temple's house, Iggy, an aging lad with a sensuous mouth and heavily lashed eyes, was there, cleaning. He wore head-to-toe black that accentuated his slenderness and matched his spiky hair. He was the only man, much fussed-over, in Fern's painting classes, and reputed to be a meticulous housecleaner.

"And wasn't it a terrible, terrible thing? A young man, cut down in his prime? Leaving such a darling family? Poor, sweet girl." Iggy swished the mop in the bucket, wrung it out, and started mopping the kitchen floor. "I love this mop. Don't my hands appreciate it, not being in water all day? How do you do it, keep your hands so smooth?"

Fern looked at me and feigned gritting her teeth. Iggy got on her nerves with his incessant chatter, no matter how charmingly delivered in his singsong drawl. We didn't dare answer Iggy's question—answers just fueled the flames of his verbal inspiration.

He leaned on the mop pole. "It was robbery, they say, but in my opinion there were others who had their motives. I love the girl, bless her heart, but he was another one altogether. A type I know too well."

This sparked my interest. "How so, Iggy?"

"I don't like to speak ill of the dead."

"Speak away," I said. Fern rolled her eyes as if to say, *now*

154

you've done it.

"I'll tell you ladies, she put up with more than most wives would. Dirty movies, and the marijuana smell would choke you."

I wondered what else Iggy might have noticed. Housekeepers are privy to all the family dirt. "Did Temple know much about his—uh—interests?"

"She knew and she didn't, you know. I think she tried to pretend things were all right. On the surface, they looked fine, didn't they? You ever see the picture they took at Christmas? The two of them, so good-looking, and the dear baby, in front of the Christmas tree? You'd say it was a storybook family from that picture. I see it's gone from the bookshelf here. Did she take all those pictures to the thrift shop? The frames were nice, I know people like nice frames."

"The pictures were stolen the day of the murder," I said, "along with personal items."

Iggy stopped mopping. "Stolen?"

"Stolen," said Fern. "Can't imagine why."

Iggy frowned. "Why steal them, then donate them to the thrift shop?"

I was puzzled. "Did you see them at the thrift shop?"

"No, I assumed she'd bought them there. You know, since they still had Temple's pictures in them. They were nice frames. I saw them yesterday, in her laundry room."

"Whose laundry room?" I asked, confused.

The first time I visited June Devon, I noticed the quiet woods, the birds at the multiple feeders, the colorful paintings on her walls. This time, suspecting her laundry room contained items stolen from Kent Mercer, I noticed the seclusion. Here and there a mailbox signaled a home back in the woods, invisible to anyone traveling on the rutted bumpy lane. I asked Iggy whether he knew anyone else living out here.

"That lighthouse mailbox, those folks are new. I do know two other families on this road. Tommy Wills coming up here on the left. He's a Burlington Wills, not a Verwood Wills. The Budds down at the end."

"George and Ursula Budd?"

"Yes. She's in your grandma's painting group, like I am."

I pulled into June's driveway. Though the trees were greening, I could see Temple and Kent Mercer's house a few hundred feet across the lake. In a few weeks leafy branches would hide the lake and those homes. Iggy stood behind me as I rang the doorbell. "I have a key, sugar, if no one comes," he said.

Ursula Budd opened the door. I had forgotten how tall she was. Her wiry hair added another two inches as it sprang up from her forehead. "Why Iggy! And Stella Lavender! What a surprise. June's out shopping. What do you want?" She still seemed nervous at the sight of me.

I showed her the search warrant. "I need to look in the laundry room. Where's Erwin? I don't want to disturb him."

"He's outside. He likes to sit on the back porch this time of day." She blocked the doorway, arms folded across her chest. "Shouldn't we wait till June gets home? I don't think I should let you poke around."

"We're here in an official capacity," I said.

"What are you looking for?" she asked.

"It's not something I can talk about," I said. "Furthermore, would you mind waiting outside with Erwin?" It was protocol—I didn't need civilians wandering about "helping."

Her tilted green eyes flashed in irritation, but she opened the door to let us in, then went out to the back porch. I peeked to make sure they were settled in. Erwin was sitting in a wicker rocker. He had a rubber ball in each hand, slowly squeezing, first the right, then the left. He turned his head to stare at me

156

with unblinking eyes. I noticed he'd had a shave and a haircut since I last saw him, remarkably improving his appearance. He looked almost well, with a glimmer in his eyes. Intelligence? Or panic and confusion?

Iggy led me through the kitchen to the laundry room. "I was waiting for a couple of things to finish drying so I could make the beds and go home. I picked up the broom and started sweeping. It gets all linty in here from the dryer. I stuck the broom behind the hot-water heater, and there's this big plastic bag. Well, I guess you'd call me nosy, but I wondered why she'd stuffed anything back there, so I looked in it and saw the pictures and little glass things, kinda nice. Here, I'll show you."

He reached for the bag, but I stopped him. "We'll need to get fingerprints, Iggy. Let me do it." I put on gloves and carefully lifted the bag out. As Iggy had said, it contained framed pictures and small objects—a glazed bowl, a carved elephant, a crystal dolphin. The pictures were family photos—some posed and professional, others candid—of the very photogenic family of Kent and Temple Mercer.

The contents of this bag had been stolen from Mercer's house the day of his murder. I rubbed my forehead. Was June involved in Mercer's death? I remembered her telling me about seeing Nikki and Mercer making love on the deck, Erwin's anger, his stroke. Would June want to punish Mercer? Underneath that book- and bird-loving mildness, was there the cold heart of a killer?

I called Anselmo. Next to finding Paige, this was the biggest break in our investigation.

I took Iggy back to Temple's, then drove to Roll's grocery store, grabbed a cart, and put a bunch of bananas in it. I wandered around until I found June Devon in the florist section. Her brown-gray hair hung damply over her shoulders. William

Shakespeare peered thoughtfully at me from her t-shirt.

My stomach roiled with pity and tension as I texted Anselmo:

Found her in Roll's, I will tail her

This civic-minded, middle-aged woman was going to be ar-rested on breaking and entering charges. She'd be grilled about her involvement in a kidnapping and murder. I wanted to take her hand, warn her that her life as she knew it—her carefully scheduled, solitary, care-giving days—would end in a few minutes. But I also couldn't wait to get her in the interview room. If she took the items from the Mercers' bookshelf, then she was there. What did she do? What did she see?

She held up a bunch of daisies. "Aren't these cheery? I'm getting them for the cleaning boy, when he comes tomorrow." She put the daisies into her cart.

"That's Iggy?" Iggy, who led me to the ill-gotten gains.

"Right. You know him? He's a wonderful cleaner, so thorough. He sees everything that needs to be done. I get impatient with his jibber-jabber, though, and last time I think I hurt his feel-ings."

"Fern says the same. Iggy does go on and on."

"Well, mustn't dawdle. See you later, Stella!" June headed toward the middle of the store. I followed, not closely, but keep-ing her in view. She was an efficient shopper, not a browser, and in a few minutes she was in the checkout line. As she rolled her cart out the door, I abandoned my bananas and followed her.

A squad car was parked in front of the store, and Deputy Chamberlain leaned against it, her hand resting on her gun. When I nodded to her, she spoke to June. "Mrs. Devon, the police want to talk to you. Come this way, please." People had stopped to gawk, excited that something was happening in the grocery store parking lot on a Sunday afternoon.

June was bewildered. "What? What about my groceries? I

have to get home. My husband needs me." She glared at two little boys who had crept close.

"Give me your keys, June. I'll take the groceries to your house," I said.

"Oh, please, don't be ridiculous. What's this all about?" June asked. Despite her question, I felt certain she knew what it was about.

One of the little boys yelled, "Hey, lady, what'd you do? Kill someone?" June shook her head slowly. She slid into the squad car and looked up to catch my eye. She glared at me with a steely anger, and mouthed something I couldn't hear as Chamberlain took her away.

After delivering June's groceries for Ursula to put away, I went to the law enforcement building to interview her. Finding the bag of stolen items in her laundry room was the first real break in this case. I *ached* to know what she knew. June had to talk. Anselmo wanted me to question her; he would watch the video stream.

In the interview room, June sat ramrod straight, twiddling her thumbs, her expression wary. I started with what I knew already—Mercer's affair with her niece, Nikki. We talked about that, and Erwin's stroke.

"He's helpless, isn't he?" I asked.

She shrugged. "Yes, basically. He's improved a bit."

"And the morning of Mercer's death, did you look across the lake?"

"I usually look out that way, watch the birds."

"See anything different?"

"Don't remember." Her face was blank, her manner calm and still.

"Tell me about the bag behind your hot-water heater," I said.

"What bag?" She was too casual. Didn't she realize the stakes of this game? Maybe this was June's way of reacting to stress—just chill, pretend nothing matters.

"How did it get there?"

"I don't know." She folded her arms across William Shakespeare and rocked, forward and back. "I have to get home. It's time for Erwin's dinner."

"Ursula's there."

"It has to be soft or he'll choke. You want that on your conscience?" Her chin jerked up another inch and she looked down her nose at me. "My lawyer's on his way. I'll be out of here in a half hour."

Outwardly I was calm, making notes, studying her face for signs of lying. Inside, my stomach knotted with frustration. "You're either a criminal or a witness or both, and I need to know what you know. Don't you want to help us solve this murder?"

She poked a trembling finger into my face, jabbing it with each word: "Whoever killed that son-of-a-bitch did the world a favor."

"Whoever it was has also tried to kill two other people."

June frowned. "I didn't know. Listen, I didn't see anything."

"What about the child? Did you see her? Take her?"

She raked her hands through her long, graying hair and pulled it back into a ponytail. "I'm saying nothing. I want a lawyer now. And a rubber band. I never got a chance to pin my hair up."

I left the room, barely able to stop myself from slamming the door, which would be unprofessional, childish, and satisfying. Anselmo noticed my expression.

"No luck?" he asked.

"She asked for a lawyer and a rubber band. Put it around her neck, would you?"

CHAPTER 22

Monday morning

I felt no closer to solving the murder of Kent Mercer than a week ago when I'd discovered his body. Terrible things had happened—grievous injuries to Lincoln Teller and Emilie Soto; the abduction of Mercer's little girl. The only break in the case was finding Mercer's stolen items in June Devon's house, but right now that led to a stone wall, since she wasn't talking. I wasn't quite ready to call myself a failure, but I sure didn't feel successful. Evidence was scant, suspects non-existent, theories empty.

I thought about Bryce Raintree. He reminded me of myself at his age—perverse, a bit lost and sad, making poor choices. Fredricks had forced me to admit that Bryce was salvageable. So why not try harder?

It had been two days since the dance, when I argued to Bryce that he'd be better off serving his country, advice he'd resisted. I knew from the recordings he was selling painkiller drugs, and he got them from the nursing home where he worked. I didn't know whether he was buying them directly from the patients, bribing a nurse to give pills to him rather than the patients, or had simply found a way to help himself without being detected. According to his phone conversations, he had only a few customers, each with a big habit he sometimes had trouble feeding.

Unemployment would curtail his source. So I made an appointment with Wilhelmina Jones, the director of Wisteria Acres, and arrived early. She ushered me right into her office and closed the door. She probably didn't want the residents and their visitors to know the SBI was paying a call.

"Call me Willy," she said. "It's easier to pronounce, and 'Mrs. Jones' reminds everyone of that song, you know which one I mean. 'We got a thing goin' on'?" She laughed. She was a tidy gray-haired woman in her sixties, with a wide welcoming smile. She wore a tailored black suit, but what caught my eye was a lapis lazuli pendant, a brilliant deep blue, hanging from a gold chain around her neck.

"Willy, you do have a thing going on," I said. "Your employee Bryce Raintree is somehow obtaining painkillers within Wisteria Acres. He's making very substantial money selling them."

Her smile vanished. "Impossible. We have a specific protocol for handling medication here."

"How strictly is it enforced? What if a patient is asleep and doesn't need that sleeping pill? Maybe it goes into a pocket."

"The aides make sure the meds are taken."

I nodded, but not in agreement. "If someone dies, what happens to their pills?"

"They're disposed of. I sign a form. The state is vigilant." Willy clutched her lapis like a rosary.

"Do you personally witness the disposal?"

She searched my face as though looking for a way out.

"I'm not accusing you," I said. "We have considerable evidence that prescription drugs are leaving your nursing home and being sold illegally. It could even be the patients hoarding their pills and selling them to Bryce." I didn't tell her the evidence was illegal recordings.

"He's buying drugs from patients? That makes our patients dealers too!" My message was sinking in. It wasn't just Bryce who would go to jail; it was Nana complaining of chronic back pain, arthritic Gramps, and Martha, the devoted nurse's aide with her twenty years of service. Wisteria Acres would make *People* for all the wrong reasons and empty out faster than the Krispy Kreme box at an SBI staff meeting.

"I'm sure you keep all medicines locked up," I said.

"Of course. But gosh, the patients come in with shoeboxes full of pill bottles. We keep all medications under lock and key, but, if it's prescribed, the patient gets it."

"Then start reviewing all prescriptions, especially painkillers, with their doctors."

"I could say we're concerned about side effects," she said. "We have a consulting pharmacist; he could take a look."

"It's possible that some of your patients were making a considerable sum of money from Bryce."

She was making notes, and looked up. "How much?"

"The market price for a forty-milligram oxycodone is about forty dollars. Bryce probably paid five to ten dollars apiece."

"And Medicare bought them originally, so it's like pure profit to these people."

"That's right," I said. "All very friendly, just a way for a senior citizen to make a little extra cash. And after being discharged from here, it was probably easier. No one counting out the pills each day. He could visit them and pick up a bottle. Or give them a ride to the drugstore."

She sat very still, waiting for my verdict.

"There are a couple of ways we can go with this," I said. "We can bring in the SBI Diversions Unit. They'll put someone in here undercover to gather evidence, then make arrests, take it to trial, and put folks in jail. That's the expensive way, both for Wisteria Acres and the State of North Carolina. It makes the SBI look smart: we're doing our job."

"What's the other way?" She slumped in her chair and fingered her pendant.

"Fire Bryce Raintree. Institute very strict controls on all medication and don't let the patients hoard any. Reduce the flow of painkillers into your buildings."

"I like the second way much better," she said. "Let me handle things."

She didn't want to shake my hand as I left but I felt positive about the interview. Not progress on the murder case, exactly, but Bryce's current business enterprise would end, and Mrs. Jones, by cooperating, hadn't forced my official hand.

I drove to Temple's to let her know we'd found the items stolen from her house, though they were evidence and couldn't be returned to her just yet.

As I pulled into the driveway, I heard voices and the pounding of hammers. I walked around to the back where Fern, Wesley, and Bryce were assembling an elaborate swing set. They'd already put up the base, a platform accessible by a wide wooden ladder and a yellow plastic slide. Underneath, Bryce was attaching a tire swing. He was shirtless, showing off his bulky muscular torso as he hefted the tire up to connect it with the chains. He nodded to me, cool but not hostile, as though we still had issues, but he'd forgiven me for our last encounter and didn't yet know I'd gotten him fired from Wisteria Acres. Here, he was Uncle Bryce, a good reason for him to be helping out.

Fern sat on the ground, a heap of wood pieces and rope in her lap. She peered up at me from under her wide-brimmed straw hat. She said. "Isn't this terrific? A present from Grandpa Wesley."

Wesley looked up from assembling a support for the slide, pulled a handkerchief from his jeans pocket, and wiped his face. "Here she comes now, our princess."

Paige started down the steps to the patio, backwards. She looked too tiny in her yellow, gingham sundress to be managing stairs, but she negotiated them easily, clambering down. I took her hand and we walked around the swing set, talking about the ladder, the swing, the slide, the hiding places. I realized her diaper was soggy. "Time for a change?" I asked.

"No!" she said. "Me do it!" And she ripped the sticky tabs open and pulled her diaper off. I laughed. Temple had her hands full with this one—a free-thinking nudist wanderer. I looked at the diaper lying on the patio, nagged by a sense of déjà vu—the diaper Merle had found in the woods below. Had Paige seen her father's body? Wandered away, to be scooped up by—whom? Without hard evidence, I suspected a Good Samaritan, but it wasn't "good" to keep the toddler for two days.

"Where's Temple?" I asked.

"She's lying down," Fern said. "Go see her, she needs company."

Temple lay curled in her bed, covered by a sheet. The baby slept beside her, a neat lump like a loaf of bread. The room smelled muggy and stale, shoes were strewn everywhere. Temple's eyes followed me as I came into the room, then she closed them. Her dark lashes looked sticky, and drool had crusted beside her mouth.

"Hey," I said gently. "I know you're awake."

"Hi, Stella. Sorry. What time is it?"

"Around ten. Were you up all night?"

"A few times. I got enough sleep. I just don't feel like doing anything right now."

"We have a break in the case. The stolen items—pictures and figurines? They've been found."

She sat up slowly. Her hair stuck flat to her head. Her body was lost in the baggy t-shirt she wore. It must have been her husband's. "Was there a picture of my parents? Very 80's—leg warmers and big hair?" Her face crumpled as she started to cry. "I don't have anyone anymore!"

I didn't know what to say. It wouldn't help to remind her she had two beautiful children and money in the bank she might even be able to keep. "You've been through a lot, Temple. It's no wonder you're down. Come outside and see the swing set. It's really nice."

"God, I need a shower first." She hiccupped a final sob. "Sorry. I'm a mess."

"Take your shower. Where are the diapers? Paige needs one."

"There's a stash in her room. First door on the left."

Outside, Paige refused my diaper offer so I left it on a deck chair and sat down to help Fern assemble a rope ladder. "Temple seems depressed," I said.

"It comes and goes," Fern said. "She can be fine one minute and the next she's worried sick over nothing. This morning she giggled for a half hour watching Paige play with her shoes. She said Kent used to get angry about it, but it was such fun to watch the baby walk around in her Kenneth Cole's. An hour later she was weeping because her shoes were everywhere."

As I wrestled with the thick rope I wondered if Temple's emotional roller coaster was due to post-birth hormones, her husband's murder, or some other trauma. Guilt? Might her husband still be alive if she'd stayed home that afternoon? Temple's involvement in his death had not been ruled out. A wave of frustration washed over me—how little I knew for certain. The few clues pointed in random, senseless directions. I couldn't connect the dots—the involvement of Lincoln Teller and June Devon; the probable murder weapon, practically handed to me in a public place; the shooting of an old friend as I stood next to her. The more I looked, the blurrier the picture got.

Temple came out onto the deck holding the baby. Still pale, she looked much better in apple-green cropped pants, matching sandals, and a colorful camp shirt. On her, that outfit was bright and charming. On me, topped by my willful, gravity-defying curls, it would frighten small children.

"This is amazing," Temple said. "What a wonderful swing set. Miss Paige, what are you doing with a bare bottom?" She sat down on a deck chair, motioning Paige to come to her.

The toddler put her hands on her hips. "No!"

"She looks like you when she does that," Bryce said to Temple. "That posture."

"Maybe this will get her to cooperate," said Fern. "Look, Paige, cookie!" Fern took one from her pocket and tossed it to Temple, who shook her head in mock dismay.

"For the past week Paige has lived off these cookies," she said. "Fern says they're healthy."

"They are! Oatmeal, nuts, raisins—good for you," said Fern.

"Sugar, white flour, butter—those aren't!" Temple held the cookie up anyway, and Paige climbed back up the stairs and dutifully lay down on the deck so Temple could put on the diaper.

Wesley dumped a bag of rubber chips at the foot of the slide. "Heard June Devon was arrested," he said.

"She's out on bail." I gave Fern an *I know you know* look, but she had tipped her head down, hiding her face behind the big hat.

Temple looked at me. "She's Nikki's aunt, isn't she? Why was she arrested?"

I told her, and she shook her head. "She had my things? My pictures? Why?"

"Excellent question. She's got a lawyer, and won't say."

Temple frowned. "I haven't seen Nikki since the funeral. Hope she's all right. Finding Kent's body must have been awful." Inwardly I cringed. Obviously, Temple didn't know Nikki had been her husband's lover. And I wasn't about to tell her, either.

"Ask Bryce how Nikki is," said Wesley. "She's over at his place all the time."

Bryce glared at him. "If you want me here, keep out of my business." The father-son dynamic I'd observed after the dance—accusations and anger—was still in place. Did they ever joke around, swap stories, go fishing?

The construction went quickly. To define the play area, the two men built a low retaining wall out of landscape timbers and filled it with more rubber chips. Finally, Fern inserted decorative flags in the corners of the platform, and the men attached a bright blue canvas tarp for shade. Paige scampered up the ladder, slid down the slide, and landed feet-first on the bouncy surface.

I asked Temple if I could hold John. He was sleepy, his eyes half-open, unfocused. It was only natural to hold him close and kiss his velvety cheek, and after a few minutes he closed his eyes. I hummed my mother's favorite lullaby:

> Lavender's blue, dilly dilly
> Lavender's green
> When I am King, dilly dilly
> You shall be Queen
> Who told you so, dilly dilly
> Who told you so?
> It was my own heart, dilly dilly
> That told me so

I wouldn't want to raise a fatherless child like my mother and grandmother had done. So holding a baby was like being a diabetic in a bakery—wonderful smells of éclairs, flans, and cheesecake but you shouldn't have any. As he rested on my shoulder, I checked for maternal feelings. They were there, low-level, but no greater than usual, so I found a rocker out of the sun and sat down. The baby slept, exhaling warm puffs at my neck. I shooed aside the guilt pangs—I needed to be working my case—but here I sat, rocking, watching a family project. Just a half hour, I promised myself. The pounding in my head stopped, replaced by a sporadic vibration like a tuning fork. It felt wonderful to do nothing.

Then my cell phone chimed. "Can we meet?" Anselmo asked. "I've got the forensic report from the Devon residence."

Anselmo and I sat in his cruiser. He held a report in a plain black cover. "Mrs. Devon is a meticulous housekeeper," he said. "She's so clean, she even washes fingerprints off doors and walls and cabinets."

"That's unusual," I said. "Not many people are so thorough."

"She vacuums well, too. But she couldn't get under the dresser where we found a cup with Paige's prints all over it." He grinned. "Furthermore, Paige put her tiny fingers everywhere. Inside a silver hoop earring we found in a jewelry box. On a brass doorstop. Inside a glass bottle filled with dried grasses," Anselmo said. "In the normal course of events, would there be any reason for the child to be at that house?"

"I don't think so. June told me she knew Sunny and Wesley—the grandparents—but not Temple and Kent. This evidence puts the child at June's." A memory startled me—Fern had stayed at June's for both of those days. I remembered Fern's not-so-innocent question—*What if someone took that child and then decided to return her. Would that someone be arrested?* Maybe Fern could convince June to talk. June had plenty to tell and it was time for her to fess up.

CHAPTER 23

Monday afternoon

"Abduction? I didn't abduct anyone," June hissed. "Don't be ridiculous." Smudges of paint decorated her hands and the front of her black Obama/Biden t-shirt. The conure clung to her shoulder. It fluffed its wings and beeped three times like a microwave timer. I smiled but ever-cool Anselmo didn't react.

"The evidence is overwhelming: Paige Mercer was here," he said. He didn't need to convince June she was guilty, only the district attorney. But he wanted her to know we had enough to get her to talk. "Kidnapping is a serious crime, Mrs. Devon. We're talking twenty years to life."

"Are you trying to frighten me?" She didn't look frightened. She looked furious, her face flushed as she nervously drummed her paint-stained fingers on the table. "No jury would convict me. I've done nothing wrong."

"Why don't you tell us what you've done, then?" I asked.

"Do I need a lawyer?"

Anselmo and I looked at each other. He nodded to me. "You're not in custody but you always have the right to one," I said.

But she barged ahead anyway. "The child was at risk. No one cared about her."

I feared saying the wrong words would silence her, so I spoke carefully. "Paige was in danger?"

"She could have wandered into the lake and drowned. She

could have been lost in the woods. She was nearly naked, all scratched up and covered with bug bites. I even found a couple of ticks in her hair, poor little thing." June spoke earnestly, apparently convinced she had done the right thing.

"Where did you find her?" Anselmo asked. He and I had talked about Paige's free spirit, that she might have wandered around the neighborhood. Her mother was not at home. Her father? We didn't know whether he was alive when Paige went missing. June could help us there.

"I'll show you." June rose from the table. We followed her into her screened porch. "Over there." She pointed across the lake to Kent Mercer's house, the blue umbrella. "At the edge of the lake. I was bird-watching and I saw her through the binoculars. Scared me, you know? A baby all alone. She was crying, nothing on but a t-shirt." She opened the screen door and went out onto the deck. "Erwin? Where are you?!" She turned to us. "He gets out sometimes."

"I didn't think he could walk," I said.

"He's desperate to walk. He's got a cane and he makes his legs go somehow. But usually he falls down and I have to find him." She scanned the area below the house, a narrow treeless acre overgrown with tall grasses, sloping down to a shrubby area skirting the lake. A path led to a cleared sandy spot where June's rowboat was anchored.

I spotted Erwin, lying by the path, almost to the lake's edge, nearly hidden in the tall grass. He had propped himself up and was pointing a rifle at us.

"Hey! Get down!" I shoved June to the floor, knocking her glasses off. The conure flapped to the floor and screamed excitedly. June swung at me and I grabbed her arm. "Whoa, easy," I said. "He's got a gun." She was tough and it took most of my strength to hold her down.

Anselmo had crouched low when I yelled, and sidled over to

a window. "He's sitting up. He means business."

"June, what's he doing with that rifle?" I asked her. I relaxed a bit, but she popped up and tried to slug me. I caught her arm. "Hey, calm down. I'm not doing anything to you."

"You pushed me!"

"I'll let go if you stay down."

She nodded. I let go and she relaxed onto the floor and folded her arms over her chest. "He'd never shoot anyone. He's upset because I was in jail. And because you're here." The bird hopped onto her shoulder and beeped again.

"Any ideas?" Anselmo asked. "Before I call for backup?" He crawled next to me, so close I could smell cloves. *Is that soap? What kind?* I wanted to ask but the moment wasn't right.

"He'll let me bring him back up here. He tires easily. Give him a few minutes."

"While we're waiting, tell me a little more about Paige. You took the ticks out of her hair," I said. "How'd you get over there?"

"I don't want to talk any more. I'm claiming my right to remain silent." June closed her eyes.

"You're not in custody yet. You took your boat and picked up the baby. Then what?"

Silence.

Anselmo peered out the window. "He's on the move," he said. "Not aiming at us any more, just using the gun to help him walk. He's got a cane, too."

"Is that your rifle?" I asked June.

"Erwin's. It's for protection, living out here in the middle of nowhere. Well, I guess it's mine now. He couldn't hit anything with it, his coordination's gone." She sat up. "I'll get him." She went out the back door and I heard her speak as she approached him on the path. "Sweetheart, you're amazing! Walking all the way down here by yourself? Dr. Newell would be so pleased!

Here, let me give you a hand. Take my arm. I'll hold the rifle. I'd completely forgotten we had that rifle."

"She's got the gun now, Stella. You can sit up," said Anselmo.

I laughed, embarrassed. "Guns make me nervous these days."

"Good. You'll live longer for it."

"I need a hand with him," called June. "This hill is too much." But as Anselmo started toward her, she said, "Not you, he doesn't like men."

I peeked out the door. June had the rifle in one hand, her arm around Erwin. They were standing about halfway up to the house, waiting for assistance. Was it irrational to want to slink away and get into my car? I didn't know how much June wanted to stop our investigation, and Erwin was somewhere south of Mad Max.

"Put the gun down," I called back.

"Sure," she said, and flung it aside. Anselmo and I flinched simultaneously; even though loaded guns aren't supposed to discharge when dropped, it happens.

I helped Erwin back into the house. Though gaunt, he was still a large man, and it was a struggle to support him as he tried to walk. He was barefoot, and his clothes and feet were muddy. He glared at Anselmo as we made our way through the porch. June took him into their bedroom.

Anselmo went outside and picked up the rifle with gloved hands. "A Remington .25-06 caliber."

"Let's take it to the lab," I said. "June can't object, or we'll add resisting arrest and assault with a deadly weapon to her family's list of crimes. He was pointing it at us in a threatening manner."

June came out of the bedroom and Anselmo asked her where she usually kept the gun.

"In the bedroom closet. Back in the corner. It's been there forever," she said.

"Wasn't here yesterday," Anselmo said. "I searched that closet myself."

"Of course it was!"

"Wasn't," he said. "I'm taking it for a ballistics test."

June shrugged. "Suit yourself."

"You brought Paige back here," I said to June, "and kept her for two days. That's the only explanation for her fingerprints and hair everywhere. Why? Why didn't you tell the police you had the baby? You sent that text, didn't you."

June pressed her lips together firmly.

The doorbell chimed. Ursula Budd came in, one of her tilted green eyes sporting a black bruise. Forestalling any questions, she said, "Tripped over the cat and fell down the stairs." She looked at Anselmo and me. "What's going on?"

"They're gonna put me in jail again, Ursula. Lock me up for the heinous crime of taking care of a little girl no one cared about," said June.

I envisioned June standing in front of a gaggle of press, wearing a starched shirtwaist dress and string of pearls, confessing she was only trying to save the sweet wee child from drowning or worse; no one on the planet was a bit concerned about the baby's welfare; anyone could see she was a kindly grandmotherly person, sole caretaker of a bedridden husband who depended on her a hundred percent. She'd get a lot of support, and Anselmo would have to explain over and over that she broke the law, that's why she was being persecuted—er, prosecuted. I didn't envy him.

"Not jail," Anselmo said. "Questioning."

Ursula patted June's shoulder. "I can stay a bit. You'll be back soon, won't you?"

"You bet. I'll call Erwin's sister, Zoë. As soon as I ask her to watch after Erwin, she'll pop me out of jail in a New York minute." She slumped down on the worn brown sofa. The bird tilted its head and made kissing noises, very cute. "Baby wants some kisses," said June. "Sweetie wants some kisses."

CHAPTER 24

Monday late afternoon

Anselmo took June to the sheriff's office, again, and I went home to listen once more to the recordings Kent Mercer had made. Merle and I lay on the floor, my head on a pillow, his on my legs. The conversations droned away, gumming up my concentration as I tried to listen for new or different voices. I carefully made notes of the participants, the subjects, and the length of the conversations, pretending it was important work, but relieved when my cell rang.

"Hello, Agent Lavender?" The woman's voice was low, precise, and familiar. "This is Zoë Schubert. I need to speak to you in private. It's very important; don't mention it to anyone."

"Certainly," I said, intrigued. Nikki Truly's mother, who'd always seemed to regard me as an unnecessary nuisance, actually wanted something.

"Can you meet me across from the Silver Hills entrance? In the grocery store parking lot? I'll be in a beige Acura in the far corner."

"I can be there in thirty minutes."

The Acura smelled so new I expected to hear "moo" as I eased onto the orthopedically-optimized leather seat. Zoë turned down the speaker volume on a samba jazz CD, but kept the engine running to maintain the car's interior temperature at exactly seventy-four degrees, according to the dashboard display next to the digitized GPS road map. She wore a soft-coral linen dress, her frothy blond hair was expensively disarrayed, and she smelled amazing—cinnamon, vanilla, honey. Edible. Zoë had come a long way from Salt Flat, Texas.

"Beautiful car," I said. "Is it new?"

"Thank you. Actually, it's William's, my fiancé. My car is why I called you."

"You said it was important. It's about your car?"

She leaned toward me, so close I could see every bead of mascara on each perfectly separated eyelash. Her voice was low, almost a whisper. "Do I have your word: you'll tell no one?"

"No," I said. As badly as I wanted to know what she had to say, I couldn't very well promise to keep a secret. "I can shield your identity as an informant, but that's about all."

"I don't know where to turn then. I can't have any publicity, not a whiff. William despises scandal." She pushed a button and her seat slipped back. As she stretched, her dress slid up over smooth white thighs.

"Help me out here," I said. "Has a crime been committed?"

"Yesterday my daughter disappeared, and my car is missing. She got her license a week ago, and I'm worried about her driving. I suspect she's with Bryce Raintree. She's been hanging out with him." Zoë rolled her eyes.

"Did you talk to Bryce's father?"

"I did. The two of us went into Bryce's apartment last night. He wasn't there."

"Do you want to report her missing?"

Zoë shook her head. "Of course not. I want you to find her."

It was my turn to frown. "I'm a sworn police officer, not a private investigator."

"No, but Nikki is crucial to your murder case. You need to protect her."

"Her affair with Mercer—is it important?"

"I think she knows more than she told you. I mean, I don't know, but she's not been herself. And William is irritated with her. We're getting married in a few weeks and Nikki is being so difficult. I wish . . ."

"Wish what?" I asked.

Zoë frowned. I knew the answer—she wished Nikki were more successful. Better grades, nicer friends, fewer piercings. Zoë seemed so fully in control of all aspects of her life that I didn't quite understand why Nikki was such a loose end. Many mothers with an irritated fiancé and Zoë's resources would have shipped a problematic daughter off to boarding school. June Devon had mentioned Nikki's intense hatred of Zoë's third husband, Oscar Schubert. Would it be any different with William Newell?

"Nikki left a note," Zoë said. "She was going camping in Pisgah Forest and she needed to be alone, not to worry. She borrowed my brother's camping gear."

"Erwin Devon?"

"Yes. He and June used to camp quite a bit, took Nikki with them a few times. She loved it."

"Seems the worst that could happen is a few mosquito bites."

Zoë sat up straight. "Like I said, I don't trust Bryce Raintree. He could be drugging Nikki. He's got her alone in the woods and I might never see her again! You can find them—I heard you have a tracking dog!" No doubt Zoë would prefer to be begging for help from a man, someone who would react to her thighs and lovely smell with a burning desire to be her white knight.

Was Nikki in danger? Probably no more than she'd been a week ago. Was Bryce a bad influence? Yes, terrible. So what would be gained if I put my time and energy into a search? I had an idea.

"I'll ask the Highway Patrol to put out an APB for your car.

No one needs to know why. We can trace any credit card usage."

"She uses my AmEx. And she's driving my Lexus."

"If I get a lead on her whereabouts, I'll look for her. But first, I want to search her room. Top to bottom."

Zoë nodded. "For clues."

"Right," I said. Clues that would lead to a murderer. I didn't care where Nikki was pitching her tent.

On the way to Zoë's house, I called Hogan and asked him to look up the numbers, then trace her credit card and car, without making waves, as a favor.

Zoë led me to Nikki's room and let me rummage. "Don't worry about making a mess. You could hardly make it worse." The ferocious little white dog, Tiny, skittered around the floor like a wind-up toy, yapping at my feet. When he nipped at my ankle, Zoë took him to another room. Merle could teach Tiny some manners, I thought.

Nikki's room reminded me of an archeological dig, with sedimentary layers of clothing, papers, shoes, books, and magazines. If I dug down far enough, I'd reach her prepubescent period, with its artifacts of Barbies and sparkly stickers and Jonas Brothers CDs. A narrow path led from the door to the bed, which is where I started, lifting the mattress, shining my flashlight underneath, and inspecting behind the headboard. I piled stuff from the floor onto the bed, giving each piece of paper a look and shaking the magazines to see if anything fell out. After twenty minutes, I was down to bare rug. Next I opened the closet, and pulled out every item—games, ice skates, make-up, balled-up t-shirts, underpants, stuffed animals, more books and magazines. I rifled through the clothes, poking into the pockets of jeans and jackets. I found three little zip-lock baggies of pot, showed them to Zoë, who flushed them.

Then I found something I didn't share. At one end of the closet, behind a pile of shoes, there was a panel, an attic access, down low in the wall. The panel gave way as I pushed it, and I snapped on my flashlight for a look into a dusty unfinished space with a partial plywood floor, a maze of air ducts and pink insulation. And just inside, an open shoebox containing four eighty-minute mini-CDs, dated with a green marker: March 15, 25, 28, 29.

Mini CDs, like the ones Kent had made of the conversations he'd bugged. I slipped them into my pocket, based on quick reasoning: (A) Zoë could refuse to let me have them, then destroy them; (B) if they were recordings of bugged conversations, they were inadmissible anyway; but (C) they had to be important. Why else would Kent give them to Nikki? Why would Nikki hide them? I crawled out of the closet and began to sift through the papers in her desk. There weren't many—Nikki wasn't a student or a letter-writer—and after a few minutes I was finished.

Zoë took me to her kitchen—a basketball-court–sized room with acres of cherry cabinets, granite counter tops, and a six-burner cooking island. She pushed a napkin-wrapped basket toward me. "Please, take a muffin. I want them out of here. I gained two pounds last week. William and I have so many social obligations, all those tempting foods."

"You seem to have plenty of self-discipline," I said, helping myself to a blueberry muffin topped with a buttery cinnamon streusel.

"I wish! This morning the scale said one fifteen. I think it was the chocolate cake at Il Palio's last night. I can't resist chocolate! If I go up a dress size, I'd have to spend a fortune on clothes!"

Lest the subject of my dress size arise, I changed the subject. "You have a housekeeper?" I heard the distant hum of a vacuum cleaner.

"He's here now, comes three times a week. June recommended him. Iggy Curran."

"Ah, I know Iggy," I said. "He's observant."

"That's right. He told me he'd discovered 'the booty' at my brother's house." She frowned as if recalling I was a working woman, not her equal, and here she was giving me muffins in her kitchen.

"Do you mind if he takes a break? I'd like to talk to him."

She disappeared into a long hallway, and soon the vacuum cleaner ceased its roar. Iggy stuck his head into the kitchen. "Why, look, it's Miss Stella!" He started to turn the twig chairs upside down on the table, another twig creation supporting a one-inch slab of beveled glass. "Care if I do a bit of sweeping in here?"

"Of course not," I said.

"You do get around! Did y'all put June Devon in jail?" he asked.

"Briefly."

"My, my. I can't imagine her in jail. I think of her painting or working in the bookstore, not sitting in a cell. What's it like?" Iggy attached a dust cloth to a pole and began to wipe down the walls. I had never seen anyone dust walls before.

"I don't want to know. How long have you worked here?"

"Oh boy, this dog hair. I pick up a bucket of it every time. Well, let me see. So Zoë was looking for a cleaning person and I was looking to add more people. So June Devon and Zoë are related, you know? June gave my name here. I try to keep about twenty people on my list. Most are twice a month, but some, like Zoë, are more than that—she wants me nearly every day. Everyone's different, you know?"

"True," I said, nodding to encourage him to move on.

"So what did you ask me? Sorry, my mind wanders."

"How long have you worked here?"

"Oh, right. It's been about a year. The way I remember is . . . this is April, right? Well March 5 is Michael's birthday—that's my friend—and he was thirty last year. So we were having a birthday celebration at Teeny's—you know the barbeque place? I was thinking the other day how we all ate the slaw, and it had sort of a whangy taste."

I waited. Iggy pulled a sponge mop out of the closet, dampened it in a bucket of water, squeezed the water out, and swabbed the oak floor. "So I thought we might all get sick and I worried about it, but no one did so I guess it was a little too much vinegar. And when I got home from dinner there was a message on the machine from Zoë, and she had the prettiest voice I'd ever heard. I played it over and over."

"Do you ever talk to Nikki?"

"Why, sure, some. But she's usually shut up in her room, watching TV or playing music. And that room—phew! It's beyond me. I have to pile everything on the bed just to run the sweeper. And the bathroom!"

Iggy dunked the mop in the bucket. "Now, I guess Nikki's left. You know—" He shushed as Zoë came into the kitchen. She had changed into a pastel-blue dress with a wide white collar, the picture of innocence. If she ordered wine with lunch, she'd be carded.

"I have to go out now," she said. "Will you get started?"

"I'll see what I can do," I said. Iggy was absorbed in his mopping, no longer talkative.

As I followed Zoë out the door, my cell phone chimed. It was Hogan. "I got a trace on Nikki Truly. She used her mother's credit card for gas in Brevard yesterday. I called the park service and gave them the Lexus plate number."

Brevard was about thirty miles from Asheville, on the edge of the Pisgah Forest. I liked the idea of a road trip. I could drive to Brevard in four hours. Listen to the CDs burning a hole in my jacket pocket. Merle could practice tracking. What else did I have to do? I would find the teenagers, bring Nikki home to her mother, and aim Bryce toward a new career.

"Thanks, Hogan. Let me know as soon as anything else turns up?"

"I will. Be careful, Stella."

"You sound like Fern. She always says 'be careful' like I'm some sort of reckless risk-taker."

I decided not to bother Richard. I'd told Hogan; that was enough. A little voice in my head nagged that I shouldn't be going on expeditions into the woods without informing local authorities. What if something happened? The SBI doesn't like surprises. I could get fired.

This is a personal trip, I whispered to the little voice, so shut up.

CHAPTER 25

Tuesday

I inventoried the contents of my backpack—sleeping bag, water bottles and filter, waterproof parka, flashlight, my Eureka Solitaire tent I love because it only weighs two and a half pounds. I added energy bars and dried fruit. Hogan had suggested a cook stove, fuel, and dehydrated meals, but I told him I wasn't hiking the Appalachian Trail—I planned to be back tomorrow. With a substantial first-aid kit—practically a mini-hospital—the pack weighed thirty-one pounds. Merle would also carry a small pack containing his dog chow and bowl. I didn't want to load him down. He had work to do.

It had been over a year since Merle's initial wilderness training. Since then, I'd taken him out in the woods every weekend to track someone, usually Hogan, and more recently, Fern, so he should perform well on this search. I had the scent article— one of Nikki's socks—in a baggie in my backpack. I even took a piece of jerky out of the freezer and cut it into chunks, to give him as a reward when we found Nikki. That's how optimistic I was.

I checked out the CDs from Nikki's closet on my computer but they seemed to be blank. Or maybe not? There was a file structure, according to iTunes, but only silence came out of my speakers. Odd. They shouldn't be blank—they had dates written on them, like the ones Fern had found, and why would Nikki hide blank CDs? I detoured to the SBI and left them on Ho-

184

gan's desk with a *please help* note.

The drive to Brevard, on I-85 then I-40, passed slowly. I had to concentrate on my driving, due to tractor-trailer monsters whipping past at eighty-plus miles per hour. In high school, I didn't pay much attention to physics, but it stuck in SBI training, especially some simple formulas about mass, velocity, and force that apply whether a bullet is exploding through a barrier, or two moving vehicles collide. I stayed in my lane at the speed limit, muttering curses as each eighteen-wheeler gusted by.

As I approached Hickory, Hogan called to tell me a forest service ranger had seen Zoë's Lexus near the Pisgah Forest entrance. Two hours later, that ranger gave me a trail map and showed me where he'd spotted the car, at the start of Brenner Creek Trail. According to the map, it ran up Brenner Mountain along an old creek bed for three miles, and then connected with several other trails. There was a primitive campground about six miles further along one of them. Nikki and Bryce might be camping out there, avoiding life for a few days. Merle would be able to tell me. The ranger showed me posters warning of black bear activity in the area and made me promise to store my food away from my tent.

I drove my car to the foot of the trail, where Zoë's Lexus was still parked. I sat on its rear bumper and dabbed on bug repellent.

"We're going tracking, Merle. A girl is missing and it's up to you." I buckled him into his harness, reached into my backpack, and pulled out the baggie with Nikki's sock. He obediently waved his nose over the sock, I took him off the lead, and Merle put his nose down for the scent, which he found immediately, to my relief. It had always been a possibility that someone else had taken Zoë's credit cards and car. Judging from Merle's behavior, the scent trail was strong. Off-lead and nose down, he trotted up the narrow trail.

I followed. The trail was little used, overgrown with brambly vines that scratched my legs. In places I had to clamber over rocks, or shove aside the underbrush to get through. We hiked for two hours, stopping every thirty minutes to give Merle some water and a rest. He was tireless, unstoppable as long as he detected the scent. I was not so tireless. Sweat dripped down my neck and back. The backpack straps rubbed my shoulders, and my legs weren't used to the climb. Each time I sat down it was harder to get up. I forced down a few bites of a trail bar that tasted like raspberry-flavored cardboard.

Around seven p.m. we reached a small clearing where the trail forked, and I called Merle back. The sun was setting as I looked at the trail map. The left fork went south, toward a pond. The scent trail led to the right fork, which continued five miles up the mountain to a campground and a spring. I envisioned Nikki and Bryce, sitting by a fire, holding hands, murmuring about their golden future together. It might take me more than two hours to reach that far, and in the dark they could be nervous about anyone approaching. I decided to wait until morning.

I had about a quart of water left, and gave a pint to Merle with his dinner. The food I'd brought went into a bag that I tossed up into a skinny tree about a hundred feet from the spot I'd selected for the tent. In case a bear got interested in the food bag, it was far away from where we would sleep. I nibbled on an apple, and treated myself to a wash with a baby wipe. It felt good to get the sticky sweat-salt off my face and neck.

I put up the tent and crawled in with Merle. The temperature had dropped into the fifties once the sun set, and though my sleeping bag kept the chill off, I couldn't sleep. My aching muscles protested the hard ground, and the noises of the forest had me on edge—a mockingbird running through his extensive repertoire, leaves rustling as little creatures scampered about.

I wondered if I would hear a bear. I worried what would happen to Merle if a bear came along and they got into a fight. Anxious, then vexed with myself for my silly worries, I closed my eyes and tried to sleep.

Then I heard a growl inches from my face, on the other side of the tent wall, its fabric so flimsy that the merest brush of a claw would slice its fibers like a cobweb.

I put out my hand and touched warm fur.

Forget about rational thought and evaluation of options. I screamed as loud as I could scream, despite the paralysis seizing me. I screamed so loud I woke myself up.

I was clutching Merle. I had turned over to face him, and the growl I'd heard was his snore, a few inches from my nose. He licked my face, as alarmed by my scream as I was by the dream.

It was a long time before my heartbeat returned to normal. Eventually I fell back to sleep for a bit, then dreamed again. In this one, Fern and I were on a ferry docking at Marseilles as seagulls screeched and sailors shouted colorful French curses. She was extolling the European way of life—the cheese, the wine, the chocolate, the lusty Mediterranean men. I was feeling dubious about it all, as I do about many of Fern's enthusiasms. Then Merle started moving around and woke me. It's hard to sleep with ninety pounds of restless dog in your one-man tent.

The dawn air was cool, humidity low. The birds were in full chorus, a din of noise. I had Merle on a lead to keep him close while I packed up. When I eased my pack onto my shoulders, my muscles started talking to me, but after Merle checked the sock and, nose down, trotted along the trail leading up to the campground, I got into the rhythm of the hike, calling Merle back when he shot too far ahead, out of sight. I hoped the spring hadn't dried up—I was out of water.

★ ★ ★ ★ ★

When I came into the clearing from the trail, there was Bryce, standing by a picnic table, rubbing Merle's back. Merle slowly wagged his tail and looked very proud of himself. I eased my pack off and found his reward, the cut-up jerky.

Bryce stared at me with sunken eyes. "You're the last person I expected." He looked grubby and smelled worse.

We were in a grassy cleared area. The only structure was the shelter, a wooden platform with plank walls and a tin roof, open on one side and enclosed by chain-link fence. Mice in the walls chattered at us to go away.

"People were worried about you."

"This is one smart dog," Bryce said. I could tell Merle was feeling like a king. Having received his reward, he sat by Bryce and allowed us to praise his doggy wonderfulness. "I never would've thought you'd find us."

"Where's Nikki?" I asked.

"In there." He pointed to the shelter, where I could see an occupied sleeping bag.

"Is she awake?"

"Ummmm," said the sleeping bag. Nikki sat up and glared at me. "What are you doing here?"

"Your mother was about to report you missing. She asked me to look for you first."

"What? She knew exactly where I was. She gave me her keys and everything."

Bryce tapped a cigarette on his thumbnail. "Yeah, this is bullshit."

It was my turn to be irritated. "Well, who do I believe? A mature woman who says her daughter and her car are missing? Or the daughter and her drug-dealer friend? Come on, kids. It's time to go home."

"Fuck this. I don't have to do what you want." Bryce lit the cigarette and started back down the path.

"He'll be back for his cigarettes," Nikki said. She slid out of her sleeping bag. "I have to pee. There's no toilets, you go in the woods over there."

"Is there water?" My throat was dry and I knew Merle was thirsty.

"Sure." She handed me a full water bottle.

"Thanks." I poured some into a cup and drank it gratefully. I blew up Merle's bowl and poured water into it. He lapped noisily, emptying the bowl. "Where's a spring so I can refill this?"

"The spring is that way—" she pointed uphill. "It's a trickle, takes forever. Did you bring a whole army of cops? They sent you to trick us?"

I pulled out my water filter. "What are you talking about? Your mother's concerned for your health and safety. She wants you with her. Why would I bring an army?"

Nikki sniffed. I decided to give her some time to adjust to my presence. I took the water filter, my two bottles and her bottle I'd emptied. A rocky path led up to the "spring," a mud hole slowly oozing water. I pushed the filter bottle into the ooze and waited for it to fill. The utter peacefulness of these woods should have been relaxing, but Nikki's and Bryce's mistrust and anger were ominous. Why did Nikki think I'd brought police? I didn't want to get into a struggle with Bryce. But he was feeling threatened and I was vulnerable. I felt exposed, and glanced up the path every minute or so just in case. But it was quiet. I heard no one.

It took thirty minutes to fill the three bottles with clear water. I added a drop of iodine to each and started back down the path. Plain communication should resolve the situation. Bryce needed to come out with his worries and I would dispel them. There was not a shred of evidence connecting Bryce to Kent's murder and certainly no one suspected him of engineering Lincoln's two "accidents," or shooting Dr. Soto. The only reason I came after them was to bring Nikki back safely.

I didn't get the chance to express these well-reasoned thoughts. When I reached the clearing, Nikki and Bryce were gone. So was Merle.

I felt stupid. My intuition had told me something was not right, but it never occurred to me they'd take off. Of course they'd take Merle, the most trusting of dogs, who'd follow anyone for a treat. They wouldn't want to be tracked wherever they were going. But how hateful, to take my dog.

I assumed they'd head for their car, but since I'd been filtering water for a half hour they'd had a head start and it was unlikely I'd catch up with them. Nonetheless I tried. I jogged the entire nine miles of brambly, log-strewn trail, stopping a few times to listen and whistle for Merle, trying to repress the ugly images that wanted to pop into my brain. I heard nothing and saw no sign that Nikki and Bryce had crashed down the path ahead of me. But when I reached the trailhead, the Lexus was gone, and they'd left me a gift—a wriggling yellow dog, tied to my car door handle.

I whooped out loud as I dropped my pack and knelt to give Merle a squeeze, shedding a few tears of relief that he licked off my sweat-salted face. I whispered "thank you" to Bryce and Nikki, wherever they were.

Then, simultaneously, I heard the crack of a rifle and felt a red-hot poker stab of pain on my left side, just above my waist. A too-familiar sensation: a bullet graze. I'd been shot. Déjà vu all over again, leaning over Merle next to my car. Where was the shooter? I dropped to the ground and scooted around to the front of the car. Each gasp of breath triggered a burning pain. A broken rib? I clutched my side but that made it hurt worse, and my hand came away red. My heart pounded hard enough to break loose. A rifle cracked again, sending a bullet to kick up the gravel at my feet, making the decision easy. I wanted to get the hell out of there. The car keys were in my backpack, on the ground by the passenger side where I'd dropped it. I reached out and grabbed it, drawing another round that tore a hole in the car door. I dug down to the bottom to find my keys.

One-two-three-Geronimo, I whispered, and crawled to the driver's side, keeping the car between me and the shooter. Crouching, I opened the door and pushed Merle into the car. "Down, down," I whispered, and he obediently lay on the floor as I started the car. Barely raising my head, I floored it onto the road. A blessed silence lasted only a few seconds, then I heard repeated gunshots. One hit the rear window, spraying bits of safety glass everywhere and going into the front seat with a thunk. Then we were out of range, and I sat up and drove about thirty miles very fast. I didn't remember much about that part of the drive.

I pulled into a motel parking lot. Thirst hit me, and I drank a quart of water, water I'd filtered up at the Brenner Creek shelter and carried down the mountain. I gingerly lifted my shirt and examined the rapidly-swelling injury, a bloody bullet track. My head felt swimmy, so I took some deep breaths and tried to focus on what I needed to do. Why was I still alive? This was the third time in a week I'd been shot at, with only a nick. Someone wanted me either dead or very frightened, frightened enough to back off. Well, it wasn't going to work. I was more angry and determined than frightened.

Who knew where I was? Obviously, Nikki and Bryce. Zoë had sent me to find them, as Iggy knew, and he was a veritable broadcast service. Bryce could have told Wesley where they were going, and Nikki had borrowed the camping gear from June Devon. A better question was, who didn't know? My boss.

That was a big problem. If I got medical help, and the doc figured out it was a gunshot injury, it would be reported. Then

I'd be fired. Not just taken off the case, but fired from the SBI, for several very good reasons: not telling the agent in charge of Brevard that I was coming into his district, trotting up and down the mountain by myself, not reporting the shooting, and not even telling Richard where I was. Obviously I couldn't get medical help.

I tended to the injury with antiseptic gel, gauze, and an elastic bandage. I found a clean shirt in my backpack and put it on. I went into the motel restaurant and got some coffee and a cup of ice. With Merle wedged tight against my hip, I sat on the ground beside my car, icing my side while I sipped coffee.

Hogan had left me a page so I called him back. "Did you find Nikki Truly?" he asked.

"I found them, but they vanished while I was filtering water."

There was a silence and I knew exactly what he was thinking, that I probably felt bad enough without his remarking on my idiocy. "I appreciate your restraint," I said.

"These things happen."

I couldn't speak. I was trembling from pain and shock, but also from feelings of guilt and failure that seemed overwhelming.

"Stella, are you okay?"

Would Hogan respect my need for secrecy? I decided, yes, he would, and told him about the sniper. "A new nick in my side. Nothing, really." I didn't want to get into a discussion about doctors.

"Was it one of those two kids?"

"Could have been. I didn't think so at the time. I guess I don't see them as gun-totin' killers. And why would they wait until I reached my car?"

"Hmmm. I'm concerned. This was a stalking."

"Hogan, someone needs to report this. And leave me out of it. Can you make that happen?"

He was silent for a moment. "I'll call the county sheriff. But whoever it is, they're probably gone."

"You don't know that. He could be picking off hikers at this very moment." I shuddered, wondering where Nikki and Bryce were. "Let's change the subject. You left me a page?"

"While you were camping, there were developments. We got a report from the lab. It was an accidental find that almost didn't happen. After Lincoln Teller's accident—well, it was no accident—the lab went over his Jag. They found blood on the driver's floor mat. It was routine to type it, but it wasn't Lincoln's type. So the technician looked at Kent Mercer's blood. Not because she was told to, but because it was the second major case in a week that originated in Silver Hills, and she had a hunch."

"Let me guess, she found a match."

"Very high probability that it's Mercer's blood on Lincoln's floor mat. Sheriff's deputies searched Lincoln's home this morning. A pair of his shoes also tested positive for Mercer's blood."

"The shoe prints at the scene," I said, feeling sick to my stomach, and it wasn't from the bullet graze. Lincoln had been lying to me.

"Lincoln's shoe prints. Stella, he was there. He stepped in Mercer's blood and tracked it to his car. It points to him as the killer."

"No. It just puts him at the scene. Don't forget: someone is trying to kill *him.*"

"Lt. Morales wants to bring him in for questioning."

"The media will be all over this," I said. "He's on the run because he knew we'd find out he was at the murder scene. It's irrational to us because we think everyone should do what we want. You know—come forward, tell the truth, ask forgiveness, go to jail."

Hogan laughed. "Neither of us would have a job then."

I took a couple of ibuprofen to dull the throbbing ache. There was no time for what I needed—real food and a hot shower. My muscles had stiffened in the hour I'd been sitting on the ground. Painfully I raised myself. Merle and I looked like a couple of arthritic turtles as we crawled into the car and settled ourselves for the drive home.

CHAPTER 26

Wednesday afternoon

As the interstate peeled away, I did some serious thinking. Why was I a target, along with Lincoln Teller and Emilie Soto? Was the killer eliminating everyone as a precaution? I didn't feel like I had a clue, but it was possible I knew something important without being aware of it. The money in Mercer's account, audio files, Emilie's sniper shooting, a bloody fingerprint, the brake tampering and morphine overdose that almost killed Lincoln—without a theory to make them hang together, these facts skittered like beads of mercury.

My side throbbed, especially when I took a deep breath. The injury had stopped bleeding but the lopsided swelling looked freakish. I tried the radio for a distraction but found only country music. I like country music—Merle's named after Merle Haggard, who's equally redneck and handsome—but today the fiddle and twang set off a resonating stab in my skull. I turned it off and talked to Merle.

"Do you know I wasn't even scared when the sniper was shooting at me? I felt like an actor in a movie, rolling around the car. So why wasn't I scared? I *should* have been scared. I'm scared that I wasn't scared. I'll have to ask Anselmo if that's normal. And you know what else? It's time for a come-to-Jesus talk with Fern. She knows something." More of this nonsense until Merle went to sleep. I wanted to sleep myself.

I was sipping my second cup of caffeine when karma—bless

her heart—made an appearance. Crossing the bridge over the Catawba River, I saw Zoë's Lexus, pulled way over to the side of the highway, one corner up on a jack. Bryce crouched, wrestling with a lug wrench, removing a tire. Nikki stood off to the side, talking on her phone. I slowed and parked ahead of them, then watched in my rearview mirror. I didn't know what kind of reaction to expect. They were dog thieves, definitely. Snipers? I decided to search the Lexus.

"Stay here," I told Merle, and walked slowly—my side was killing me—to their car.

Nikki saw me and shook her head. "I don't believe it. Listen, I'm sorry about the dog. Bryce said—"

"Shut up, Nikki." Bryce stood, holding the lug wrench. He was a muscled lump with a solid piece of metal, and I was not feeling at my best. I stopped at a distance. "What do you want?" he asked.

"I want to search your car." I held out my ID. This stop was official. I didn't want to tell him what I was looking for.

"Yeah? Go ahead. I need a smoke anyway." He dropped the lug wrench, I was glad to see, and joined Nikki. They sat on the ground, smoking. I looked under the seats, in the trunk, in the spare tire well. No rifle. And, oops—no spare tire, either.

"Thank you," I said. "Now, Nikki, we're going to talk to your mother." I called Zoë's number and told her I'd found her daughter.

"Where?" She sounded pleased.

"Brevard, camping. She says you gave her the car keys, that you knew where she was."

"Nikki and the truth have a tortured relationship. Where is she? I want my car back."

Fatigue, pain, and frustration nearly pushed me to say something I'd regret. I heard cheeping overhead and looked up at a mess of sticks on top of a light pole, an osprey nest. Lots of cheeping; parent must be feeding chicks. I didn't answer Zoë, and the silence grew.

Finally, she said, "I'm grateful to you. Really."

"Really? Well, here she is." I handed my phone to Nikki, and crooked my finger at Bryce. "Come see this." I showed him the empty tire well.

His shoulders slumped. "Dammit. This is just not my day."

"Ask Nikki's mom what to do. It's her tire." I was done with Zoë Schubert and her offspring. I retrieved my phone from Nikki, and trudged back to my car.

I reached Temple's house around seven p.m. and rang the bell but no one answered. The door was unlocked so I let myself in. Upstairs the baby wailed. Through the French doors I saw Fern sitting at a table on the deck, doing something crafty. Paige stood on a chair beside her.

"Oh, dear girl, you look so pale," Fern cried out at the sight of me.

Gingerly I leaned down and kissed her cheek. "I'm just tired. I spent last night in a tent. What are you doing?"

"Decorating eggs. For the Family Safety Center flea market." Using a pin set into a cork, she was dotting a wax design onto each egg, then dipping the egg into colored dye. The process was repeated several times, achieving a batiked effect. Several dozen exquisitely decorated eggs nestled in cartons, ready for sale.

"They're gorgeous. Can we talk?" My reservoir of patience was nearly bone-dry.

"Just a minute, we're almost finished. Here, Paige, put this one in the blue." The child delicately lowered it into a cup of deep-blue dye. Then she counted, "one, two, fwee, seben, eight, ten!" Fern took the egg out of the cup with a spoon. The egg was now blue with yellow pinstripes and pink stars.

"Magical," I said. "Wish I had time to help out."

Fern took the hint and led Paige upstairs while I wandered around. I went down the hall to Mercer's office, a small room but not claustrophobic, with two skylights and a wide window. It hadn't been occupied at all, it appeared, since Chamberlain, Anselmo, and I had searched the desk and file drawers. I sat on the leather couch and waited for Fern.

I made myself a to-do list—go through the contents of Mercer's desk again; review the reports of interviews with neighbors and alibi witnesses, again. Sit with Hogan and review Mercer's financials, again. Devise an action plan for Bryce. Buy some aspirin. The baby was still crying as I fell asleep on the couch.

Fern returned and woke me. "Sorry I took so long. I had to give John a bottle and put Paige to bed. With stories it takes a while."

We went back outside to finish the eggs. A warm breeze fluttered the daffodils and swayed the lofty loblolly pines against the sunset's blazing orange clouds. "How's Temple?" I asked.

"She has good days and bad days. Today she stayed in bed."

"Post-baby blues still?"

"She needs rest and good food. I'm tending her." Fern was good at that. She patted my arm. "Looks like you could use a little tending yourself. What happened?"

"Just a couple of long days." She didn't need to know about the shooting, my bruised rib. "Listen, Fern, remember last week, you were asking me about Paige, what would happen to the person who took her?"

"Mm-hmm," Fern concentrated on decorating another egg.

"I know it was June Devon. I need you to tell me everything you know."

"Why? It's not relevant." She dipped the egg into yellow dye for a few seconds, then retrieved it and blotted it dry, revealing a school of tiny fish.

"How do you know? And what isn't relevant?"

She gave me an exasperated look. "Where Paige was, of course."

"How is it not relevant? She's Mercer's baby; she disappeared at the same time he was murdered. There has to be a connection."

"I mean, June didn't murder Mercer." She lowered the egg into pink dye, rolling it to obtain an even color.

"You have to tell me everything," I said. "There've been two attempts to kill Lincoln Teller, Emilie Soto nearly died, and I'm a sniper's target. So keeping a secret isn't an option for you." I picked up an egg and started making stripes on it with crayons. I would make up in color what I lacked in finesse.

Fern looked surprised at this. "You know June had Paige. Why do you need me?"

"She's not telling us what she did, what she knows. To get her to talk, we need leverage. A witness would be perfect."

"She's my friend!"

"You know she'll say she was taking care of the baby . . . it's all a misunderstanding. She'll call Harry Edwards and she'll get off."

Fern nodded. "Harry's a good lawyer. And you're right. She was worried about Paige's welfare. The father was a louse and June thought the mother couldn't be any good, leaving her baby with him. June was going to call social services until she heard about the murder."

"Was Paige at June's house the entire two days?"

"Yup," Fern said. She dipped her egg in a brilliant turquoise. This time she'd made a dozen tiny butterflies, complete with segmented bodies and elaborate wing markings. Mine was starting to look like a Peruvian blanket.

"So were you."

"Oh yes." Fern managed to look both defiant and guilty.

"Who else knew? Your entire painting class? Even Iggy?"

"Not Iggy. Just Ursula Budd. Ursula is very good at secrets. She's got more secrets than Merle has fleas."

I decided she wasn't insulting my dog, just being colorful. I pondered my next step. "If the DA learns about this, you and Ursula could be arrested as material witnesses."

"How silly. What good would that do?"

"It's called justice, Fern, not goodness. Laws were broken." I took my egg out of the purple dye and patted it dry, pleased with the crude, vibrant results. "But I agree, basically. I want June to talk. And Harry will advise her to cooperate, once he knows we have witnesses. So my problem is, how to let him know, without going through the sheriff or the DA?" As I posed the question, the answer was obvious to both of us.

"I'll call Harry," said Fern. "You go home, you look terrible. Do you want to take your egg, or should I sell it?"

"I'll take it, thanks. I need a little color in my life."

Before I collapsed into bed, I checked my email. The Firearms and Tool Mark Section had completed a ballistics analysis on the rifle Anselmo took from Erwin Devon on Monday.

Erwin's gun had fired the bullets injuring Emilie Soto.

The shooter couldn't be Erwin. He was too disabled. His wife, June? What possible motive could she have? Nikki, their niece, was in and out of their house frequently. Had she taken the gun?

Two other guns still to be identified: the 9mm pistol that shattered a mirror in Emilie's office, and the sniper's rifle from today. I could probably find its bullets lodged in my car seats. But I didn't dare take them to the SBI Lab for analysis. Maybe Hogan's call to the county sheriff would pay off with ballistics evidence.

Anyone in North Carolina can buy a rifle, no permit required. Over a half-million state residents have permits to carry a concealed handgun.

So be nice, people. You don't want to piss off someone in my state.

As I seemed to have done.

CHAPTER 27

Thursday morning

Hogan and I sat in Richard's office. My side was bandaged and bound. It hurt only when I breathed.

Richard wanted an update. He was dapper in a muted gray suit, shirt, and tie, enlivened by a bright orange pocket square in an origami fold. He held a cigar in one hand and a guillotine-like cigar snipper in the other. "Lincoln Teller is missing," he said.

"How can you lose someone that famous?" Hogan asked, looking up from his phone. "Call *Entertainment Tonight* and tomorrow we'll have a hundred sightings." Next to Richard, Hogan looked drab in wrinkled chinos and a polo. Neither of us enjoyed ironing.

"Stella, where's your man?"

"This is the first I heard he was missing, sir. He's not at the sister's in Durham?"

"No. She said he took off early this morning," Richard said. "What's going on with him?"

I shrugged. "Avoiding our questions? Or, after two attempts on his life, he's afraid. Or, Clementine has kicked him out and doesn't want to admit it."

"Or, foul play?" Hogan was texting, probably love notes to his latest online conquest. "Three strikes and he's out."

"Let's not go there," I said.

"Why not? Are you the only one allowed to have theories?"

Richard waved his unlit cigar in the air. "Now, children, play nice."

"Think how difficult it would be to take Lincoln against his will and leave no trace," I said.

"No trace? You haven't even looked for him," Richard said.

"I'll start right now."

Hogan put away his phone. "I'll help. No problem."

I smiled. "No problem" was how Hogan replied to every request.

Clementine greeted me at the door of her sister's condo. She looked as smooth and put together as ever, her hair caught by a red headband matching the flowers on her linen shirt. But her puffy, dark-circled eyes revealed her exhaustion.

"We're miserable," Clementine said. "There's no space for the boys to run around. I'm terrified they're going to break something." She was right. The condo wasn't a suitable place for two rambunctious little boys. Porcelain collectibles, flowers in vases, and dozens of framed pictures were arranged decoratively on many little tables.

"Actually they've already broken stuff. I asked Peg if I could put things away while we were here, but she wouldn't hear of it. So I'm going home today. No one's trying to kill *me*, and Lincoln's disappeared."

"When did you see him last?" I asked.

"He left real early this morning, saying he needed to get out," Clementine said. "When he came here from the hospital, he was too quiet, not really himself. He didn't want to talk to me or the kids. I thought it was the shock of the accident, the surgery, and the attempt on his life in the hospital, you know? But there must have been something else bothering him, something he didn't want to talk about. He took my car, which, needless to say, has left me stranded."

"Give me a list. Friends, relatives, places where he fishes or hunts or plays golf."

"He wouldn't be playing golf or fishing after that accident."

I felt depressed. I realized how much I liked Lincoln, how he represented what a husband and father could be, how he respected and loved his wife and helped her with the children. If he had walked out, then any man could—as Fern had always preached to me. *Come home, Lincoln,* I thought, *and prove Fern wrong.* And talk to me about Mercer's blood on your shoes.

Hogan called. "The four CDs you left for me Tuesday? I turned them over to computer guys in the Digital Evidence Unit. The files were encrypted, that's why you heard nothing. I found the encryption software purchase in Mercer's credit card statements and contacted the vendor with a subpoena."

The "computer guys" turned out to be Libby, a young Asian-American woman. When we reached her office, two floors up from Hogan's, she handed us each a CD case. "A copy of the decrypted files," she said.

"Wow." The SBI computer guys always impress me. "Was it easy?"

"Uh, define 'easy'?" She laughed. "Without getting too technical on you—I needed two keys. The vendor supplied one, then I chucked a dictionary at the login, hoping Mercer had used a dictionary word. Most people do. It worked, and I was able to decrypt the files."

I scanned the document she gave me, a transcript, organized by the four dates.

"They're recordings of voices, some phone conversations. Original files plus lots of altered copies—spliced or patched. Here's an example of splicing." Libby inserted a CD, moved the cursor to "preview," and clicked the mouse.

Temple's voice suddenly filled the room. I had heard her

speak these words before, from the CDs in Paige's closet. She was reading to Paige from a children's book. "It was a happy little train, with such a jolly load to carry. Where's your bathing suit?" The second sentence had been pulled from a different conversation.

"How's this done?" I asked.

"There's software for editing audio files. I'll show you." She opened a new program. "The file is displayed as a waveform, see?" She pointed to a jagged graph on the screen. "The lumps are words. Here, I'll play this bit again. Watch the marker move across the waveform."

We heard Temple say, "Where's your bathing suit?" as a vertical line moved across the screen, crossing a blob with each word.

"It's like editing a text document," Libby said. "You can cut and paste, insert, delete. You can reduce background noise, add sounds."

"Can you make a new sentence? For example, could you make her say 'Let's go surfing'?" I asked.

"Not quite. If the individual words were recorded somewhere, you could splice them together. But the intonations and emphasis of the words would be all wrong."

"So it wouldn't sound like a spoken sentence," Hogan said.

"Probably not." Libby clicked on the file to close it.

I had told no one except Hogan about these CDs, and even he didn't know where I'd gotten them. I recoiled at the thought of listening to them, suffering through hours of eavesdropping on Lincoln's and Ursula's commonplace calls, Bryce's drug deals, Kent's stories, Paige's singing. But I had no choice. These might contain additional recordings or evidence I had missed earlier.

Hogan gave me a lead on Lincoln's whereabouts. He'd headed north, using an ATM in Richmond and buying gas with a credit card in Fredericksburg. He'd registered at the Cumberland Hotel in Reston, Virginia, just an hour ago.

I pondered my next move. I could ask the Reston police to take him into custody, then send a marshal up there to bring him back for questioning. They knew him around there—he'd played for the Washington Redskins as a rookie right out of Gardner. If he chose to resist, it could get ugly. Lincoln's enormous size could be threatening to some cops, who'd be afraid of trying to physically restrain him and might use their guns instead.

I decided to go to Reston myself, convince him to turn himself in and explain Mercer's blood on his shoes. I could be there in two hours by air. I left Anselmo a voice message but I didn't want to talk to my boss, Richard, about it. He'd want to go by the book and notify the Reston PD, we'd argue, and he'd win.

I took Merle to a doggie day-care center he loves, The Bone-A-Fido. It's a ranch where the dogs roam together all day. Merle gets re-socialized as a pack animal, reminded that he is a four-legged creature with extra-special communication skills. If he could grin, he would've, as we turned onto the road leading to The Bone.

Chapter 28

Thursday afternoon

A nice man sat next to me on the flight from Raleigh-Durham airport to Dulles. I should never have admired his smart watch. He showed me its many clever little features, then asked me to sleep with him—not in those exact words, but that's where he was going. I seriously considered it.

Steven was about my age, spoke intelligently, and had a soft, russet beard I was dying to pat. We talked shoulder-to shoulder, sharing recycled air, for the hour-long flight. He traveled five days out of seven, managing a consulting contract with the postal service.

"What about dinner?" he asked. "I've enjoyed talking with you and I hate to eat alone. I'm staying at this boutique hotel in Alexandria with great food." He handed me his card and a brochure for his hotel. "I'll be here all week."

When I say I considered it, I mean my intellect flashed up red stop lights as my libido tore through them. I looked wistfully at the photos: a canopy bed, double whirlpool surrounded with flickering candles, and the breakfast options—pecan French toast, mimosas, spinach-mushroom strata. I wondered briefly why I wasn't offended by his offer of champagne, fine cuisine, a night of energetic sex followed by a fantastic breakfast. I decided it wasn't offensive enough. "I like that tub," I said, handing the brochure back to him.

"So, how about it?"

"I have to work tonight."

"You're a US marshal, right? I noticed the holster."

"Department of Justice." He didn't need to know.

"You're after a suspect?"

I nodded. "Wanted for questioning, as they say."

"So, you'll be working."

"I will. I probably won't even stay overnight if I can find him quickly."

"What happened to your head? Someone shoot and miss?" He chuckled at his little joke. I'd tired of artfully pinning my hair up and reverted to my usual braid, which didn't hide the gauze-covered lump very well.

"Actually, yes."

"Are you all right?" He put his warm hand over mine. Inside I felt a slow turning begin, like the coiling of a spring. I barely heard the static-filled blare of announcements as the plane descended. "Sea-blue eyes," he said. "You don't ever blink, do you?"

The flight attendant leaned over Steven to rudely tap my tray. "Tray up, please," she said. I complied, still bemused by his touch.

The plane landed and taxied to the gate. "Well, I'm sorry you're busy," Steven said. "If circumstances change, give me a call. I'd love to get together." He put away his papers and checked his watch for messages. I stared out the window at the luggage handlers, feeling tired and depressed. My case, stalled for so long, had been cracked open by a lab tech's curiosity. The number one suspect in Kent Mercer's murder was now Lincoln Teller. Finding and questioning him—as I was about to do—would earn me a gold star.

But I was rooting for his innocence, even if it meant the gold star would shatter into rusty shards.

★　★　★　★　★

I drove east on the Dulles Toll Road in a rental car. A few miles later I exited onto Fairfax Parkway, a ten-lane mega-road crammed with SUVs piloted by harassed-looking moms issuing commands into cell phones as they hauled their kids to Suzuki lessons and Little League games. The traffic reminded me why I live in Verwood. I reached Reston and pulled into the Cumberland's underground parking lot.

I took the elevator to the fourteenth floor and knocked on Lincoln's door. No one opened it, and I didn't have a warrant so I decided to wait in the lobby. I picked a seat with a good view of the lobby doors, the elevators, and the restaurant. Wafting toward me were wonderful smells from the open-air kitchen, accompanied by the sounds of many diners merrily enjoying today's special, salmon with grilled polenta. My stomach growled.

While I waited, I watched the people, a homogeneous group of government contractors—women and men in dark suits, sensible shoes, short styled hair and manicures. Perhaps because I was so clearly out of place in black jeans and a red leather jacket, a middle-aged man felt empowered to hit on me.

"Ah, a pretty girl, all alone," he said, folding himself down on my couch. He had a black mustache and matching soulful eyes that crawled all over my body, finally settling on my hand as if to take it in his, perhaps kiss it. "I am Hasan. I think you are wanting company, no? Did you have an accident and get a boo-boo on your head?"

"I'm sorry, I'm waiting for someone." I didn't mention my company might not be back for hours.

"I am doing business with AOL. What is your business?"

I looked at him calmly. "Law enforcement."

"Oh-oh-oh. Are you FBI? Are you going to arrest me?" He scooted a few inches away.

"Not if you go away right now."

"Okay, of course. Nice to meet you." Hasan rose and sauntered through the lobby. What was it today—did I have a *lonely, please take me home* sign on my back? I watched Hasan chatting up the bell captain. Probably asking him where to find compliant women who would be impressed by his AOL connection. In my irritation, I almost didn't see Lincoln Teller come out of the restaurant.

He went through the revolving door just as a valet pulled up in his car, the Volvo wagon Clementine usually drove. He tipped the valet and drove off. I had to know where he was going, but it would take fifteen minutes to get my car out of the parking garage. So I jumped in the first cab lining the circular driveway, and told the driver to "follow that Volvo, the silver wagon."

"Lady, you make my day," said the cab driver. "Is this a bust?" He was an elderly fellow with pictures of his terrier dog pinned around the windshield.

"Sort of," I said. "I want to know where he's going. What's the dog's name?"

"Puffy. She's my soul mate." We talked about our dogs as he followed Lincoln, a few cars back. Lincoln didn't get on the toll road, but crossed under it, then drove about fifteen minutes on a winding two-lane road. After a few more turns, he pulled into a parking lot.

"Don't follow him in, just drive by," I told the cabbie. I looked at the sign on the four-story brick building—Anxiety, Phobia, and OCD Clinic of Northern Virginia.

Well, I felt like the punchline to a sorry joke. *Hotshot agent executes trans-state search and daring car chase, corners celebrity criminal.* Finish the sentence—*consulting his ailing wife's doctors.*

I paid the cabbie and walked over to Lincoln's car. I sat down on the concrete parking barrier. It was hard, and my bottom started to hurt, which served me right. Sitting that low was awkward, so I took my boots off. When it started to rain, I scampered into the doorway, where I waited about a half hour until Lincoln came out of the building.

"What the heck?" he said. "You're everywhere, like an Elvis sighting. How did you find me?"

"I followed you from the Cumberland." I got to the point. "The SBI wants to interview you again. I thought maybe you'd come back with me, explain some things. And Clementine was worried." My arms were folded casually across my middle, though my right hand, hidden inside my jacket, gripped my gun firmly. I held my breath, unable to predict Lincoln's reaction.

"You came all this way? Where's your car?"

"I flew."

"Well, I'll drive us both home. You can collect the mileage if you want, you don't have to pay me. Hop in."

I started breathing again and he laughed, his perfect white teeth gleaming as he boomed, "Ha, ha, ha! You thought I was gonna try to escape?"

I didn't think it was funny, but waited until we were seated in his car to tell him why. "Lincoln, when forensics looked over your Jag they found something."

He turned his head slightly to look at me. "What?"

"Kent Mercer's blood on a floor mat. It looks suspicious. You have to come in for questioning."

Lincoln banged his hands on the steering wheel. "I've done nothing! I'll tell you what happened!"

This is why I got on the plane and flew to Reston, exposing myself to the predations of strange men, snarled traffic, and the fury of a certain Special Agent in Charge. I prayed silently that Lincoln would indeed tell the truth. I got out a tissue to pat my damp hair, which had bulked up to twice its normal size in the ninety-nine-percent humidity.

Lincoln was silent.

I waited.

Finally, he said, "Stella, I guess I'm glad you found out. 'Cause it's been very difficult carrying this around. Yes, I went to Kent's house. But he was dead when I got there."

"What time was this?"

"Man, I don't know. Two forty-five?"

"You didn't tell anyone."

"I saw two possible outcomes. First one: I'd be charged with the murder. No matter what evidence, the fact I was there and the man was dead would be enough to charge me. Happens all the time if you're a black man, I don't care how famous. Second outcome: I don't get arrested 'cause the police don't have evidence, but I'm a suspect. People find out Kent's been stealing from me. The press makes up trash about me. Soon I'm a tabloid joke.

"Now it doesn't matter to me what people say, I know who I am. But it matters to my family. It matters a hell of a lot. You ever been hounded by the press? There's nothing worse."

Lincoln was right. And wrong. He was involved, always had been, but he had withheld crucial information from the police.

"Can you go through that afternoon at Kent's? Every little detail."

We were stopped at a light, and he turned and looked at me. "Let's see. Okay, Kent was supposed to call me around two, arrange to meet. He stood me up, the bastard. I called him but he didn't answer. That didn't mean he wasn't home. He never answers his phone. So I drove over there. He doesn't answer the doorbell. The door was unlocked so I went in and looked for him. The sliders were open to the deck, I walked out, and there he was, on the patio. Man, that was a horrifying sight."

I watched Lincoln for signs he might be lying. He met my gaze directly, though tiny muscles around his eyes quivered with tension. "He was lying on the patio. So you went down the steps?"

The light turned green and Lincoln eased ahead. Traffic was heavy; it was almost five o'clock and the office buildings were emptying out. "Yeah, on the chance he might still be alive. I checked the pulse in his neck, but he was dead. Guess that's when I stepped in his blood. I did my five seconds of thinking and cleared out of there, like my mama taught me—walk away from trouble. Went home. The rest is like I said before."

"Did you see anyone?"

"Nope."

"Not even the little girl?"

"Nope. If I'd seen the kid I would've spoken up, you know? Helped out any way I could. I was mighty relieved when she was found. I heard your name was pinned to her clothes."

If Lincoln told the truth, he'd arrived right after the murder. Perhaps the killer saw him there and felt threatened. I could understand why someone wouldn't want to attack a man Lincoln's size with a purple bird's-beak paring knife. But why engineer a car accident for him? Risk being seen in the hospital, giving him an overdose?

On the other hand, Lincoln admitted to being on the patio and stepping in the blood. He could have killed Mercer and discarded his clothes, but forgotten to clean his shoes and the floor mats. But surely he hadn't cut his own brake lines, engineered a morphine overdose. And that wasn't his bloody fingerprint under the deck.

"So if it wasn't you, who killed Kent Mercer?"

"He must've been into some bad trouble."

Did Kent's bad trouble—bugging phones, selling prescription drugs, and having sex with the babysitter—add up to murder? I couldn't share all that with Lincoln.

He let me out at the Cumberland to get my rental car. He

followed me while I returned it to the airport, then drove us both back to Raleigh, a five-hour trip. We talked, a conversation strained by mistrust. I was investigating a murder, he was involved, and the complications made us both tense even though the topics—our dogs, football, his kids—were neutral enough.

Lincoln told me about Clementine. Her compulsions and phobias tended to flare up when she was under stress. They'd first appeared after she and Lincoln were married. She'd been working as a legal secretary and going to law school nights. They were worried about money as Lincoln was still in college, playing ball. Her father had moved in with them for a few weeks, a difficult time for Clementine since he wanted money for gambling. One day Lincoln saw her freeze at the front door, unable to leave the apartment until she tapped the frame sixty-four times, eight times eight. She had already been using tapping to alleviate anxiety, but it was surreptitious—toe-tapping during a test, head nodding before she paid at the grocery store.

"Sometimes I pick her up and set her on the other side," Lincoln said.

"Doesn't that freak her out?"

"No, it's fine. She appreciates it. Going through, someone carrying her—fine. Walking herself through, now that's impossible."

"What helps? Meds?"

"And therapy. Her old doc in Reston cured her. The kids, the pro football life, practicing law—she could handle anything. But when we moved back to Verwood and I bought the restaurant, she started to unravel. Dr. Emilie Soto was helping her, but then—you know—the shooting—so I went up to see the doc we'd used before, get his opinion. He wanted a face-to-face."

"You didn't tell Clementine where you were going?"

"Yeah, now that's a problem. Clementine doesn't always want to be helped. She thinks she's managing, you know? Only she can hardly leave the house, and it's really hard to watch her struggle with it. So I had to consult her old doc. He gave me the name of a therapist in Raleigh we can try." He sighed. "Between my wife and the restaurant and finding Kent's body—it's been too much."

I didn't say anything. It was a challenge to drum up sympathy for someone so wealthy, famous, and respected.

"The restaurant's on my mind all the time. By the way, are you coming to the engagement bash—Zoë Schubert and Bill Newell? At Clemmie's tomorrow night?"

"No. Lots of people?"

"Around two hundred. Starts at eight with cocktails. Then a sit-down dinner and ten-piece dance band."

"Nice party. Good business for you, Lincoln."

"Yeah. Though that Zoë is a piece of work."

"How so?"

"Talk about anxiety! She worries every detail to death. Man! What kinda oil in the salad dressing? Which ranch is the beef from? Who makes the goat cheese and how often do they wash their hands?"

I tried to laugh, until my cracked rib sent a stabbing reminder—someone with a rifle was trying to kill me.

CHAPTER 29

Friday morning

My phone's gentle chimes woke me. My head throbbed, my side hurt like hell.

Sam asked, "Are you okay?"

"Uh, just woke up. I'm fine."

"Sorry to be calling so early but my cell doesn't work out at your grandma's place. I've been meaning to tell you—I really enjoyed myself last Saturday."

I had to think fast—enjoyed what? Too much had happened. "Mmmm," I said, hoping for a clue.

"Too bad you had to leave so quickly," Sam said.

Aha—the dance at Essex Mills. I remembered the pleasurable feeling of his hands on my waist, his graceful and gentle maneuvers around the floor, occasionally brushing up against each other in a comfortable accidental way, in the shadowy room with the starry lights. The too-short kiss, broken by Hogan's tap on my shoulder. It seemed eons ago.

I got up, stretched slowly, careful of my injuries and mountain-climbing muscles. "I had a good time, too. A very good time." Up until the knife in the cheese.

"We're finishing the work at your grandma's tomorrow. She's invited a crowd for a party in the afternoon. Hope you'll be there?"

"Wouldn't miss it." I meant it, tried to sound confident. Sam and his work on Fern's house were the one happy corner in my life.

Do the hard thing first. Somewhere I'd read that was a practice of successful people, and dammit, I was tired of failure. I made a pot of coffee, slid the CD of decrypted recordings into my computer, and tried to pay attention—Temple reading to Paige, the gravelly voice of Bryce making his deals, Lincoln calling home to find out what time he was supposed to pick up Sue after her violin lessons. Silly splicings. I was nearly weeping from boredom until suddenly a new conversation came out of my computer.

Or not new, depending on how you define "new." It was bits of Lincoln Teller (taken from calls he'd made to Clementine) in a dialogue with Ursula (ditto, to George). It was meant to sound like they were talking to each other. It didn't quite work.

> Lincoln: Hey, how're you doing?
> Ursula: Good, good. Are you busy?
> Lincoln: Can't wait to see you tonight.
> Ursula: I should be done here about five. Can you pick me up?
> Lincoln: Sounds good.
> Ursula: We've waited too long.
> Lincoln: You know it, baby.

I laughed out loud. Merle looked up. He didn't hear me laugh very often; that was something I needed to work on. I recognized all of the dialogue from previous recordings—Ursula asking George to pick her up; Lincoln greeting a golf buddy with "Hey, how're you doing?" "We've waited too long" came from a call Ursula had made to her son's school, to complain about the lack of services for his learning disability. Mercer must have spent hours listening to the mundane and trivial conversations he'd recorded, trying to find the pieces that could be spliced together in a suggestive way. What had Mercer done with this file? It certainly sounded faked to me, because I'd heard the originals it was taken from. Could Ursula explain it to her husband, who, according to Fern, "fixes cars"? Had George been fooled enough to "fix" Lincoln's Jaguar?

"Here's a scenario," I said to Merle. "Let's say Kent Mercer tries to blackmail Ursula, which won't get him much—she's not wealthy. She isn't the source of the fifty thousand in his bank account. But go with it: suppose George finds out, and believes what he hears on the CD, the implication Lincoln is having an affair with Ursula. George tries to kill Lincoln, twice. But why would George kill Kent Mercer? George's jealousy could be a motive, but usually it's the wife or lover who is killed. And why shoot at Dr. Soto? It doesn't scan, buddy."

Merle's tail swished in agreement.

"Try it another way. Mercer tries to blackmail Lincoln, who is wealthy enough to be the source of the cash. Even though this recording is faked and not credible evidence, Lincoln pays him off and then kills him. Somehow, Clementine hears the recording, and is so furious she tries to kill Lincoln, twice."

Merle's pumpkin-gold eyes searched my face for a hint that this conversation might lead to a snack.

"What's wrong with these scenarios, you ask? June Devon and the missing baby. Dr. Soto doesn't figure. And Clementine can't even walk through a doorway. How could she commit murder? She would rant, maybe throw something, but she's a civilized woman."

Merle's tail thumped.

"Okay, I know, civility is on the surface. Corner a human and you'll get a vicious animal. Present company excluded, Merle, and thank you for listening." I gave him a cheese cracker.

I clicked "play" and listened to the last audio file—another version of the Lincoln-Ursula dialogue, this one even sillier. Frustrated and impatient, I shut the computer down.

Anselmo called to tell me Lincoln was coming into his office for questioning and I needed to be there. "Ten o'clock."

"Can you keep it confidential?" I asked.

"He's tough, Stella. He's used to being banged around."

"Maybe," I said. "But the media will treat him like just another celebrity who uses violence to get what he wants. Fodder for the tabloids. He'll be ruined."

"You're exaggerating. And what if he's guilty? He deserves whatever he gets."

"Right now all you have are footprints. Those aren't proof of murder."

"The sheriff isn't going to handle him any different from any other material witness. Let's agree to disagree on this."

An hour later I drove downtown. A few blocks from the law enforcement center, traffic slowed. Dozens of cars were circling, searching futilely for parking spaces. A bevy of reporters milled in front of the building, including video crews from the network news affiliates. The irresistible combination of a Silver Hills murder and Lincoln's celebrity drew the media like Japanese beetles to Fern's roses.

Now, seeing the media swarm in the parking lot, I realized I needed to avoid them, too. Fern would be thrilled to see my face on the *News at Ten,* but my boss wouldn't. The only publicity the SBI likes are exact quotes from heavily edited press releases. I drove a block away, parked in an elementary school lot, then walked back to the center and knocked on a side door. For five minutes.

Finally Deputy Chamberlain opened the door a crack. "No press," she said firmly, trying to close it, but I'd already inserted my right foot, left hand, and right shoulder.

I smiled sweetly. "I'm not press, I'm here to see Lt. Morales, and don't you remember me?"

She peered through the opening. "Sure. Your face looks much better." She let me in, then pushed the door closed and tested the lock.

"Is it crazy here?"

"You don't even know." She chuckled. "And you're in for a surprise."

"Tell me." I knew Lincoln would be interviewed, but I thought I knew what he'd say.

"I don't want to spoil it. But you'll be glad you stopped by."

I walked down the hall to the first interview room. Lincoln wasn't there. Instead, I saw June Devon, looking decorous in a black dress and pearls, her hair in a tidy twist. Next to her was her lawyer, Harry Edwards, a dapper gent—that's how I'd always thought of him—holding an unlit stogie in one hand and June's paint-speckled fingers in the other. He was whispering to her. All my grandmother's friends loved Harry. In his seventies, three times divorced, now single, he bedded many women. He didn't pursue them so much as hang around and admire, offer to give a back rub, prune the roses, and make a cup of hot chocolate. Before long, treating a woman like a valued treasure instead of the person who picks up his dirty underwear, he was the friend most men wouldn't be. This according to Fern; Harry hadn't worked his way down to my age bracket yet.

Nonetheless, Harry was a decent lawyer, and since June was guilty as hell, he'd have done his best to persuade her to work with us rather than face the ordeal of a trial and a potentially lengthy jail sentence.

June straightened in her chair as I entered the room. "You still have that bump," she said, pointing to my head.

"Hi, Harry," I said. He stood and gave a little bow.

"I've come to confess," June said. "Your buddy Morales

talked with the DA."

"Well, dear, not confess, exactly. *Explain*," Harry said. "We're negotiating a plea bargain."

I suppressed a grin. Fern had done good work, convincing June to come clean. "What's the offer?" I asked. So far, the DA had charged June only with breaking and entering. An abduction charge was being considered, offset by the fact that June had rescued Paige from a dangerous situation.

"Drop the B and E charge; she'll plead guilty to theft. She needs to care for Erwin. He won't survive if she goes to jail." Harry patted June's arm lovingly. June beamed at him.

I didn't quite agree. Erwin looked tough enough to survive in the desert eating mashed-up scorpions. But I could understand June's dilemma—Erwin needed on-site management. "In return for full disclosure, of course," I said.

"Why, yes," said June. "I'll leave nothing out. Spill the beans. Tell all."

Anselmo came into the room, raised his eyebrows. "Busy day. We can't decide who to arrest for what." He beckoned me into the hall. "You saw the ballistics report? Her husband's gun was used in the Soto shooting?"

"Are you charging her?"

"Not for anything connected to the gun." He handed me a tape recorder. "You'll need this. The video recorder isn't working." He opened the door to the interview room and motioned me in. He turned to June and Harry. "Mrs. Devon, the DA accepts your offer. He'll withdraw all charges except misdemeanor theft. He'll ask the judge to grant immunity from further charges in this case and sentence you to ninety days' house arrest. Now I'm going to leave Agent Lavender in charge. She'll record your interview." He winked at me, raising my body temp a degree. I wrenched my attention back to June and Harry, and turned on the tape recorder. I'd record for Anselmo's benefit. The SBI would want a written report, so I would also take notes.

"Mrs. Devon, even though you've told this story before, we need your statement to be complete. Please start at the beginning, the day of Kent Mercer's murder," I said.

June seemed relieved to be there. Her anger had vanished, and she told her story calmly. "Monday, I was watching a Cooper's hawk through my binoculars, in the trees across the lake. It was around one o'clock 'cause Erwin had finally turned off the TV. He watches *Dora the Explorer* while he does his exercises. Anyway, right away I saw this tiny child, almost to the lake, in the underbrush. There's snakes . . . a terrible place for a baby. I could tell she was crying." June shook her head and Harry squeezed her hand.

"I didn't see anyone around so I figured I'd have to do something. I rowed across the lake, scooped her up. Poor little thing had lost her diaper and all she had on was a t-shirt. She had a firm grip on her boom box, though. She went nowhere without it, as I discovered. I wrapped her in my jacket and climbed up to the closest house, the Mercers' house."

"Did you think she lived there?" I asked.

"I wasn't sure. I knew the Mercers had a little girl that Nikki took care of, but I'd never actually met her. So I went up the steps to the deck and looked through these glass doors. I could see this disgusting porn movie on the TV, and a man lying on the couch. He was—you know." She squinched up her face.

"I don't know," I said. "For the record, please?"

"Masturbating. Gross. Well, I didn't have a good opinion of him anyway. He had seduced my niece. I knew he was a repulsive jerk. But that baby could have drowned in the lake. He didn't deserve to be her father. So I pounded on the door, and when he finally stood up and came outside I gave him what-for. But it didn't seem to register; he was stoned—he kept smirking at me."

June paused and looked at Harry for reassurance. He nodded. "You're doing fine," he said.

"So then I got angry. I sort of challenged him, you know, walked toward him. I was holding the baby, and he didn't seem to care she was cold and scratched and mosquito-bit. I pushed him, he stepped backwards, away from me, and fell down the deck stairs. His reactions seemed slow, maybe because he was stoned, and he landed real hard on the patio."

"Was he hurt?" I asked. Had the mystery of Mercer's concussion been solved? Maybe.

"It was a hard fall. His head made a thunk on the flagstones and he just lay there unconscious. I felt his chest, his pulse. He was still breathing."

"You didn't call for help," I said. "Medical help."

"I thought he'd wake up in a few minutes. With a helluva headache. I sort of panicked. I didn't want anyone to know I'd been there. So I stuffed a few items in a pillowcase to make it look like a robbery attempt, throw the police off the scent. I wasn't thinking very clearly."

"And Paige?"

"First I put her in her crib, but she started crying so I picked her up again. I couldn't leave her there. Thought I'd take her home for a few hours until someone responsible could take over. I got some diapers, and made my way back to the rowboat. I rowed home. I—"

"Excuse me, you took the child and the bag of stolen items with you?" From what I knew of Paige, it might have been difficult to restrain her in the boat.

June nodded.

"Could you please answer for the record?" I asked.

"Oh, sure. Yes."

"Now the child is in your boat. Life jacket?"

She flushed. "No. I hadn't exactly planned a fun-filled out-ing. I put her in the bottom of the boat and she stayed there. With her boom box."

"How long did it take you to cross the lake?"

"Ten—fifteen minutes. It was after two when I got home. Erwin was real excited when I brought home a baby! She liked us—we played for a while—then I fed her. When she fell asleep on the couch, I carried her into the spare bedroom. She'd had a terrible morning and I thought she needed a good nap. We all did. Then Iggy Curran called and told me Kent Mercer had been murdered. I thought I'd done it! Even though it was an accident, I freaked out."

Ah, Iggy. A better information distribution network does not exist. "How long did you keep the child?"

"Until I left her in the supermarket. You know about that. But I sent you a text so everyone would know she was okay." She sank against Harry as he squeezed her shoulder. She sighed, then straightened. "Are we done?" she asked.

"Do you have the phone you used for the text?"

June dug in her purse for the simple mobile and handed it to me. Her story was a huge piece of the puzzle, like a big piece of fluffy cloud in a picture of blue sky, but I didn't know where it fit. Assuming she told the truth—a presumption at best—Mercer fell, hit his head, and lost consciousness. So someone else could come along and kill him, apparently.

I had one more question for her. "Why did you decide to return Paige?"

There was a long silence as June fondled her pearls. "Two things, I guess. First, I read in the paper that Kent Mercer hadn't died from the fall, but from knife wounds. It was a big relief and I felt a lot better, not so crazy with guilt. The second reason was, I wasn't great at taking care of her—we never had children. I couldn't get her to eat anything except cereal and milk and she fussed and it was wearing me down to the bone.

Between her crying to get what she wanted and Erwin grunting to get what he wanted, I was not doing so well, mentally speaking. When Fern suggested letting you find the baby, it was like the lights came on. Of course."

Harry and I winced simultaneously when she mentioned Fern. Maybe the DA would ignore it in the interests of inter-bureau harmony. I asked June if she had rifled through Mercer's office, and she denied it. I thanked her, and clicked off the tape recorder.

June's statement placed the time of Mercer's murder after two. Her behavior even had a certain logic. I was no closer to identifying the killer than I had been two weeks ago, but a sequence of events was beginning to emerge.

We walked into the hall and Harry leaped ahead to open the door for June and escort her from the building. Anselmo leaned on the wall, his arms folded across his chest, his expression royally pissed.

"What's the matter?" I asked.

He scowled. "You didn't tell me you'd been shot again."

I thought, *you didn't ask,* but realized he was genuinely troubled and a smart-alecky retort would spoil the moment. As I murmured, "Just a graze," he took my arm and pulled me into the nearest interview room.

"Ow." I pulled away. "That's my bad side."

"Why didn't you tell me? What happened?"

I gave him a brief version of the sniper attack at the Brenner Creek trailhead. "How'd you find out, anyhow?" I'd told Hogan and Fern, no one else.

He ignored my question. "Dammit, Stella, you're not always going to be so lucky. You're not bulletproof!"

I tried not to sound defensive. "I was tracking teenagers. Didn't know they'd brought a sniper."

"Third time you've been shot at this week. What are you doing about it?"

"I'll avoid open spaces, okay?"

His eyes searched my face, questioning. He shook his head. "Well, before you almost die again, let's go over what we have. Tomorrow morning at ten." He put his warm, strong hand on my shoulder, and if I turned just so, I could press against him and . . . wherever I was going with that thought ended as Anselmo handed me a folder and opened the door.

"Be careful," he said. He closed the door, leaving me alone in the interview room.

I hoped I wasn't blushing. I wanted to go home and talk to Merle about this futile adolescent crush on a married man. Also my other crush, the one on the wealthy, single-dad contractor Sam. And the lingering feelings for Hogan, the jealous pangs every time I saw him with Jasmine. Three lovely men. Merle might not understand, being a one-woman dog. But he would listen.

I opened the folder. Lincoln's statement. I read it three times before I realized what bothered me. It was nearly word-for-word what he'd told me on the drive back from Reston except for one thing I hadn't heard before, that he hadn't mentioned. On the day of the murder, when he arrived at the Mercer home, he'd seen Kent's car in the driveway. That's how he knew Kent was at home.

But, when Nikki and I arrived there, an hour or so later, Kent's car was in the garage.

I thought about that car the rest of the day. Who moved it? Why? It was such a small detail, but I couldn't ignore it, and couldn't decide what it meant.

CHAPTER 30

Friday afternoon

It was time to execute my plan for Bryce Raintree. I drove north to Wesley's house, where Bryce lived in a room behind the garage. His Mustang was gone, so Bryce probably wasn't there.

Wesley was up on his roof, blowing leaves from the gutters. He wore ear protectors and didn't hear me pull into his driveway. I sat in my car until he noticed me and climbed down.

"I want to talk with you about Bryce," I said.

He motioned me into his house. Before we sat on his squishy chintz chairs, he wiped his feet carefully and brushed off his clothing, still respecting his dead wife's housekeeping rules. I told him my plan. "I'm going to arrest him, with you right behind me offering an alternative."

He nodded. "I'll try anything," he said. The tense muscles of his face showed strain. "But why do you care? What do you get out of it?"

Excellent question. Bryce was a pestilence at this point, an unwanted and unnecessary complication. Since I knew he was dealing, I had to do something, though I couldn't arrest him based on illegal recordings. And, in my opinion, an investigation would be a waste of resources.

"I want it to end. Let's get his attention and make him stop," I said.

"Like you'd train a puppy," Wesley said.

"Exactly. Aim him at the straight and narrow, give him a

227

good shove."

Wesley grinned. "I like it. When do we start?"

"How about today?"

When Bryce's Mustang pulled up, we went outside. Nikki had been driving. She walked around to the passenger side and pulled Bryce out. He stumbled to his apartment door and leaned against it, his eyes closed.

"Mr. Raintree, Bryce isn't feeling very well," she said. I felt embarrassed for her; she was wearing a stretchy red tube top and might as well have been half-naked. Wesley stared at her, spellbound, as she took out her phone, then looked back at us. "Gotta run. See ya." She sauntered out onto the street.

"Can I give you a ride anywhere?" Wesley called after her.

"Naw, thanks." She waved at us and disappeared around the corner, probably to hitch a ride. I couldn't stop her—I had another project at the moment.

"Shall we help him inside?" I asked.

"His room's off-limits. That's the agreement I hammered out with Dr. Soto." He gave Bryce a nudge with his shoe. "I should just leave him here."

"I think this is a mitigating circumstance."

"Yeah, okay." Wesley unlocked the apartment door and we managed to get Bryce upright. We aimed him, like steering a refrigerator with wobbly legs, inside.

"Whaa? Whassit?" Bryce made it to the kitchen nook, fell to his hands and knees, vomited up a neat little puddle, then lay down on the floor. He was quite alive but moaning about it.

Wesley gave him a push with his foot. "Might as well look around since I'm here," he said.

What he found didn't surprise me. In the middle drawer of a small desk, dozens of little plastic bags each held a few to a dozen pills—blue, yellow, white, orange, all carefully labeled—Xanax, Vicodin, Klonopin, Tylox, Ketamine, Oxycontin. Different dosages of each. A veritable pharmacy. Wesley picked up all the pills and I didn't stop him. "This was Sunny's desk," he said. "Is he taking them or selling them?"

"Possibly both," I said. We looked back at greenish-tinged Bryce lying on the floor. When Wesley yelled in his ear, Bryce opened his eyes and sat up.

"Go to bed, son. We'll talk when you're more alert. Remember this—I took all your pills and you will thank me." Bryce looked dazed, his eyes red and watery. Wesley helped him out of his stained sweatshirt and went through his pants pockets. No pills. After Bryce fell onto the bed, Wesley searched the kitchen and found six small bags of pot in the freezer. He flushed them down the toilet. "Now what?" he asked.

"I'll come back when he wakes up," I said. "Call me and don't let him go out."

"I'll be right here. I have zero tolerance for this."

When I left Bryce's apartment, about fifteen minutes had elapsed since Nikki walked off. I drove toward Silver Hills, hoping to catch her. About a mile up the highway, I spotted her walking. I pulled up and she hopped right in.

"You weren't hitching, were you?"

She gave me a sour look. "I can take care of myself. I turned down one ride already. The guy was sketchy. But you're no risk."

Well, not that kind of risk. But I didn't give her a ride without a motive. "Are you going home?" I asked.

"Yeah, I guess. Unless—where you going? Near the mall?"

"As a matter of fact, I'm going there right now," I said. Shopping is a bonding activity. Away from her mother's protective control, Nikki might unburden herself of a few secrets. We passed the turn-off for Silver Hills and headed north.

"Something special you're looking for?" I asked.

"I might get this DVD. A Justin Timberlake concert."

"He's really talented."

"I love him. You should see my room, like, I have his picture everywhere."

I remembered the enormous poster of JT's scruffy visage that hung over her desk. "I think Kent Mercer looked like JT, don't you?" I asked.

There was a long silence. I hoped I hadn't pushed her too far. I looked over and saw tears. "I'm so sorry," I said. "You really cared about him, didn't you?"

"Yeah." She scanned her chewed-up nails for another bit to gnaw on.

"It must be hard, not having anyone to talk to, now that he's dead."

"We were going to be together," Nikki sighed. "He had to get enough money."

And divorce his wife, leave his children . . . It was unclear to me how Nikki could think it was likely to happen. But as soon as she said "money," I was very interested. "Where did he plan to get the money?"

"He had some ideas. He was a good businessman. I learned so much from him."

This was a subject I wanted to explore. "Here we are," I said, pulling into the mall entrance.

I offered to buy her lunch, hoping to prolong our chat. We took our tacos to a table in the food court. Three hairy boys in baggy pants and ball caps sat down at a table next to us. "Nice hooters," one said, and the other two snickered, grunting like chimpanzees.

I opened my jacket to give them a glimpse of my shoulder holster and, in my special agent voice, suggested they might want to give us some space right now, that this wasn't a good time for meeting new people. Like cooperative citizens, they ambled away with only a few grumbles.

"Young guys are, like, totally lame," Nikki said. She'd un-braided her hair so it covered most of her face and some of the red tube top.

"Totally," I agreed. We munched away companionably while I wondered how to keep the conversation going. Her remark about "lame guys" gave me an opening. "That's another reason you liked Kent, isn't it, he was more mature."

"He was so nice. He was never, like, gross."

"I want to find out who killed him."

She nodded, her mouth too full to talk.

"Who would have a reason?" I asked. "He was well-liked, responsible. Of course, he was secretly recording people. Maybe someone didn't like that."

Her eyes grew big and she put down her taco. "You know about the recordings? No one knew. How did you find out?"

"He burned some CDs. Office calls. Bryce's phone conversations."

"Oh. My. God. Does Bryce know you know?"

"I'm not sure. Nikki, do you know of anyone else he recorded?"

"People who worked there. But listen: I think George Budd killed Kent."

"Who?" I asked.

"You know, Ursula's husband? The big guy? She's the book-keeper at Clemmie's?"

"I'm listening."

"Because she had affairs and Kent found out. That's why."

Not the most logical motive for murder, but I was intrigued nonetheless. "Affairs? More than one?"

"With Lincoln Teller, Kent was sure of it. Plus, she gave away a baby girl when she was my age. Now the girl is hanging around, wanting to know who her father is. Ursula talked on the phone to George about it, whether she should warn the father that this girl was looking for him. She called the father TJ something. They were in high school together."

"Did Ursula warn him? TJ?"

"I don't know. The thing is, Kent thought TJ might be someone important. So it would be like a scandal if people found out? And TJ might pay to keep it a secret? Man, that was the best idea." Nikki wiped her face with a napkin. I helped her clean taco sauce and sour cream out of her hair. I knew about the recordings of Ursula and Lincoln that Mercer had tried to splice together, but I didn't remember one where Ursula talked to George about someone named TJ. The "baby" was Lauren, the young woman I'd seen with Ursula in the grocery store.

I also realized there must be audio files I hadn't heard. "Do you know where those recordings are?" I asked. "Maybe there are some clues in them."

"Uh . . . nope. Listen, I got to get going. Thanks for the ride and lunch. Good luck with, you know, the investigation and all."

I wondered whether she was thinking of the CDs I'd taken from her closet. I was certainly not going to mention them. "How will you get home?"

"I'll find a ride, don't worry. See ya!" She pushed back her chair and I watched her walk away, a solitary figure in the crowd of stroller-pushing moms, mall walkers, packs of pre-teens squealing over the latest hallway melodrama.

Pretty, lonely, lying Nikki.

CHAPTER 31

Friday afternoon

The high school librarian, Mrs. Garland, remembered me. She was a friendly woman famous for her arguments with the administration over sex-ed books in the library. They told her to get rid of them. She claimed the students needed the information. Most parents were too apathetic to make a fuss, so the books stayed, at least until a student stole one, which happened so frequently she had a carton of remaindered replacements.

"Stella Lavender, you look exactly the same!" she burbled. "Your hair still has that bounce."

"Uh-oh, time for a makeover," I said.

"Oh no, you look wonderful. Except for—" She patted her forehead.

"Well, thanks, Mrs. Garland. May I look at some yearbooks? Twenty-one, twenty-two years ago?"

"Looking for someone in particular?"

"Her name was Ursula. I don't know her maiden name."

"I know exactly which one. Here it is," she said, handing me the 1993 volume of the yearbook. "Someone was in here a few weeks ago looking for Ursula, graduated twenty-some years ago. He spent a couple of hours going over these yearbooks."

"Let me guess," I said. "Blond crinkly hair, blue eyes, a tan, mid-thirties?"

"Now it's my turn to be surprised. You know him?"

"You might have read about him in the papers. That was

233

Kent Mercer, right before he was murdered."

"Well, that takes all. And now you're tracing his steps. I heard you were with the SBI."

"I'm wondering who else he was looking for in this yearbook. Can I sit down with it for a while?"

"Of course."

I found Ursula's picture in a few minutes. She was a junior in 1993, with the same orangish, kinky hair and tilted eyes, but a lot more baby fat. Then I starting looking for the mysterious TJ, assuming he was also a high school student. I got lucky right away. There was one in her class—Tyler Jenkins Benjamin.

Only now they called him *sir. Mr. Benjamin, sir.* He was my boss, the attorney general of the state of North Carolina. A wizard lawyer, politically connected, ambitious. You didn't think "scandal" when you thought Tyler Benjamin. You thought "straight and narrow" with charisma and southern charm. Whispers of ambition for the governor's job followed him everywhere.

I stopped breathing as I realized how poorly my boss Richard would react if I associated Tyler Benjamin with an illegitimate baby, blackmail, and the murder of Kent Mercer. Was Tyler Benjamin the "someone important" Mercer had mentioned to Nikki? Did Mercer approach Tyler Benjamin, or threaten Ursula that he would? How could I find out? I decided to go to the one person who might know.

Ursula answered my call to her cell phone on the first ring. "I've been expecting this call for two weeks. Come on over. I'm at Clemmie's."

She was in the restaurant office, at the computer, surrounded by bills and folders and bank statements. Her black eye had faded to rust and green. We could almost be a matched pair.

"Just trying to keep this place going," she said. "You know

Lincoln hasn't been around much. And he hasn't filled the manager's job. So lots of things are falling through the cracks. I spent all morning with the chef, going over invoices."

"Lincoln must be glad to have your help."

"Lincoln will have to pay me. But the good news is, he can. The restaurant makes money. Why did the cops pull him in this morning?" She picked up a stack of papers from the floor and stuffed them in a trash can.

"Lincoln didn't kill Kent. But that's not why I'm here. Did you know Kent bugged this phone?"

"What? No."

There are many signs that someone is lying. The mouth narrows, the forehead wrinkles. Ursula fidgeted, looked down at the desk as she spoke, then sighed deeply.

"He recorded your conversations with George. Did Kent approach you about Lauren's biological father?"

Another deep sigh. "The deadbeat, you mean. Lauren has a perfectly good father in Oregon—the man who adopted her."

"Kent heard you say the deadbeat was someone you called TJ. Did Kent ask you about him?"

"No, he didn't." This time Ursula looked me in the eye. "The son-of-a-bitch asked George. Took the recording to the repair shop and played it for him. Asked him did he know about my mistake, who fathered the baby."

Just as Nikki had said. "Was George surprised?"

"He knew I'd had a baby and given her up for adoption, long before he and I even met. That's all. It didn't matter to him."

"So why did Kent ask George who the father was? Why not you?"

"Kent didn't like me. We'd had our run-ins at the restaurant because I accused him of stealing. He asked Lincoln to fire me a couple of times, but Lincoln trusted me and wanted me to keep an eye on things. I bet Kent thought George would be mad, get it out of me, find the guy for him."

"How did George react?"

She giggled. "George got mad all right. He has a terrible temper."

"Did he threaten Kent? Attack him?" I asked.

"George told me—" speaking gruffly, imitating her husband— " 'that Mercer fellow asked me a question about Lauren's father. I paid him a visit, and he won't be asking us no more questions.' "

I frowned. "What did he mean?"

"Knowing George, I think he scared the bejesus out of Kent. He probably manhandled him a little. You know, nothing that left marks, just enough to show Kent he was serious. My husband doesn't rile easy, but when he does, watch out."

"When did this visit happen?"

"The week before Kent was killed, in case you're thinking George did it. He didn't. He was at the shop all that day. You can check."

"And the recording? What happened to it?"

"George said it was an invasion of privacy and destroyed it."

I had one more question for her. "You called Lauren's biological father TJ. Was he Tyler Jenkins Benjamin? He was in your class in '92."

Her tilted eyes grew large and she gasped. "What? Tyler Benjamin?" she laughed, choking. I patted her on the back until she calmed down and wiped her eyes. "Oh my," she said. "Tyler Benjamin and me. No, no, no. I go for the common man. Like George."

"Who is TJ then?"

"No one. No one you need to know."

"Ursula, this is important. Kent may have tracked him down, asked for money."

"It's Lauren's business. I'll have to get her permission to tell you. Give me a day."

Arggggh.

The dinner crowd was filling up Clemmie's as I left. I went home and when it got dark—hoping my personal sniper didn't have a night-vision scope on his rifle—I took Merle out for a run. I ate a peanut butter and fig jam sandwich with a glass of milk, an attempt to mimic the nutritional pyramid.

Wesley called me and said Bryce was still sleeping. I thanked him for keeping me posted and we updated our plan. I found a bottle of white-out and changed the date on the fake arrest warrant, and he called the recruiter to reschedule Bryce's appointment. Tomorrow morning would be soon enough. A good night's sleep would help Bryce appear clean, in every sense of the word.

I wanted a good eight hours myself. I checked that my doors were locked, though my best protection was Merle's deep woof. Maybe sleep would unknot the lies, more lies, and audio recordings that had woven a tangle around my brain. It felt like a logic puzzle, the kind where Tribe A never lies, Tribe B lies all the time, and you get one chance to figure out who's who. My current acquaintances all belonged to one tribe, everyone lying some of the time.

CHAPTER 32

early Saturday morning

Wesley unlocked the door to Bryce's apartment and I marched in, holding my Sig with both hands, planting myself in the isosceles stance. It was 5:20 a.m., and Bryce still slept, wearing the same clothes we'd left him in thirteen hours ago. The bedroom smelled like fermented fruit, stale sweat, cigarette ashes. I shook Bryce's shoulder. "Wake up," I said.

"Wha?" He opened his eyes and saw my gun. He couldn't know it wasn't loaded. "What the fuck?"

"Turn over and put your hands behind your back." I'd brought over-sized handcuffs, but even they were tight on his wrists. I told him to sit up and laid the faked warrant on his lap. "Bryce Raintree, I'm arresting you on charges of narcotics theft, possession of illegal substances, illegal sale of narcotics, and trafficking in narcotics."

As I reviewed his Miranda rights, he slumped back onto the bed and closed his eyes. At each "do you understand?" he groaned assent. "I want a lawyer. I'm saying nothing to you."

"Fine. Mr. Raintree, you have a family attorney?"

Wesley frowned. "He's an adult, right?"

"Legally," I said.

Wesley folded his arms across his chest and stepped back. "He can get his own lawyer. I can't afford lawyers for him."

Bryce flinched. "Betrayed by my own father. Jesus."

"You did it all yourself, son. I just found the pills," Wesley said.

"You turned me in."

"No, your brother was responsible for that," I said.

"Those fucking recordings," Bryce said. "Where are they? Do you have them?"

"Don't shift the blame to Kent. You stole narcotics, you sold narcotics." Wesley leaned down and looked Bryce in the eye. "A man takes responsibility for his behavior!"

Bryce seemed to be considering this advice. "Like when you killed Mom?"

Wesley slapped him hard, and Bryce kicked his father's knee. Wesley pulled his hand back to hit him again, but I grabbed it and pulled him away. "What's with this, hitting someone in handcuffs?" I hissed at Wesley.

"The implication that I . . . I . . ." Wesley exhaled loudly in frustration. "I can't even say it."

"Listen," I said, "this is very serious. Bryce is going to prison for, I don't know, ten years. That's if he can plea bargain down to dealing, forget the theft."

"Ten years? For selling a few pills? That's bullshit!" Bryce's cheek was bright red from the slap, and he looked like he might cry.

"What a way to spend your life," said Wesley. "While your friends go to college, start careers, build something, you'll sit in a jail cell."

"Maybe you'll get into the prison farm," I said. "It's outdoor work, picking tomatoes and broccoli. Seasonal, but you'll get a good tan. Come on, now, let's head out." I motioned them toward the door, but Wesley held up his hand.

"Wait," he said. "Let's wait a minute. Son, I'm sorry I hit you. No call for that."

Bryce nodded, glaring at him, accepting the apology without

giving an inch.

"Your mother would say I failed if I let you go to prison. Failed in the most important job a man has. And she'd be right. Agent Lavender, how about some coffee and a civilized chat about our options here."

"What options? I have a warrant," I said.

"Look, it's dawn. The judge won't be in court for hours. Just a cup of coffee."

Agreed, caffeine would improve my disposition. "Coffee would be nice," I said.

"I'll make it," said Wesley. He went into the kitchen nook. Bryce sagged in silence on the bed. I leafed through a copy of *Cycle News*, chock-full of articles on racing stars, motorcycles, and very cool padded leather clothing.

"Do you have a motorcycle?" I asked.

"I've got a really hot bike, a Ducati 996."

"Do you ride it much?"

"Some. It's a racing bike. I was gonna get a racing license. There's a school in Maryland that qualifies you. Shit, I was going this weekend."

"Too bad. Guess your father will sell the bike," I said. Bryce was silent.

Wesley came back with three cups, milk and sugar on a tray. I uncuffed one of Bryce's hands and linked the other to the bed frame. Bryce sat down on the floor.

We sipped the hot brew. "Agent Lavender," said Wesley, "how far along is this arrest thing? I mean, is it irrevocable?"

"It's never irrevocable until sentencing. Even then, there's appeal."

"So even though you have evidence . . ."

"Lots of evidence," I said. "From the nursing home, from the narcotics found in his apartment, from the recordings. Plenty of evidence. Open-and-shut case."

"Still, it's his first offense," Wesley said.

"It's a shame to trash a young man's life this way, I agree," I said. "And he may not adapt well to prison."

"What do you mean?" said Bryce. "I can adapt!"

"You may be tough, but mentally it gets you," I said. "No cars, no girls, lousy food. You're surrounded by a bunch of idiots with turnips for brains." I sipped my coffee. "This is good coffee. What kind is it?"

"Nothing special," Wesley said. "Son, at least you can defend yourself."

Groaning, Bryce lay back and pressed his face into the mattress. We ignored him. I put *Cycle News* back on the table and smoothed out the cover. "Can I take this subscription card?" I asked Bryce. "I have a friend who'd love this magazine. He might even want to buy your bike. How much do you want for it?"

"Dad, can't you do something? Help me!"

"Like what? It's up to Agent Lavender. She's in control, not me."

"Take her gun! Uncuff me! You'll never see me again, I promise!" He rattled the cuff against the bed frame.

"So you want me to join you in jail? No, thanks," Wesley said.

I stood up. "Shall we move along? Let's stop at the public defender's office, see if anyone's there. There are two lawyers, but Marie's out on maternity leave. You may be able to see Womble on Monday, I guess. No, wait, he's in court. Tuesday, maybe. Depends on his caseload. With Marie out, he's really backed up."

I unlocked Bryce from the bed frame and cuffed his hands in front. His shoulders sagged and he hunched over his hands as he started toward the door. He turned and looked at me, then at his father. "Is it too late for that Navy thing?" he asked in his gravelly voice.

Wesley controlled his expression admirably, all except his eyes, which glistened. He blinked a few times and cleared his throat. "The military isn't a place to park societal misfits. They don't want felons," he said.

"They weren't illegal drugs or anything. And who has to know?" Though his hands were cuffed Bryce managed to extract a cigarette from his shirt pocket and light it with a Bic.

The smoke made me sneeze. I waved the fake warrant in the air. "Excuse me? Arrest? Let's get going."

"Listen, I know you have a lot to do. But can we talk privately?" Wesley asked me. "Let's step outside, get a bit of fresh air."

"Fresh air, sure. I can spare five minutes," I said.

Bryce exhaled a puff of smoke at the ceiling.

Wesley and I went outside and sat on two lawn chairs, part of a grouping around a fountain, a stone fish eternally spouting water into the basin. The gurgle of the fountain, the cool April dawn air, and the pink-orange glow on the eastern horizon made a magical scene.

"Will he survive boot camp?" I asked. "Is smoking allowed?"

"No smoking in boot camp. He'll be fine. Bryce is tough."

Reassured, I asked Wesley why he had joined the Navy, mostly to kill a few minutes while Bryce stewed, but also because it was a topic dear to him. He sat up straighter and talked about the Naval Academy, his first six-month deployment out of Norfolk on an aircraft carrier, returning to get married in Washington, DC. As he spoke, his voice relaxed and a real smile replaced the crooked smirk he usually wore. I imagined him in his Navy whites, walking with his bride, Sunny, under the cherry trees, proud of her and his uniform, optimistic about his life, ready to handle all challenges. Maybe Bryce would redeem himself and give Wesley something to be proud of again.

We went back into the apartment. Bryce had lit another

cigarette. He stared at the floor as he smoked, as though unable to look at our faces.

"Your father's very persuasive," I said. "I've agreed to give you one more chance. This is the last one though, be certain of that."

"Thank you," Bryce mumbled. "Thanks, Dad."

I unlocked the handcuffs. "I'll leave you two alone to work out the details." I'd already reached my deception threshold for one day, and providing a reference for Bryce Raintree to an armed services recruiter would tip me right over it.

As I left the apartment, I heard Bryce ask his father, "I want to be a pilot. Does the Navy have jets?"

"Yes, sir, the F/A-18, a fighter," Wesley said.

"Cool." Bryce said, his hopeful voice like a rasp across sandpaper.

An hour later, I met Anselmo in the Essex County evidence room, a cavernous dusty basement furnished with metal shelves bearing hundreds of cardboard boxes and plastic evidence bags. Anselmo pulled six cartons out and placed them on a wheeled cart. He pushed the cart into a service elevator and we rode up to an empty conference room on the second floor.

I hadn't mentioned my early morning's work to Anselmo. He wouldn't approve of my methods. And Bryce and Wesley were related to Kent Mercer, making them unsuitable playmates for me.

"You're the investigator. Where do you want to start?" he asked. He started tapping the cartons. "We've got Mercer crime scene, Mercer child abduction, Lincoln Teller auto tampering, Lincoln Teller morphine pump tampering, Soto shooting, Soto office break-in and shooting. Anything else?"

Neither of us mentioned the sniper attack on me. There was no carton, probably just a slim report in a file in the Transylvania sheriff's office. Hogan said they'd found a couple of bullets at the trailhead, .30 caliber, but that was all. I'd dug one out of the seat of my car, too.

Anselmo wore jeans and a plaid flannel shirt and smelled like spicy soap, an ordinary guy with impossibly broad shoulders. In other circumstances I'd be wondering how it would feel to press my face into the flannel, inhale deeply, and snuggle. But the six cartons anchored me firmly in the reality of a murder and four attempts, all presumably related and the work of one person, who showed no signs of being done.

"Box one," I said. "Let's look at every bagged item, every scrap of paper, every interview, and every lab report."

"Let's do it," he said.

We worked all morning. I reviewed Mercer's autopsy report and the forensics analysis of the crime scene. The interview files contained hundreds of reports from his neighbors and acquaintances, as well as more detailed interrogations. Phone records. Analysis of fiber, DNA, and hair. A purple bird's-beak knife, Paige's clothing. The sheer mass of data smothered me. Lost in minutiae I couldn't afford to ignore, I tried to focus on the key questions: Why was Mercer killed? Why the double attempt on Lincoln Teller's life? Why try to murder Emilie Soto?

Anselmo was restless; he stood frequently to stretch, sip coffee, or gaze out the window. A few times I caught him looking at me. "What?" I asked.

"Nothing," he said, a most aggravating response. There was something, obviously, but I couldn't read his expression.

"The usual motives don't seem to apply, do they? Where are greed and revenge in this picture?" Anselmo tapped his pen on the table. "Are the recordings important? How many are there, anyway?"

I froze, then turned away as my face grew pink and warm. "Uh . . ." How did he know about the CDs?

"I'm on distribution for this case. SBI Digital Evidence sent me a transcript and I scanned it. Where did you get them?"

I decided quickly to ignore that question and answer the previous one. *How many are there?* An excellent question.

I knew the answer. Or at least where it was. I rummaged through the carton of evidence taken from Mercer's home until I found three large manila envelopes holding the contents of his desk. I'd leafed through the envelopes twice, not seeing anything useful. But as I considered Anselmo's question, I remembered a small notebook, practically unused, spiral bound, with graph paper inside. On the first page was a list of eleven dates, the earliest February 10, the latest, April 2. Eleven dates. Eleven dated CDs?

I showed it to Anselmo. "Might this be a list of recordings? Look, some of the dates match up with the ones on the CDs."

"Four CDs I know of," he said. "Are there more somewhere?"

I turned away and retrieved one of my own files. "Yeah, I know about five more. My grandmother found them in a box in one of Mercer's closets. Hold on, let me look at my notes." I was starting to feel entangled in my own sticky web.

He laughed though he didn't sound amused, but incredulous. "Your grandmother found them? When?"

"I listened to them. They weren't helpful. Here're my notes. See? One is a bug on his brother's home phone. The rest contained conversations between Mercer and other people—he must have worn a lapel mike and just recorded anyone he spoke to. And an hour of random office phone calls. And the dates match up." I checked off the five dates.

Anselmo was so pleased with this discovery that he dropped the question of how many CDs, when I first heard them, why I hadn't told him, and whether he wanted to listen for himself. He looked at the list. "The dates are all accounted for except for March 18 and April 2? Two missing CDs?"

I nodded. "I learned about one of them yesterday from Nikki. Kent Mercer had recorded his bookkeeper Ursula talking to her husband about a baby she gave up for adoption twenty-one years ago. On the recording, Ursula calls the baby's father TJ. Mercer wanted to find this TJ, possibly for blackmail. He approached Ursula's husband, George, who didn't cooperate—in fact, he destroyed the CD."

Anselmo looked at me thoughtfully. "You've been busy. When were you going to tell me?"

"I'm telling you right now," I said. I felt defensive; after all, it had been less than a day since I first heard about the mysterious TJ.

"That's it? One missing CD? Anything more?"

I shook my head. I wasn't going to 'fess up to my doings with Bryce, no matter how guilty I felt.

Fern had always explained that guilt was good. It meant my conscience was working.

CHAPTER 33

Saturday midday

After Anselmo left the conference room, leaving me amid the jumble of cartons, I called Ursula's cell phone and found her in Paradise Keep, spending the day helping her seniors. "Sure, come on over, I need a break," she said. "I'm in 715. Take the elevator to seven and go all the way to the end."

Apartment 715 was crammed with dusty furniture. I squeezed past a china closet displaying about a hundred glass figurines and into a living room dominated by a six-piece, turquoise damask "suite." It was hotter than Hades. "I know, I know," said Ursula. "She keeps it at eighty degrees. Sit here by the window. I've got it opened a crack."

"She" was Olive, a tiny bird of a woman with puffy ankles, perched in front of the TV. "Don't touch anything. I told her you could come in but don't touch anything," Olive said with a dark look. I folded my hands obediently and sat down next to Ursula.

"See what I have to do to survive?" Ursula whispered.

"Let me get out of your way, then, so you can finish." I was starting to sweat. "Tell me who TJ is."

"I need to ask Lauren."

"Why is it her responsibility? Look, this is a loose end I have to tie up."

Ursula squinted her green eyes. "Well, I guess . . ."

As I waited, I could almost feel the hairs on my head swelling

247

as they absorbed the damp, warm air.

"It's not really my secret to tell. But look at the yearbook. He was two years behind me. The picture's not great but . . ."

I nodded good-bye to Olive and was in the hallway ten seconds later, jogging toward the elevator. Ursula called down the hall to me. "Go easy on him, okay? We were only kids. And Lauren hasn't called him yet."

I nodded, realizing the complications. Well, TJ was doubtless a big boy. He could handle it.

Tobias James Allen, class of '96. Cute, lots of dark hair, and a big grin with a little gap between his front teeth. He'd have been sixteen when Ursula got pregnant, making him thirty-six today. I pointed his picture out to Mrs. Garland, who was intrigued to be summoned into the school library on a Saturday.

"Lives in Simms Fork. Want his phone number?" She pointed to the computer.

"I'd rather have his address," I said. "I'll just drop by."

"Easy." She typed in his name. "He lives at 990 Bells Lake Road. Here's a map."

"You're a treasure."

I pulled into TJ Allen's driveway in Simms Fork, a mill town about a half-hour's drive from Verwood. He lived in a doublewide up on cement blocks, with mildewed lattice work nailed to the bottom. Pine woods surrounded the trailer, though fifty yards away the highway roared. I went around to the back. Four beagles in a kennel barked hysterically when they saw me. I pulled myself up to look in a window, and saw a rumpled bed, clothes on the floor, and a pile of shoes, dishes, and beer cans. It was nearly five p.m. and I figured TJ would be home soon.

In twenty minutes, a dirty red Ford Ranger pulled up next to my car. TJ didn't look much like his picture—his hairline had

receded about six inches, and his waistline had expanded twice
that much. He still had the gap-tooth grin.

"Howdy," he said. "Do I know you? I'd for sure remember if
we'd met. You're cuter than a speckled pup." He walked toward
me until I had to back up to keep a foot between me and his
beer belly. He carried a six pack and a large pizza box giving off
warm oregano smells.

I quickly put my ID into his face. "I need to ask you some
questions."

"Whoa there, Nellie! What's this about?"

"I need to verify some information. If it checks out, you won't
ever see me again."

"Now that would be too bad, wouldn't it? Come on in. I'll
get you a beer." He kicked the door to his trailer open and I
had no choice but to follow. He seemed good-old-boy harmless
enough, but I'd heard even Ted Bundy was charming. I kept my
arms folded, ensuring quick access to my Sig.

I declined the beer and sat down on the couch. The dog hair
made me feel right at home. TJ settled into a sagging recliner
and turned on the television. I had the impression the TV would
be on until he went to bed, and it didn't much matter which
channel.

"Now, what do y'all do at this state bureau place? Are you a
census taker?" TJ popped open a beer. "Pizza?" He offered me
the box, and when I shook my head, took a piece and put it
halfway in his mouth.

I explained what the SBI did, and the light in TJ's eyes
dimmed a bit. "You're a cop? Listen, the state has already
garnisheed my paycheck till there's nothing left. Here, I'll show
you. You take this to Brandy and tell her she won't get no more
blood from this turnip." He dug around in his pocket and held
out his pay stub.

"No, no, this has nothing to do with Brandy—" I started to

explain, but he interrupted.

"You mean Layla's after me, too? I was up with her payments. See, that's my other job." He frowned. "You won't tell Brandy I got another job, will you, 'cause she'll ask for more."

"You're supporting two women?"

"Yeah. Well, three kids, two moms. Child support. Here's their pictures." He pulled a couple of dog-eared photos out of his wallet. Two little TJs grinned out at me from one, and a blond doll in a pink dress smiled sweetly from the other. "But I'm living alone now. How'd you like to move in here? Save you some on rent, I bet. You got a boyfriend?"

"Cute kids," I said, "but this has nothing to do with child support. I want to know where you were on Monday, April 9?"

"Why?"

"I'm investigating a murder. Man named Kent Mercer."

TJ stopped chewing and frowned. "Never heard of him. Got nothing to do with no murder. Anyhow, Monday's my day off. I would have took my dogs and went and shot some squirrels. People don't eat much squirrel any more but it makes a good stew." He gestured toward a walnut cabinet in the corner. "Wanna see my guns?"

Did I? Yes and no. He was the first person I'd come across in this case who professed a working relationship with guns, and I'd been shot at three times by someone with a decent aim. If he'd been shooting at me, would he offer to show me his guns? Was it a ploy—another opportunity to finish me off?

My desire to look outweighed my caution, but to be safe, I asked him to give me the key to the cabinet, then step back to the opposite wall. "Not that I don't trust you, TJ, but I prefer to be the only one in the room with a weapon," I said. He raised his eyebrows, but gave me the key.

I unlocked the solid walnut cabinet. It appeared to be quite old, and was beautifully crafted. I wondered how it, and the guns, had escaped the auctioneer's gavel as Layla and Brandy squeezed their due out of TJ. Inside were three rifles and two shotguns. TJ moved toward the cabinet and I slammed the door shut. "Stay back," I said.

"Ain't none of them loaded," he said. "I'll tell you about them. They're most all my daddy's."

"Tell me from there," I said.

"Sure. Calm down, would ya? You're jumpier than a polecat. That one's a Krag bolt-action army rifle. Used for deer and bear. And the double-barreled shotgun's for turkey and pheasant. But the rifle's better; it's a Browning semi-automatic. And a collector's gun—the Winchester model twelve."

I'm no expert but I thought the Krag might use .30 caliber ammunition, like the sniper had used at the Brenner Creek trailhead. I picked it up. "I'm going to borrow this for a few days. For tests."

He bristled and moved toward me. "You can't take my gun. Don't you need a warrant or something?"

I shut and locked the cabinet. "Nope, it was in plain view and you invited me in. Now back off."

He sat down, red-faced and defeated. I had the feeling that repeated legal bouts, and no doubt a few run-ins with the law, had taken the fight out of TJ. I would ask Hogan to do some due diligence on him, check for prior convictions, particularly gun-related.

However, he was certainly not the source of the fifty thousand dollars in Mercer's bank account. And while the existence of a grown daughter might be a big surprise to him, he wasn't going to see it as a social embarrassment, a liability to be hushed up. Still, it wouldn't hurt to run his gun, and a bullet I'd dug out of my back seat, past ballistics.

CHAPTER 34

Saturday afternoon

Fern didn't need my guacamole for her house-warming party. She had enough friends bringing potluck to feed fifty people. All I had to do was show up.

"Where are the ruts? The holes?" I wondered aloud to Merle as my car rolled smoothly down Fern's long lane, now evenly graded and covered with a layer of gravel. Someone had whacked down the brambly blackberry bushes but left the azaleas, blooming profusely in every hue of scarlet, pink, and purple.

The lane curved around a stand of black walnut trees. And there was the new porch. Gone were the two-by-four barricades blocking off rotted steps, the buckets to catch leaks. The once-sagging floor was level and painted dark green. The porch rail and balusters gleamed shiny white, and two fans swirled lazily from a sky-blue ceiling, pushing a breeze down onto white rocking chairs. Pots of red geraniums decorated the steps. The scene lacked only a dog and a pitcher of lemonade, and I had brought the dog.

The lemonade was inside on a new red countertop. Fern spun with open arms. "Ta da!" She'd sewn herself a sundress in the same apple green as the kitchen walls. Tied round her waist was a black and white scarf in a checkerboard pattern matching the new vinyl floor. But the most amazing sight was the new stove, an ordinary four-burner gas stove. I felt like kneeling and kissing the little glass rectangle in the oven door, caressing its knobs, fondling each burner.

"I know, I know," Fern said. "You like the stove."

"I want to marry that stove." I gave her a long hug, ignoring the complaints from my aching rib. She smelled like lavender from the soap she'd always used. When your name is Lavender, that's what your friends give you. "Show me the rest," I said.

I oohed and aahed over the smooth, golden boards of the refinished pine floor in the living room, admired the gas-log fireplace. Fern pointed out the floor vents that would carry cool air into the room come July. "Of all the changes, that's my favorite," she said. "No more noisy window units!"

The second-floor bedroom used to be mine. I'd spent my childhood there, dreaming, dozing, peeling away layers of floral wallpaper. At fourteen, in a decorating frenzy, I'd painted over the entire mess in bubblegum pink, found a remnant of black carpet for the floor, and tacked an Indian bedspread to the ceiling to hide water stains. Pink, black, and batik.

Now, I couldn't believe it was the same room. The walls were smooth and pale blue, with creamy white paint on the trim and beaded-board ceiling. Sunshine poured through newly glazed windows. Above the bed hung Fern's painting of my old toys.

"Is the bedspread new?" I asked. The thick white chenille was inviting and soft as a basket of kittens.

"I found it in the attic."

"It's beautiful." Money *can* buy happiness. The improvements had entirely changed my perspective on Fern's living out here by herself. No longer would I worry about Old Ironsides blowing up, or an AC window unit frying the knob-and-tube wiring, or food poisoning from egg salad stored in the old refrigerator that shuddered at the end of each cooling cycle. Fern wouldn't step through a rotten porch floorboard and snap her ankle. She would be warm in the winter and cool in the summer. For a few moments I forgot about my case and savored a rare peace of mind, purchased for only twenty-eight thousand dollars.

More guests arrived. Joseph, the art appraiser who'd made all this possible, squealed "Eeeks!" as he smooch-smooched my face. "Ziss plass er mervlus! Und zoo er zexy!" He slid his hands around my hips and squeezed.

"Eeeks yourself," I said, removing his hands. "What's in the bag?"

He handed me a loaf of dark bread and a chunk of cheese. I pointed him in Fern's direction and went back to the kitchen to find a slicing knife and a platter. I was sawing away at the bread when Iggy Curran, my favorite inquisitive house cleaner, came in.

"Bless your heart, Stella, working away in the kitchen when everyone's outside having fun. Where's the sugar?"

I handed him the sugar bowl. "Who else is here?" I asked.

"Painting-class people. Zoë Schubert. Ursula Budd. Temple with both her babies. And Joseph—do you know him? He's so weird, isn't he? I think he's a man, with a name like Joseph. But he could be a woman, the way he looks. Except he's so tall, like a man. He kissed me—can you imagine?"

"Where?"

Iggy giggled. "On the cheek. Both cheeks."

"Oh well, he's European, that's the custom. And he's definitely a man."

I took a chocolate sheet cake from Ursula Budd. She and George had brought their son, Phillip, with them. He had probably been a cute child once—he had beautiful, long-lashed brown eyes—but puberty had given him bulk, zits, and stiff hair he'd pinched into spikes with gel. His t-shirt bore a scary image of a scythe-wielding creature with dripping teeth. If clothes make the man, Phillip was a bat-eared ghoul. I gave him the pitcher of lemonade and told him to walk around and refill glasses.

I spotted Sam Norris, also with his son. This child was adorable, about three years old, with a crew cut and chin dimple. "Garrett, say hello," Sam said. Garrett didn't speak, just chewed on a finger. Sam looked a little sun-burnt, and I was about to ask him if he'd been fishing when Hogan walked up and put his arm possessively around my shoulders.

"Uh, Hogan, you remember Sam," I said, sliding from under his arm. After TJ and Joseph, Hogan was the third man to invade my space this afternoon and I was getting tired of it. "Sam did all the remodeling work on Fern's house."

"Great job," Hogan said. "Looks terrific." I was thankful he didn't mention the interrupted kiss.

"Where's what's-her-name? Begonia?" I looked around for her little stick figure.

"Jasmine. She had a Tai-Bo class."

"I have a job for you," I said. "Background check on someone."

"Sure. Give me the name."

I wrote "Tobias James Allen" on a card and slipped it into his pocket. "Fern's over there, go say hello." I pointed to the apple-green-clad figure across the yard. I wanted to flirt with Sam and Hogan was a hindrance. Hogan took the hint and wandered off.

I asked Garrett if he wanted some ice cream. He nodded, keeping his finger firmly in his mouth. We three went into the kitchen. Iggy had brought a tub of homemade strawberry ice cream, and I fixed three cones. "The house looks beautiful," I said. "And you finished so quickly."

"It was a matter of scheduling the crews," said Sam. "They enjoyed it, working on a nice old place like this. It has real character."

"It goes back five generations. My great-grandmother was

born here. Now it's renewed."

"For future generations?"

"We'll see," I said.

"Here's hoping," he said, and raised his cone to me in a toast. I licked mine and tried not to be annoyed at his assumption that I planned to reproduce. Even loveable Sam was getting on my nerves today. It had been a long day, starting with the pre-dawn raid on Bryce, then all morning in the evidence cave with Anselmo, followed by visits to Paradise Keep, the high school library, and TJ Allen's mobile home. I was tired. And I still had a murder to solve, a missing CD, nagging questions about Lincoln Teller, a bruised forehead, and a cracked rib.

"Whose idea were the happy wall colors?" I asked Sam.

"Fern chose them. I've got no color sense."

"Your clothes always look nice, though—coordinated." He wore a taupe silky knit polo and perfectly creased charcoal slacks.

"I get help. Emma used to shop with me. Now there's this salesman I always go to."

What's the part of the brain that retrieves memories? The hippocampus? Mine woke up when he said Emma picked out his clothes. Who else had his wife's help with colors? Lincoln Teller had told me Clementine picked out the colors in his restaurant because he was color blind.

It mattered, but how? Carefully I turned this puzzle piece around. Lincoln said he had seen Mercer's car in the driveway the afternoon Mercer was killed, but later, when I arrived, it was in the garage. But what if Lincoln had seen someone else's car and being color blind, hadn't realized it was a different color, hence a different car? What if that someone else had watched him discover the body, assumed he would remember and identify the car, and decided he was a threat?

Mercer's car was a burgundy Infiniti SUV. Lincoln wouldn't

have noticed the color. But would he have noted the model? Would he remember? I gave my ice cream cone a final lick and tossed it into the trash. I wanted to put Hogan to work, and tell Anselmo what I was thinking.

"You busy tomorrow?" said Sam. "I'm going out on my boat. Want to come?"

I was torn. What did I need more: an afternoon with Sam on the sparkling lake, a couple of beers, and a few knee-buckling kisses? Or hours with Hogan and Anselmo pouring over car registrations and Silver Hills gate records? "I'd love to, but I have to work."

Sam wiped a drip off Garrett's shirt. "On Sunday? You and Emma, both workaholics."

Ouch. He'd likened me to his ex-wife. "Rain check?" I asked. "When I'm done with this case."

"Next weekend?"

I nodded a definite yes—something had to break in a week—and Sam seemed satisfied. I hoped he wouldn't find someone else to boat with in the meantime.

I found Hogan with George Budd, both drinking Coronas, eating barbeque, and laughing like long-time buddies. I took him aside and told him my hypothesis about the car in Mercer's driveway but Hogan didn't seem impressed. "Everyone drives SUVs these days," he said. "Even if Lincoln Teller can identify the model, you haven't got much."

I must have looked deflated because he added, "But it explains a lot of things. I like it. Points to someone else being there."

I asked him to find out what kind of cars everyone even remotely involved in this case drove. "The butcher, the baker—everyone."

"Sure. Tomorrow soon enough?"

It wasn't but I let it go. Unlike me, Hogan had a personal life.

Fern wandered over, Wesley at her heels. "There you are," she said. "This gentleman is taking me out to dinner, to celebrate." She and Wesley exchanged shy smiles. As I'd predicted, Wesley was the newest member of my sixty-two-year-old grandmother's fan club.

Zoë Schubert joined us, wearing white skinny jeans and a sheer jacket over a navel-baring crop top. What almost-forty-year-old woman exposes her middle? She carried a strawberry trifle in a glass bowl. She raised her eyebrows when she saw me. "I'd forgotten you were related to Fern," she said.

"Where's Nikki?"

She shrugged. "Right at this moment? She's supposed to be doing homework." I wondered whether Zoë knew I'd driven her daughter to the mall yesterday and quizzed her about Mercer's secret recordings. I remembered how she and Nikki had sat wedged hip to hip when I interviewed them the day after Mercer's murder, looking like sisters, with the same petulant expression, dark-lashed gray eyes, each gripping the other's hand. But had she lied to me about Nikki's expedition with Bryce to the mountains? It was hard to believe Zoë was aware of her daughter's blackmailing "business plan" with Mercer.

Fern linked her arm through Zoë's. "Did you know Zoë's an amazing fundraiser? The arts council is actually solvent this year."

"My friends are generous." Zoë held the trifle bowl out to us. "Want some? Real whipped cream."

Zoë's *monied* friends. *Silver Hills* friends. Money talk triggers an unattractive seething in me, the aftermath of an impoverished childhood. I pushed the feeling aside, reminded by Fern's beaming face that today she lacked for nothing, and picked up a spoon to inhale a bite of the trifle—a mix of pound cake, strawberries, sherry, vanilla custard, and whipped cream. "Oh my. Good."

Fern leaned into us and whispered. "There's a problem and I don't know who to ask. It's Temple. She wants to go home, but she shouldn't be alone."

"I thought she was better," I said.

"She's started medication, but she still has bad days."

"Where is she?" Zoë asked.

"I'll show you." Fern led us both to the art room, where Temple sat on a stool in the corner, leaning against the wall with her eyes shut, twisting a strand of greasy hair around her finger. On her lap, the baby fretted, gnawing on his hand. Paige had dragged a box over to the sink and turned on the water to "wash" various brushes and bottles. She was soaking wet, her diaper hanging sodden below her soiled t-shirt.

"You're missing a great party," I said.

Temple opened her eyes. "Do I look like a party? I'm on anti-depressants so I can't nurse and my boobs are dripping like a leaky faucet. I don't know why we came."

What could I say? She was beautiful in an exhausted maternal way, though she wouldn't believe me if I said so. At least she wasn't weeping. She lifted John, but he banged his nose on her shoulder and started to cry. "There, there." She patted his back. "We're going home, as soon as I get water baby away from the sink. She's liable to pitch a screaming fit."

"Let me help." Zoë efficiently picked up toys from the floor and stowed them in Temple's tote bag.

"I should be able to handle all this," Temple said. "I have to sooner or later. Fern's been a godsend, but she's moving back here tonight and then I'll have to manage by myself. You know what really bothers me? Kent's killer hasn't been caught. I keep thinking he'll sneak back into the house." She walked around the room as John wailed.

"Why would he sneak into your house?" Zoë asked.

"Why not? Who knows? No one knows why Kent was murdered, do they? It seems completely random. Yesterday I even bought a gun. Got the permit a year ago, but couldn't be bothered until now. I still don't know if I want it in the house." She lifted Paige off the stool onto the floor. "Sweetie, we have to go. It's almost bedtime."

Paige shrieked "No! No!" then started to yowl, adding her cries to the baby's. Their racket put me on edge. I found an old frayed towel and wiped up the water puddled on the floor.

"Maybe they'll quiet down on the ride home," Temple said.

"Let me go with you," Zoë said. "William can get me later."

Temple looked at her. "Are you sure?"

Zoë nodded firmly. She picked up the tote bag and Paige's boom box, then walked outside to help Temple fasten the children into their car seats. I watched the minivan roll away, feeling uneasy about the cosmic shifts in my universe: Zoë was being helpful, Wesley was sleeping with my grandmother, Lincoln had lawyered up, and Bryce wanted to join the military. What was next?

I needed to think. I went back inside the farmhouse, climbed the stairs to my old bedroom, and lay down on the kitten-soft bedcover. Stared at the ceiling. I tried to visualize Mercer's last morning, the SUV in the driveway, the murderer hiding under the deck. I scrolled through my phone until I found the photo I'd taken of the bloody fingerprint. That bloody fingerprint was useless until we had a suspect. Who was desperate and cold-blooded enough to carve the flesh of an unconscious man?

I slid the facts around like letters on a Scrabble rack. Someone had taken Mercer's computer, his phone. Where was the missing April 2 CD? Betrayal, knife, blackmail, abduction. Jealousy, fear, revenge, anger. If I could just find the right order . . .

CHAPTER 35

Saturday late afternoon

I went back to the scene of the crime.

The guard waved me into Silver Hills. After almost two weeks of driving through these streets, I no longer ogled the turreted mansions. The only people I saw were crews spraying weeds and blowing pine needles off driveways, small brown men who probably felt as out of place as I did.

No one answered Temple's doorbell, but the house was unlocked as usual so I let myself in. I locked the door behind me, a habit of mine, one I wished Temple would adopt, at least until we found her husband's killer.

Chaos reigned in the kitchen. John whimpered in his baby carrier. Paige sat on the floor amidst spilled Cheerios, putting them into her mouth one by one. In the family room, Zoë crouched on the floor, sorting and straightening Paige's toys and books. I supposed Temple would appreciate the order, but it wasn't my priority. "Where's Temple?" I asked Zoë.

"Upstairs," she said. She'd found a carton and was filling it with stuffed animals and dolls.

I went upstairs to Temple's bedroom and knocked on the open door. "You okay?"

"I'm in here. The only place I'm ever alone," she yelled from the bathroom.

"What can I do?"

"Give the baby a bottle. There's one in the fridge. Warm it in the microwave ten seconds, then shake it."

"I can do that. Why don't you stay up here, relax? We'll be fine." I hoped this was true—I had no experience with week-old infants. But John's whimpers slowed when I settled with him on the couch, and he latched onto the bottle like a pro. It felt natural to tuck his blanket snugly around him and cuddle him close. Success.

Zoë was organizing a toy kitchen that seemed to have a hundred pieces—pots, pans, cups, dishes—as well as a veritable grocery store of wooden food items. She arranged everything neatly, then lifted the carton of stuffed toys and dolls. "I'm going to take these to the playroom," she said, heading into the hall.

Paige followed her, returning with toys to bombard me with noise. First she paraded around the room pushing a diabolical popping toy, shouting "pop-pop-pop-pop." She squeezed Barney's purple plush paw as he sang "I Love You" in a growly voice, over and over. When that got old, she pushed a button on Elmo's foot. His red arms flapped and he began a high-pitched song—"Elmo wants to be a chicken, Elmo wants to be a duck." Paige accompanied him on a drum. After about eight repetitions, I hated Elmo and wished him dead.

In spite of the commotion, John sucked enthusiastically on the bottle with a pause now and then to catch his breath. Halfway through I thought a burp might be in order. I propped him in a sitting position and he obliged, spitting up milk. I wiped him off, told him he was a good baby. I could actually hear myself. Paige had abandoned noisy toys and put on headphones, a brilliant invention. Now she was trying to jam a CD into her boom box. She squealed in frustration.

"Bring it here," I said. "Look, there's another CD in there already. We have to take that out first." I reached to help her with my free hand.

"No!" She mashed the "play" button and closed her eyes to concentrate. No wonder June Devon abandoned her in the grocery store. I'd been alone with her for ten minutes and felt like reporting myself to the child-abuse hotline as a precaution.

"Daddy," she said.

"Daddy?" I leaned toward her and peered through the transparent plastic at a spinning homemade mini CD, Memorex 80 like the others Mercer had recorded. I reached out to take the headphones. "Let me listen, sweetheart."

"No, no!" she screamed, and pulled the boom box out of my reach. She ran into the kitchen. SBI training didn't include seizing evidence from a toddler, but I knew what worked with Merle—distraction, preferably food. I put John back into his carrier, dashed into the kitchen, and rummaged through the cupboards. Temple was a damned crunchy mom. I found only organic-this and whole-wheat-that. Finally, in the freezer, a box of frozen fruit bars.

"Look, Paige," I said, "pink popsicle!" I put the stick end in her hand as I snatched the boom box and headphones away. She screamed anyway so I flicked on the TV and scrolled through the channels until I found a trio of squeaky-voiced pudgy creatures. Paige turned to the screen. The popsicle dripped onto the floor. I sat her on the couch and put a towel in her lap. Temple would forgive me.

I lifted the CD out. *April 2*, it read, the date of the missing CD, number eleven of Mercer's homemade collection.

"I'll take that." The voice behind me was soft and low.

I turned around. Zoë Schubert stood in the doorway. Her face was ashen, not so young. "I've been looking for that CD everywhere," she said. "And it was in the kid's boom box all along?" She laughed and held out her hand. "Give it to me, it's mine."

The tiles lined up, the puzzle pieces slid into place. Zoë, who grew up shooting squirrels for stew. Who once owned a garage, working side-by-side with her husband. The nurse Zoë, in the hospital on the day of Lincoln's overdose. Who owned an SUV and sent me to the mountains to be a sniper's target. Who had enough money to buy Mercer's silence.

I didn't know why, but the answer had to be on this CD. "What's on it that's so important?" I asked.

Her eyes glittered. "What do you want? I can write you a check right now. Five thousand dollars."

"A confession? A secret?"

"Ten thousand. Please. I have to have it."

I didn't have my gun or handcuffs and I didn't want to get physical with the kids around. I needed to call for backup to arrest her. But as I took a step toward the hall, where I'd left my phone, she reached into her handbag, brought out a gun, and pointed it at my throat.

Zoë with a gun. Had she shot Emilie, grazed me, shattered a mirror scattering shards into my face, sent sniper fire raining down on me and Merle at Brenner Creek? As adrenaline spilled into my bloodstream, my breath grew shallow. She was extremely dangerous.

"Slide it over here. Now." Her voice was harsh.

"Looks like a Glock 19," I said to Zoë. "Uses nine-millimeter ammo, right?"

"I want the CD, nothing else."

I could charge her and grab the gun but I didn't want to risk a scuffle—Paige sat a few feet away, still absorbed in the television, and the baby was close by too, not to mention my own precious self. I tossed her the CD. She put it in her pocket. Paige was still glued to the TV and hadn't noticed a thing.

"Get down on the floor," Zoë said, gesturing impatiently. Reluctantly I sat. My mind raced, looking for a way to stop her.

"My show! My show!" Paige wailed. A commercial had come

on. She looked away from the TV and saw grim-faced Zoë holding a gun. She looked at me for reassurance. I smiled but that wasn't enough and Paige started to cry, "Mama mama ma—"

"Make her lie down with you." Zoë's voice was steely.

Behind Zoë, the stain of a shadow moved on the wall. A bare arm, a body wrapped in a towel, Temple's pale face, dripping hair. I tried ESP: *stay there, Temple, don't come any closer.*

"Come here, Paige," I said. "Sit by me." I patted the floor.

"No! Mama mama mama . . ."

"Don't come after me," said Zoë. "I'm taking the baby," Still pointing the pistol at me, she picked up the baby in his carrier with her other hand, backed out of the room, and disappeared into the hall.

Paige stopped crying. She looked at me for an instant. "*My* baby," she said. She ran after Zoë. I lunged across the floor to stop her, but missed. She dashed around the corner.

"Goddammit all to hell!" I heard Zoë cry, her voice no longer soft and refined but shrill with a nasty twang. Paige howled and a gun went off, the explosion reverberating through the house as I instinctively covered my head. Terrified of what I might see, I jumped up and scrambled into the hall.

Temple stood there, a gun in her hand. "Did I kill her?" she whispered. She didn't mean Paige, who clung to her legs, furiously sucking her thumb. John cried angrily from the shock of being dropped, carrier and all. Temple pulled off her towel, knelt down, and dabbed blood spatters off the baby. "There, you're all right," she said. She picked up the baby, jouncing him. She didn't seem to care that she was naked.

Zoë lay face down, motionless. Black powder circled a hole in her sheer jacket. I eased the gun out of her hand, felt her wrist. No pulse.

I found a raincoat in the closet and helped Temple put it on. "What happened?"

She swayed side to side, holding the baby close. His button eyes were serious but he had stopped wailing. "When I got out of the shower, I heard Paige crying for me, so I came downstairs. I saw Zoë had a gun. With my children in the room! I went into the closet to get my gun and then she came out with the baby. I didn't even think about it. I let her walk by the closet, stuck the gun in her back, and pulled the trigger."

The bullet had entered Zoë's back. Blood seeped out the wound, staining her jacket. A tangled froth of blond hair clung to her face. I lifted her hair gently. Under perfectly shaped eyebrows, Zoë Schubert's gray eyes stared blankly at nothing.

CHAPTER 36

Saturday early evening

Someone had to tell Nikki her mother was dead.

I called June Devon, Nikki's aunt, and gave her a summary of the evening's events. I suspected Zoë had killed Kent Mercer, and had attempted to kill Lincoln Teller and Emilie Soto. "Can you break the news to Nikki?" I asked her.

She was silent for a moment. "It will be difficult."

My turn to be silent, knowing there will never be an easy way to tell a child her mother is dead.

"For a long time, all they had was each other," she said. "They were close. Maybe too close."

"Nikki has you, and Erwin."

"Of course we'll take her in. But she's almost old enough to be on her own."

Two weeks ago, after I'd discovered Kent Mercer's body, I had questions for Nikki the babysitter. Tonight, I had very different questions for Nikki the killer's daughter. Did she know that her mother had murdered Mercer? Did she know why?

"Can you ask her a question for me? I don't want to interview her officially. But I need her to confirm some facts."

"You think she knows something?"

"Wouldn't Nikki do anything for her mother?" Until she hooked up with a blackmailer.

June sighed. "This will break her heart." Her voice was weary, overlaid with conure chatter. I could almost see it perched on

267

her shoulder.

My heart was cold, frozen solid by a bloody conch shell necklace, a smashed Jaguar, Paige's face as she listened to her dead daddy's voice reading bedtime stories. "Get her to talk to you about her mother. There's no longer a need for secrets."

"What do you want to know?"

"Ask her why she stuck the purple knife in the brie."

"Say again?"

I repeated the request.

"Why should I help *you*?" Belligerent, the side of June I knew well.

"It will help Nikki, to confide in someone safe. You're safe. Besides, I kept you out of jail, remember? Call me after she answers the question."

For the second time in two weeks, an ambulance arrived at 1146 Fair Oaks Lane to transport a body to the medical examiner's facilities in west Raleigh.

It was nearly eleven p.m. before the sheriff's deputies finished their interviews and evidence collection. Temple had put her children to sleep. Still wearing the raincoat, she sank into a chair to answer police questions in an exhausted monotone. She showed a spark only when they questioned her use of force. "What was I supposed to do—ask her nicely to please hand my baby back? When she probably killed Kent? That's nuts. I'm sick of people taking my kids. I've had enough. I'm going to bed." She pulled herself wearily up the stairs.

I confronted Anselmo, trying to appear calm though my temper simmered. "It's self-defense, plain and simple."

Anselmo repacked his camera into an evidence kit. "Intentional homicide. Temple shot her in the back. The DA might want to charge her."

"With what?"

"Manslaughter."

"You'll look like a fool. Someone breaks in—"

"Zoë Schubert didn't break in. Temple invited her in." He counted over the clear plastic evidence bags arrayed on the floor and compared them to his log list. Methodical, literal, and annoying.

I took a breath, tried to sound calm. "My point is, she entered with malicious intent, to search for that CD. She threatens an SBI agent and two children with a gun. She snatches up the baby and starts to leave. If you arrest Temple, you'll have every parent in North Carolina calling their legislators. Oh, and don't forget she's a murderer."

Anselmo looked at me. In spite of the late hour, his eyes were clear and calm. "Two things. First. Thanks to you, neither Lincoln Teller nor Bryce Raintree nor June Devon is in prison. Second. You don't know Zoë murdered Kent Mercer."

Bryce in jail? Oh, yeah. Anselmo had read transcripts of the encrypted files. I put my hand on his wrist. "Wait until the morning. Temple's asleep now."

He pondered a moment. "All right. I'll talk to the DA. Now you owe me two."

"Two?"

"I never wrote you up for that accident." He motioned to Chamberlain to take the evidence bags out to the car.

"I owe you two then." I tugged on his wrist. "I'm sure Zoë murdered Mercer. I just thought of something. Don't pack up that fingerprint kit. Let me see her Glock."

Anselmo frowned. "What for?"

"It will have her prints. Let's do a quick match with the latent." I quickly scrolled my phone photos to the latent print found under the decking the day of Mercer's murder, where someone had rested a bloody hand.

"We'll get her prints from the ME tomorrow."

"I know." I studied the photograph. "This one's a partial, a pocked-loop type."

He opened his fingerprint kit and carefully brushed a small amount of black powder onto the Glock. A mess of overlapping fingerprints was revealed. "On the barrel, here, isn't this a pocked loop? Looks like a left thumb." He grinned.

I compared the two pocked-loop fingerprints. I wasn't an expert, and I didn't want to force a match, but they looked the same. Zoë had crept under the deck and rested a bloody hand against a joist, praying not to be noticed. She'd watched Lincoln Teller feel for a pulse, step in Mercer's blood. It was her SUV in Mercer's driveway.

He slid the gun back into its evidence box. A puff of black powder drifted into the air.

"She wasn't a suspect," said Anselmo. "She barely knew Mercer. Was she angry about his affair with Nikki?"

"The answer should be on this." I held up the CD I'd taken from Zoë's pocket, the eleventh CD, and inserted it into Paige's boom box. It was a poor recording of a phone call, broken and staticky in places. The woman's voice was shrill and angry.

"Who is it?" Anselmo asked.

"Listen." I started it again.

Anselmo shook his head.

"It's Kent Mercer and Zoë Schubert. That's the way she sounded when she was furious. She reverted to West Texas. Monophthongs."

"What?" Anselmo was amused.

"Like 'watt' for 'white'. 'Give me a baat of that thur paa.' " I turned up the volume. It lasted less than a minute.

"I can see why she wanted this CD," he said. Using tongs, he took it out of Paige's CD player and slid it into a plastic bag.

"Yes," I said. "It proves her motive. She needed to shut him up."

CHAPTER 37

Sunday early morning

In a tailored midnight-blue suit, starched ivory shirt, and a tartan-plaid tie, Richard was ready for the busy day ahead. He looked much more alert than I felt; dawn had barely cracked and I'd been up all night. June had called me around three a.m. with Nikki's answers to my questions. Nearly all the puzzle pieces were now locked in place, so I could paint the picture for my boss.

I inhaled deeply to capture any stray caffeine molecules emanating from Richard's coffeemaker. "About a year ago, Zoë Schubert murdered her third husband with an overdose of insulin," I said. "Her daughter, Nikki, knew, but didn't tell anyone until Kent Mercer started looking for someone to blackmail. Nikki saw a perfect blackmail opportunity: her wealthy mother had gotten away with murder."

"The daughter set up her mother for blackmail?"

"Yup. Mercer and Zoë meet. He tells her he knows she killed Oscar Schubert and demands money to keep quiet. Zoë's angry, asks him how he found out. He says Nikki told him."

Richard's chair squeaked as he swiveled. "This was on the eleventh CD."

"The following day, Zoë pays him—that's the fifty thousand deposited in his bank account. But then she finds out he's recorded their brief conversation. She goes to his house to get that recording."

271

"To kill him?"

"Maybe not at first. But Zoë must have been furious. She's paid Mercer fifty thousand dollars but it's only the beginning of his blackmail. When she gets to his house, he's unconscious, the perfect victim. She grabs his computer and cell phone, which might have copies of the recording. Then, to ensure his eternal silence, she finds a sharp knife in the kitchen and severs arteries in both his arms. Lincoln Teller drives up and finds the body as she hides under the deck."

"The daughter must have known what happened all along."

I nodded. When June had asked Nikki my question—*why did you stick the purple knife in the brie?*—Nikki wept. Secrets poured out, lies were recounted. Nikki confessed to her aunt, and June—once I assured her Nikki wouldn't be considered an accessory or charged with obstructing justice—had shared Nikki's statement with me.

I now shared it with Richard. "When Mercer is killed, Nikki makes the connection—Mercer's blackmail has backfired." *My mother has murdered my lover and it's all my fault.* "Nikki begins to search the Mercers' house, looking for the recording, but I stop her. Later in the afternoon, in her mother's car trunk, she finds Mercer's laptop, his phone, the purple knife—still a bit bloody—and her mother's blood-smeared clothing. Horrified, Nikki pockets the knife. She's ambivalent—emotionally tied to her mother, complicit in the blackmail, wanting Zoë to be stopped, yet unable to bring herself to turn her mother over to the police. Nikki brings the knife to the dance, and stabs it in the cheese. A small cry for help but a lousy clue."

"The previous murder? Zoë's husband?"

"Nikki says Zoë deliberately overdosed him with insulin. Oscar Schubert was cremated, but Lt. Morales has requested his autopsy report."

The coffeemaker huffed steam, smelled divine. Richard

selected a mug, poured himself a cup, and added a drop of cream. "What about the attempts on Lincoln Teller's life?"

"Zoë thought Lincoln saw her car in the driveway and might describe her car to the police. But it turns out Lincoln's color-blind. He did see the car, but he thought it was Mercer's. To him, they were the same gray color."

"She knew how to cut brake lines? Not something most women—or men—could do."

"Zoë had scrabbled up the social ladder, but she had lots of practical knowledge. Her first husband owned a garage, and Zoë worked right alongside him. She could find brake lines with a hacksaw. And she'd been a nurse, knew all about IV equipment. I even saw her in the hospital the day of Lincoln's morphine overdose. But the evidence is circumstantial."

He took a cigar from his drawer but left the wrapper on. "The Soto shooting?"

I closed my eyes, unable to speak, stunned by a sudden memory of Emilie's eyes as she'd struggled to breathe.

He waited. "Stella?"

I took a deep breath. "I don't know how to link her to that. But I think she did it. We know the gun came from June and Erwin Devon, but Zoë was in their home occasionally. And she was a good shot. She hunted for food as a child."

"What's her motive for trying to kill Dr. Soto?"

"When Zoë learned Nikki was having sex with Mercer, she sent Nikki to Dr. Soto for a private consulting session. Then, after Mercer started the blackmail, Zoë realized Nikki wasn't keeping the Schubert murder a secret between them. She panicked—she thought Nikki had also blabbed to Dr. Soto. Zoë shot Dr. Soto to silence her. And to frighten me."

"You think she was the Brevard sniper?"

I froze. I knew guilt was written on my face.

"Some agents—most agents—follow protocol."

I recognized sarcasm. Should I apologize? "I didn't want to cause you any trouble," I said. "That's the truth."

"Not quite. You didn't want to ask permission. A very different thing."

"If you don't know, you won't worry. I didn't want you to be responsible for me."

"Are you crazy?" Richard stood, like he might vault over his desk and throttle me.

"Sir, I apologize. Sincerely. Yes, I do think Zoë shot at me in Brevard. She knew where Nikki and Bryce were camping because they'd told her. It was a place Nikki had been before. So Zoë followed me. She waited near the trailhead for me. I doubt she enjoyed sleeping in the woods, but there was nothing fragile about Zoë Schubert."

Richard sat down again. His rage had vanished as quickly as it came, like a ten-second thunderstorm. I knew he was processing what I'd told him, thinking about ramifications, the press coverage, the attorney general.

"Nice work, Stella."

That was unexpected. Richard was notoriously stingy with compliments. "Thank you, sir, but I know it's not a tidy resolution."

"Never is. Have some coffee." He picked up the black carafe and poured me a cup. I sipped it gratefully, savoring its earthy flavor, a symbol of his approval.

Wired on excellent coffee, the adrenaline of the night's events, and the elation of solving my case, I drove to Fern's to help her clean up after the party. When I reached her mailbox, I had to pull aside to let another car out of her driveway. Wesley Raintree threw me a jaunty wave as he pulled onto the road.

I parked in front of the porch, its gleaming white balusters beckoning me onto the bounce-free floor. The rooster crowed,

Bill and Hillary brayed a greeting.

Fern opened the screen door. "You've just missed Wesley."

"I saw him. Nice man." I followed her inside and picked up a dish towel. "Do you ever think, 'what if?' " I asked as I dried plates, a motley collection, some of them surely older than Fern, with darkly crazed surfaces and worn gold edges. "What if Mercer had been kinder to Temple? She wouldn't have gone out shopping that day. Or what if he'd kept a closer eye on Paige and not let her wander off? There were so many ways he might not have died."

"You can think 'what if' all you want. Things happen for a reason."

"What's the reason for murder?"

Over her coffee cup, she blinked at me with true-blue eyes. "To teach us a lesson."

"And . . . the lesson is?"

"You have to figure it out. That's your purpose in life, to learn your lessons."

I didn't, and never would, accept any reason for murder. But I didn't contest Fern's platitudes. They helped clear away the muck of her bad memories, stirred up by my work.

We went onto the porch. The air was cool, the sunshine warm. A bluebird fluttered his bright wings from his perch on top of the birdhouse, inviting the girl birds to check out his real estate. Questions swirled in my mind. Would Clementine get the help she needed? I hoped that Lincoln—back with his family—would see his dream of a successful restaurant realized. What path would Nikki follow, now that she was orphaned, wealthy, and on her own? Would the Navy take Bryce? Would he strengthen or crack in the forge of military life? I marveled at Temple's strength and courage, the rage that overcame her natural gentleness and helped her pull the trigger of her gun. Perhaps her children would teach Grandpa Wesley their tender ways, so he, in turn, could show them anthills, stars, and rivers.

Fern smoothed aside my hair and kissed my forehead. "The swelling's gone down," she said. "You'll probably always have a scar." Zoë's mark.

Through the fallen cloud of morning mist that lay over the field, I could see Merle digging furiously. He froze, then attacked the ground in a different spot. His purpose was clear and he was learning his lessons, light-years ahead of me, as usual.

ABOUT THE AUTHOR

Karen Pullen is the author of *Cold Feet* (Five Star, 2013), the first book in the Stella Lavender series. Her short stories have appeared in *Spinetingler, Ellery Queen Mystery Magazine, Sixfold, bosque (the magazine), Phantasmacore, Reed, Every Day Fiction,* and several anthologies. She edited the Anthony-nominated *Carolina Crimes: 19 Tales of Lust, Love, and Longing* (Wildside, 2014). She earned an MFA in popular fiction from Stonecoast at the University of Southern Maine. She lives in Pittsboro, North Carolina, where she owns a bed & breakfast inn.